The

Beekeeper's
Cottage

BOOKS BY EMMA DAVIES

The House at Hope Corner

The Little Cottage on the Hill
Summer at the Little Cottage on the Hill
Return to the Little Cottage on the Hill
Christmas at the Little Cottage on the Hill

Lucy's Little Village Book Club

Letting in Light
Turn Towards the Sun

Merry Mistletoe
Spring Fever
Gooseberry Fool
Blackberry Way

Emma Davies

The Beekeeper's Cottage

bookouture

Published by Bookouture in 2019

An imprint of StoryFire Ltd.

Carmelite House
50 Victoria Embankment
London EC4Y 0DZ

www.bookouture.com

ISBN: 978-1-78681-845-4
eBook ISBN: 978-1-78681-844-7

To Mother Nature – You're doing an amazing job, don't give up on us.

Prologue

Grace's mother always joked that she should have christened her Grace Anne Decorum, not plain Grace Anne Jones as she was back then. It was a teasing reminder that a high-spirited child like her should practise Grace And Decorum at all times… or at least whenever possible. Now she was much older, Grace often wondered if this mantra was her mother's way of helping her cope with all the blows that life had dealt her. She hoped so; Grace needed all the help she could get.

Her mother had taught her many things as a child: how to laugh, how to sit still for hours watching the baby rabbits on the lawn, how to creep out on a bright frosty morning to see the miracle of cobwebs in the hedgerow, the same hedgerows that a few months earlier had yielded bursting blackberries for her taste buds to explore. She'd taught her how to love hot buttered crumpets by the fire, and the feel of the wind in her hair, the tang of salt from the sea on her skin and the gentle caress of the sun-warmed air. Above all, she had taught Grace how to value each and every thing in her life, because one day they might not be there. Her mother had died when Grace was only twenty-two, and so many years had gone by now, some days it was a real struggle to remember her at all.

Not today though. Today, Grace could see her mother everywhere in the garden; in the tall Michaelmas daisies whose friendly heads bent gently in the breeze, in the tumble of leaves playing joyously along the patio, and in the air itself which enfolded her with the kindest of touches. And she was glad, because today she really needed her mother's help. She needed someone to remind her what was important in her life.

Grace was sitting in her favourite spot, just under the apple tree, on a bench that had seen better days but which was still the most comfortable place to sit. With a cup of tea and a biscuit with her for moral support, she contemplated her options, although, in truth, there was only one. A friendly robin came to join her momentarily, and she wondered if it was these little things that she would remember most about this day in time to come, or whether they would pale under the enormity of what she was about to do.

Fortunately, she didn't have too long to wait, and the sound of tyres on gravel soon cut through her thoughts. She drained the last of her tea and, rising, brushed the crumbs from her skirt. Then she began to walk slowly back inside the house where she would greet her husband and bring an end to their thirty-two years of marriage.

Chapter One

Amos clutched the loaf of bread to his chest with one hand, savouring its smell. In the other hand he lightly swung a carrier bag, trying not to snag it on the roses that lined the pathway from the village shop. Their scent was heady this late in the day, and he breathed it in, feeling the same sense of peace and contentment that had drawn him to the village in the first place. Finding the little shop had been a pleasant surprise, but discovering it was open until eight o'clock in the evening had been nothing short of miraculous. But then Amos had always believed in the miraculous.

Bill, the shopkeeper, had been very helpful. Not wary like some folk were when they first met Amos, who, with his dungarees and bright-red Doc Marten boots, would be the first to admit that his appearance wasn't all that conventional for a man of his age. Listening carefully as Amos explained that he was looking for a place to camp in return for any kind of work he could offer as payment, Bill didn't make any promises but suggested that Amos have a look around the shop for a few moments while he made a phone call; he knew someone who might be glad of an extra pair of hands.

Only when the deal was done had Bill given him a name and address and Amos had understood perfectly. You couldn't be too careful, not in this day and age. He'd paid for his bread, a bottle of water and some apples before taking his leave. With any luck, he would soon be in a position to properly repay Bill his kindness. In Amos's world, that was just the way things worked.

Taking the little lane up by the church, Amos followed Bill's directions, enjoying the rustle of the wind in the big horse chestnut trees along the way. He would have liked to see them in the autumn too, but he knew he would be long gone by then. Stopping for a moment he looked up at the cloudless blue sky and frowned slightly, knowing from just the sound that the car coming towards him was driving far too fast. He stepped safely onto the wide verge in good time as a dark-blue Lexus roared past him, sending a shower of dust and noise up into the air. Amos stared after the car for quite some time, thankful that there was no one else walking the lane, someone whose reactions were a little slower than his. It must be sad, he thought, to be in that much of a hurry on such a beautiful day. He rubbed the back of his neck absent-mindedly.

After walking steadily downhill for some time, the sharp bend he had been told to look out for appeared ahead of him in the distance, but Hope Corner sounded like the kind of place that should be savoured and Amos was in no rush, so he decided to relax and enjoy his walk. It would be a few hours yet before the sun set, and it really was the most beautiful evening. The hedges that bordered the lane were thick with wild dog roses and honeysuckle, and their scent drifted along beside him.

Rounding the bend at last, Amos drew level with a red-brick wall. It was far too high to see over, so he could only imagine the kind of house that lay behind it. He trailed a hand along the wall's rough surface, marvelling at the variety of foliage that had sprouted there, and waited to see what else his senses would pick up.

He stopped for a moment and placed the bag of apples inside his rucksack, tucking the bottle of water into a pocket on the side. His intuition told him he was not far from his final destination and, knowing from Bill's directions that the sweep of wall would eventually give way to the lane up to the farm, he picked up his pace, his heart beating a little faster as he drew level with a sunny-yellow sign that read 'Hope Blooms'. And he smiled. Whether the pun was intended or not, if that wasn't an omen of good things to come, then he didn't know what was.

A little further along was another board, which told him he had arrived at Hope Corner Farm and, as he walked through a double five-bar gate into a wide yard, a distant bark told him he had been spotted. Bracing himself, Amos prepared to be greeted by the elderly black Labrador that lumbered up to meet him, followed by a woman wearing a sky-blue dress underneath a red apron. She had flip-flops on her feet and her mass of curly black hair was left loose to cascade over her shoulders, but it was her smile, stretching from ear to ear, that truly caught Amos's eye.

'Hello!' she called.

Amos waved and waited until they were within speaking distance, smiling down at the dog and offering a hand to meet its wet, inquisitive nose.

'It would seem you've passed the test,' said the woman, still smiling. 'Although to be fair, Brodie makes friends first and asks questions later.' She frowned. 'I probably shouldn't be telling you that…'

Amos lifted both hands in the air. 'Friend, I promise… although to be fair I probably *would* say that.' He lowered his hands and smiled. 'Are you Mrs Jamieson… Flora?'

'I am. Hello. And you must be Amos?'

She smiled again, and Amos felt the subtle change in the air between them.

'You found us all right then?' she added. 'Bill said he'd give you directions…' She paused and Amos knew she was wondering how best to bring up the subject of exactly why Amos was there. Trying to be tactful. 'And he explained that you were looking for some work in return for a place to stay for a while, is that right?'

Amos nodded.

'So, are you… homeless then?'

Again, Amos nodded, waiting while she looked him up and down, taking in his appearance. It was a crucial moment, they both knew that, and there were a lot of things that Amos could say to make his way of life sound rather more appealing, but he often preferred to see how this particular piece of information was received before explaining anything further. Not a test exactly, but revealing nonetheless. It let Amos know where he stood.

Flora's appraisal continued for a few more seconds, her face tilted against the evening sun. At fifty-two, Amos wore what he pleased and if his clothes or his wild black curly hair meant people judged him poorly, then so be it. But only time would tell whether Flora was prepared to see beyond a first impression or, better still, reserve judgement until she knew him better.

'Right,' she began. 'Well, first, you'd have been welcome to come and camp here for free, unless you pitched tent in the middle of the flower field – then of course I would have had to shoot you. And second, I've just this morning been let down by a couple of university students who were going to come and give us a hand for the summer but got a better offer of a month in Greece. So, as far as you working for us in return, I'm only just stopping short of biting your arm off!' She extended a hand towards him. 'Welcome to Hope Corner, Amos.'

He grinned. They were going to get along like a house on fire.

'Thank you. It's very nice to be here.' He let his gaze rest just over her shoulder where he could see a range of red-brick buildings and a patch of garden which was massed with summer flowers.

'So,' he said. 'Hope Blooms.'

'Yes, it does,' she replied. 'Or at least we like to think so. Now, would you like a drink first, before I show you around? That way you can meet everyone at the same time.'

'Only if there's nothing you need doing straight away. There's still plenty of light left in the day.'

Flora narrowed her eyes. 'I think we could let you off work this evening, as you've just arrived, but I do still have all the flowers to water and that takes *ages*.'

'Then I will gladly help,' replied Amos, ruffling the dog's fur. 'Hello Brodie,' he added.

The dog lifted his paw which Amos shook, laughing. 'That's a neat trick,' he remarked, looking back up at Flora, only to find her staring at both him and the dog.

'I've never even seen him do that before!' She laughed again. 'Come on then. Brodie, lead the way.'

Amos realised he was still clutching his loaf of bread and he held it out. He'd been planning to have it for his supper, but that was before he'd met Flora. 'A contribution,' he said. 'It's the least I can do.'

But Flora shook her head. 'Not necessary,' she said. 'But I'll take it anyway, otherwise you'll be carrying it around everywhere and feeling foolish. We can talk when we get inside and work out how we're going to do this, but don't worry for now though.'

The farmhouse kitchen was a big square room, clearly the most used in the house, with a well-worn sofa against one wall and a traditional scrubbed pine table occupying its centre. Seated at either end of this were a much older couple who met Amos's wave with polite interest, but no smiles he noticed. Not yet.

'Amos, this is my mother-in-law, Hannah, and father-in-law, Fraser. Have a seat and I'll get you a drink. What would you like?'

'Just a glass of water if I may, thank you.'

He took the chair nearest to him, closer to Hannah who gave him the briefest of smiles and then nudged her glasses up her nose.

'Are you hungry, Amos?' she asked. 'Only I'm afraid we've already eaten.'

She had a kind face and neatly cut grey hair, and was wearing a colourful floral tee shirt with jeans. Older than him, certainly, but not that old. He shook his head.

'Thank you, but I brought a loaf from the village, so please don't go to any trouble.'

Flora put the bread down on the table.

'Some cake then?' she said. 'Fresh honey cake, made this afternoon…'

'Well, I must admit to having a rather sweet tooth so that would be lovely.' He nodded his thanks.

'Coming right up. I'll just go and fetch Ned. If he hears there's cake and doesn't get a piece, he'll be very upset.'

She smiled and left the room while Amos sat a little awkwardly waiting for the inevitable. The seconds ticked by.

'So, what brings you here then, lad?' asked Fraser somewhat gruffly from the end of the table.

It was a question that Amos never knew quite how to answer. He usually thought that honesty was the best policy, but saying 'a guilty conscience' would have him shown the front door in a matter of minutes. So, instead, he settled for a vague version of the truth that usually sufficed.

'I'd been doing some work not too far from here. It's a beautiful place and as I was passing through I thought perhaps I might like to stay awhile. Flora said you could have need of an extra pair of hands.'

Fraser's eyes narrowed. 'Aye, we do that right enough. What sort of work do you do?'

'Odd jobs mostly, but I can turn my hand to many things. Farms are busy places and I've worked on quite a few before now.'

There was a nod and the steady appraisal continued, but that was okay, Amos expected no less. He could hear Flora returning through the hallway and he looked up just as she arrived, a burly red-headed man close behind. He could see the family resemblance straight away; Fraser was a less hearty-looking, paler version of his son. His red hair was now faded with age to a soft sandy colour, but there was no mistaking where Flora's husband got his looks from.

In contrast to his parents, however, Ned wore a bright grin and immediately strode across to where Amos was sitting, his hand extended in welcome.

'I'm Ned. Flora's been telling me all about you. It's so nice to meet you.'

Amos got to his feet. 'And you. I hope I can be of help. You've just been let down, I gather.'

Ned rolled his eyes. 'Your arrival could not be more perfectly timed. I'm sure we can find you plenty of things to do.'

There was a slight sniff. 'Yes, well, first things first,' said Hannah. 'Now, are you sure a glass of water is all you want to drink, Mr... er...?'

'Fry,' Amos supplied, smiling. 'And thank you, that would be perfect.' He couldn't blame her for her wariness. He'd feel exactly the same way under the circumstances.

*

Half an hour later they were back outside again and Amos's head was buzzing with thoughts. The conversation had become a little less trying as time passed and they'd discussed the many jobs there were to be done on the farm, but Amos couldn't help but feel his instincts had brought him here for a different reason. Past experience had proved that his hunches weren't usually wrong, but only time would tell. The answer would come to him in due course, it always did, he thought as he followed Flora towards a low line of buildings a little further down the courtyard.

'So, this is where we were going to put the students,' said Flora, her hand on the solid oak door to one of the cottages. 'As you'll see, it's very much work in progress. Which is short for, we haven't the time or the money to finish it right now. But we had envisaged the students would take their meals with us, in the main house, so it's just a place to sleep really. And have a little privacy.' She lifted the catch and pushed open the door. 'It's rather basic though, I'm sorry.'

Amos smiled at her concern. The fact that it hadn't even occurred to her this was far better than he was used to made him like her even more. He didn't tell her that the state of the cottage mattered little to him, and that his creature comforts were not to be found *inside* a house at all, because a kindness was a kindness and Amos was very fond of the phrase *you reap what you sow*. It had stood him in good stead over the years.

'It's no problem. I'll be working all day so I just need a place to come inside if it's wet.' He looked around the room that he guessed, in time, would become the kitchen but for now contained no more than an old fridge and a small table pushed up against one wall with a kettle, a toaster, a tray of cutlery and a collection of mugs and glasses on top. Another table stood in the middle of the room along with two mismatched chairs. 'Would it help if I fixed this place up for you?' he asked.

'Can you even do that?' asked Flora, astonished.

Amos smiled, deducing that now might be a good time to explain a little more about himself.

'You asked me earlier if I was homeless,' he said. 'And, strictly speaking, that's not true. I do have a home, I just choose to let someone else live there and instead I travel… I meet amazing people, who have amazing stories, and mostly I find that they need help of one sort or another, and so I fix things… buildings mostly—' He broke off. He'd almost said 'and people too', but stopped himself just in time. 'Or I do odd jobs, whatever is required. But, like I said before, I can turn my hand to most things. I'd be happy to have a chat about anything you'd like doing.'

Flora took her time looking around her as she weighed up Amos's offer.

'It sounds as if you're prepared to stick around for a while then?' she said eventually, dropping her gaze to the floor before lifting it again and meeting Amos's look square on. 'Only, we can't afford to pay anyone,' she added. 'We'd like to, and work like this *should* be paid for, but the simple fact of the matter is that board and lodging is about it, I'm afraid.'

'That's all I ever ask for,' replied Amos. 'And I can stay for as long as you need me.'

'What, like Mary Poppins?' quipped Flora.

Amos smiled and said nothing.

She was watching him again and, as a gentle smile slowly transformed her face, she shook her head. 'Do you believe in fate, Amos?' she asked. 'Only it was just this morning that our students let us down and I was wondering how on earth we were going to manage. And then you turn up out of the blue! Makes you wonder, doesn't it?'

Amos ran a finger along the grain of the wooden table. 'Don't ever stop wondering, Flora. Life would be very dull if we didn't.'

He straightened up, drawing in a breath, and shrugging his rucksack from his shoulders, placed it onto a chair. 'Right, I'll pop my stuff here for the minute and then I think you mentioned something about some watering that needed doing.'

Flora smiled. 'Come with me,' she said, beckoning with her finger.

Amos followed her out of the cottage and back towards the main house, turning off onto a path that led through to the gardens. The evening air was soft and still balmy from the heat of the day, insects darting here and there as Amos and Flora walked through an area of longer grass towards a patio surrounded by flower beds and bright with huge tubs of flowers. Beyond the patio was a line of bigger bushes and trees, and it was towards a ranch fence among them that Flora was headed. Amos reached out a hand to push aside a low-hanging willow branch which bordered the edge of the garden, and felt his heartbeat began to quicken. All of a sudden it became very obvious what Flora had brought him down here to see.

In front of him, and stretching out both to the left and the right, was a field filled with more colour than Amos thought he had ever seen in his life before. Flowers, massed in rows – pinks, purples, reds, yellows, vivid oranges, soft blues and heathery purples, all laid out in riotous glory before him. He turned to Flora open-mouthed.

'You'd better get used to eating honey, our local bees have had somewhat of a party,' she said, grinning.

He struggled to find his words as a swell of emotion washed over him. He had never expected to find such beauty so close at hand, and he was utterly unable to speak.

'I know,' said Flora. 'It fair takes your breath away, doesn't it?'

Amos could only nod.

'Hope Blooms,' she added, in case any further information was necessary.

It took a few moments for Amos to gather his wits, his eyes sweeping from side to side. 'And you planted all these?' he asked. 'By hand?' He scratched his chin. 'I'm no expert on flowers but, from what I do know, these grow mostly from seed, would that be right?'

It was Flora's turn to nod. 'Grown from seed, pricked out, and planted out, every single last one of them. Weeks and weeks of back-breaking work… We must be mad…'

Amos shook his head. 'And that's your reward,' he said, turning to look at her. 'No wonder you'd do it all again in a heartbeat.'

He saw a slow smile spread across her face as she acknowledged the truth in his words. And he could see just how she was feeling; her pride in what they had achieved, her awe and profound love of the flowers that had grown as if from her own fingertips.

'And now of course, they need to be watered, and cared for, plant by plant…' he added.

'Yep.' Flora breathed out in an excited rush. 'And picked… ready for our brides, our shops, our birthday bouquets, our anniversary surprises. You wouldn't think, would you, that at the beginning of the year Hope Corner was a dairy farm?'

Amos stared around him. 'A dairy farm?'

'Yep, wall-to-wall cattle…'

'So how did you…?' He shook his head in amazement. 'That's quite some transformation.'

'It had to be. We'd reached a point in time where things needed to change; dairy farming wasn't working for us, so we had to have a sharp rethink. And the flowers were it.'

'And let me guess… this was your idea, Flora. Ha! Even your name fits!'

'Yes, well… but you're right, I am to blame – quite how much remains to be seen. But so far so good.'

It made absolute sense. Amos could see how much work was involved and his arrival would seem to have been perfectly well timed but, still, there was something missing… Something buzzed at the back of his mind and he thought back to Flora's earlier words, suddenly coming to full alert.

'So, the bees?'

'Ah, yes…' She angled her body slightly, and pointed to her left, up high, to the hill which swept up from the edge of the fields. 'That's where they live,' she said. 'Our neighbour keeps them.'

Amos laughed. 'I would imagine they feel like they've died and gone to heaven with all these flowers,' he remarked.

'I should imagine they do,' replied Flora. 'Grace will know. She talks to her bees all the time. She says they know *everything*,' she added, laughing.

Do they now, thought Amos. Do they indeed.

He glanced up at the sky. 'You mentioned before about the watering...' He trailed off, staring out across the field and wondering quite what he had let himself in for.

There was a peal of laughter from beside him. 'Oh, don't worry, not *these* flowers... Blimey, I wouldn't want to water this lot by hand. No, it's just the ones in pots up around the house, although that's bad enough.' She looked at him, shaking her head in amusement. 'I still don't quite believe this... you... but I'm not going to argue. Come on, I'll show you what's what.'

It didn't take too long with them both working at it, but Amos could see that, without his help, the task of watering all the flower pots and troughs that lined the walls of the courtyard and stood outside gates and doorways all over the farm would have taken Flora quite some time. It was her last task of the day and Amos was glad that she would now have the opportunity to go and enjoy the rest of the evening with her family.

He wandered back out into the courtyard once they were done, staring up at the sky. Dusk was still an hour or so away yet and, having checked first with Flora that it was okay for him to take a walk and get a feel for the lie of the land, he began to stroll towards the fields where they had been earlier. The reason why he was really here would come to him, it always did. And if by some rarity his intuition had let him down, well then, there was still plenty to keep him occupied on the farm. Surely there was no nicer place to be for the summer. Reaching the gate into the field, he eyed the foxgloves which lined the hedges to his left and then he followed the hum of the bees.

Chapter Two

Grace added two spoons of sugar to the mug of tea she was making and stirred it thoroughly before passing it to her husband. 'Paul, please keep your voice down, people will hear.'

Paul glared at her for a moment before snatching the cup away sulkily. 'Is that all you're worried about, that people will hear? Well, so what? This is my house, my kitchen, and if I want to shout then I bloody well will. In fact, I think I'll shout some more... Who's going to hear anyway? We're in the middle of nowhere and those country bumpkins next door are probably glued to *The Archers* by now, sucking their rich tea biscuits and sipping their cocoa.'

'Those "country bumpkins" are my friends, Paul. Besides, I really don't think calling them names is going to make any difference to the situation.'

'Hah!' snorted Paul, his face twisting. 'Is that what you call it – "a situation"? You tell me you want a divorce and then call it a situation. Well, that's not the word I'd use, honey. "Betrayal", now there's a word, or how about "ungrateful cow", or are you going to get all pedantic on me and say that's two words?' He took a slug of tea, his jaw working as he thought up his next missile.

Grace eyed him calmly, noting that he was still quite happy to drink the tea she had made him. 'I am neither ungrateful, nor a cow, Paul.

Before you throw your next insult at me, let me just tell you yet again why I want a divorce.' She took in another steadying breath.

'Firstly, let me tell you that making a marriage work usually involves a little effort, and it certainly involves a little monogamy! Your protests would go down a lot better if you hadn't just come home from entertaining your latest fling. Secondly, I have today, as most days, washed and ironed and cleaned and cooked for you without so much as a thank you or a helping hand. I have also entertained your countless slimy colleagues and their gossipy wives over the years in the name of your career and, as well you know, have done all these things without question, as your wife. Yet not once do I recall you *ever* asking me what would help *me* or make *me* happy.'

Grace could feel the heat rising up the back of her neck as she summoned up a steely glare that she hadn't even known she was capable of. Her voice sank even lower as she continued.

'Today though, Paul, you reached a new low, even for you. Earlier this morning I received this email from your assistant, Barbara, and would be very grateful if you could explain to me just how you thought you were going to get away with this.' She handed over a single sheet of paper with a shaking hand, willing it to stay steady.

Paul snatched the paper from her. His eyes, which had narrowed further and further over the last few minutes, were now mere slits. She drew no pleasure from the fact that his face, usually a perma-tanned mahogany, was becoming paler by the minute. A colour that usually meant only one thing; she readied herself for the explosion.

'The stupid cow,' spat Paul. 'She is *so* fired!'

'Yes, I thought she might be,' Grace replied calmly. 'Incidentally, so did she. Which is why, while you were busy cavorting with the TV station's weather girl this afternoon, she cleared out her desk in preparation for a new job that starts tomorrow. As you know, PAs of her calibre are very hard to come by. So, now I know that Barbara is out of harm's way, I'll ask you again: just how did you think you were going to sell this house out from under me?'

Paul's fist was white at the knuckle around his mug of tea. 'Oh clever, *very* clever,' he snarled. 'But the house is in my name, it's mine to do with what I please. I've always hated it; it's so horrifically *twee*, like everything in this godforsaken village. So while you're in your *twee* little shop tomorrow, with your *twee* little pots of honey, having *twee* little conversations, I will arrange for an estate agent to value it and tell me just how much I can sell this heap for. You can have your divorce, darling, but you'll be looking for a new place to live too.'

Grace gulped down the ball of anxiety that had lodged itself in her throat. She had known for a long time that the end was coming, that one of these days Paul would present her with the final straw, but it didn't make it hurt any less. It was time to play her final card.

'You might think me many things, Paul, but I'm not a fool. I know about the money you have stashed away in accounts you thought I never knew existed. I know about the flat too, your little bolthole in London. So, you need to listen to me very carefully now. I am not leaving this house, Paul. It's my home, and I have loved and cared for it over many years, just as I have you. Living here is the only thing that has kept me sane in this sham of a marriage and you owe me this one courtesy after everything I've done for you.'

She paused, taking a big breath to steel her nerves. 'I will make no claim on any of your assets if you walk away now and leave me the house. If not, then I will be forced to use select pieces of information given to me by Barbara to take my rightful share of *everything* you have.'

'You wouldn't bloody dare, Grace. Not little Grace who wouldn't say boo to a goose. Why do you think I married you, sweetheart? Because you knew on what side your bread was buttered, and you still do. You won't create the kind of fuss you're talking about, you don't have it in you. Nice try, darling, but you're fooling no one.' He handed the mug back to her. 'See you tomorrow, Grace.'

'It's with my solicitor,' she blurted at his retreating back, her resolve almost gone.

Paul turned slowly towards her once again. 'I beg your pardon?'

'The information from your PA. It's with my solicitor in a sealed letter addressed to Dominic, your Head of Programming. If I don't call my solicitor by five p.m. tomorrow he will email Dominic with the contents that evening and have the letter couriered over the following morning.' She held her breath. Dominic was the last person she wanted to contact, especially given what had happened, but she really needed Paul to believe her.

A nerve twitched in the side of Paul's jaw. He shook his head slowly. 'Well, well, Grace. If I'd have known you had this much fight in you, I would have made much more of an effort, especially in the bedroom… Wouldn't that have been fun? You'll be hearing from me, Grace. Me *and* my solicitor. Don't think this is over.' And with that he stalked from the room.

Grace waited until she heard the spin of gravel on the driveway before letting out her breath, slowly at first and then in great gulping gasps. By the time her legs had buckled from underneath her and she'd sunk to the floor, her breaths had given way to choking sobs. It was tempting to stay that way but the minute the thought entered her head she realised she could not. A sudden revulsion swept over her and she held a hand over her mouth for a moment before rushing up the stairs and into their bedroom. She stared at the bed, a place she had often slept alone, assailed by memories of the past few years. And then she pulled off every stitch of clothing she was wearing and stuffed it all in the laundry basket. She had never felt more dirty than she did now.

She stood in the shower for quite some time, scrubbing furiously at her skin and her hair, washing herself repeatedly as she sought to remove the poison of her words before they sank so deep they could never be cleansed. But then, as her breathing eased, she let the silky coolness of the water mingle with her tears and wash it all away. The tears were not about the end of her marriage, not really – she had shed enough of those over recent years to know that her grieving process was almost at an end – but rather they were a reaction to the depths to which she'd had to sink to protect herself, and her home.

It had taken her a long time to plan what to say to ensure she only had to say it once. She had rehearsed her lines over and over, until it had become a part that she could play just like an actor; convincing, but not real. Not *her* words, not the real Grace, just the mantle she'd had to assume to get her through the evening.

She switched off the water and stepped from the shower, wrapping herself in a plain white towel before walking back through to the peace and tranquillity of the room she had designed for exactly that purpose. The window overlooked the garden and she stood looking down on it, just as she had on countless other occasions, except that tonight she felt just a tiny bit closer to making the peace absolute. Who knew what tomorrow would bring, but she had spent a long time preparing herself for what was to come. Tonight she just wanted to enjoy her garden without worrying what mood her husband would be in when he got home. Even this small pleasure was enough to lift her spirits as relief settled gently around her like the soft evening air.

Taking a clean pair of pyjamas from a drawer, she dressed quickly, pulling the towel from her hair and letting it fall halfway down her back in long grey tendrils. And then she turned and looked at herself in the full-length mirror. Her eyes were a little puffy, but her skin was still clear and almost unlined, her body slender, her limbs graceful. Grace And Decorum, she thought to herself, smiling softly as she remembered her mother's words of long ago. Perhaps it wasn't too late after all. Maybe there was still time to bring back to life the confident and vital woman she had once been. Her hopes and dreams might have been squashed by her husband's bullying behaviour but there was a new future settling ahead of Grace, full of possibility, and she would navigate it as best she could. She could ask no more of herself.

The air was especially fragrant tonight, a slight breeze carrying the scent from Hope Farm's flowers up towards her and, after the heat of the day, the grass was now cool as she walked barefoot across it. She didn't even think about where she was going, the hum of the hives drew her as surely as if she were being reeled in on a line. It would be good to talk to the bees, to put their minds at rest.

'Good evening,' she whispered as she neared the first of the hives. 'It's a beautiful night.'

After a moment, she lowered herself to the ground and sat cross-legged on the grass, well out of the bees' flight path, but close enough that she could see them, still busy about their work even at this hour. There was something about keeping bees that Grace always found particularly soothing. Not that they really needed her help of course, and she never thought of them as belonging to her, more that she belonged to them. She was an honorary member of the hive, tolerated as long as she abided by their rules. Whichever way round it was, Grace enjoyed the sense of belonging that it gave her. And her bees had forever changed the way she viewed the world, and for that she would be eternally grateful.

She stilled herself and tried to empty the last of the angry and negative thoughts from her head. Some people said that bees could sense prevailing moods and, while Grace wasn't sure whether that were true or not, she always made sure that when she invaded their space she was as calm and serene as possible. They reacted to her almost instantaneously whenever she lifted the lid of the hive. When removing the combs for inspection, it was as if a wave rippled through them, a change in their movement, a tonal difference in their humming, the machinery of the hive shifting a gear. And there were times when Grace would keep her distance, when something told her that it wouldn't be a good time to disturb them, a darker note.

Tonight though, there was something else. She listened, sifting through the sounds she heard and discounting those that belonged outside of the hive – the birdsong, the rustle of leaves – until there was just the sound of the hive itself. They were busy; summer was at its height and the hive was hot, they had lots of nectar to cure into honey. Grace was used to this noise, the hum of a contented hive, but tonight the tone was raised up a notch; not unhappy, quite the reverse in fact. If Grace had to put a name to it, she would say they sounded excited…

*

Away down the slope of the hill where Grace's garden met the field, Amos had stopped, his face turned to the sky. After leaving Hope Farm he had simply set out to walk the edge of the field, to see up close the flowers that grew there and get a feel for the space around the farm. But, as he had walked further and felt the prickles at the base of his neck, he knew he had been drawn to this particular place by something.

Sitting there for a little while, he had heard voices; not loud enough to make out individual words, but there was no mistaking the anger in the sounds he heard. Dark, almost like thunder. Amos could feel them cut through the soft summer air outside the house. He had felt torn and misplaced, almost as if he were trespassing – even though he knew he had every right to be where he was – but at the same time completely rooted to the spot.

Now, though, the air was calm once more. Whatever, or whoever, had shattered the peace was gone, but it had still left its mark on Amos. He rubbed the back of his neck. Now it was all beginning to make sense.

Chapter Three

The dream was always the same. As Amos awoke drenched in sweat and clawing at the images in his head, he was grateful that while it was still a nightmare, the intensity of it was less than the last time. This dream was his weather vane, the thing that drove him onward, telling him that it was time to seek out somewhere new, someone else with a problem that he could solve to assuage his guilt. Now that he had arrived at Hope Corner he hoped its occurrence would lessen for a while.

He rolled over, shivering in the cool of the early-morning air, and got to his feet. He had slept in the field, under the edge of the hedgerow. After a bit of a walk to stretch his legs and shake off the last vestiges of the dream, he was just coming through the garden on his way to the cottage when he caught sight of Ned's father leaning against the wall of the house. He raised a hand in greeting.

'Good morning,' Amos called. 'It's going to be another beauty!'

Fraser turned to him, lifting the mug he held in his hand as if in salute. 'I confess I don't much mind what the weather does these days,' he replied. 'Having thought at one time I wasn't going to see another sunrise, just as long as they keep coming, I'll keep being grateful.'

Amos gave him a quizzical look.

'Heart attack,' replied Fraser, succinctly. 'Five months back, followed by a double bypass.' He touched a hand to his chest. 'I've got a scar from here… to here… And every morning when I get up and every evening as I go to sleep it reminds me to make the most of what I've got left.'

Amos nodded. 'It gets you like that, doesn't it? Nothing like a dose of your own mortality to keep you in good health.' He joined Fraser, feeling the warmth from the brick at his back even at this early hour.

'And what would you know about mortality?' asked Fraser. 'A young 'un like you?'

Amos slid him a sideways glance. 'I'm older than I look,' he said as evenly as he could. The dream was still all too fresh in his mind and hiding the truth was not always that easy. He and mortality had been very well acquainted for a number of years now. 'Anyway, how are you doing?' he asked, changing the subject. 'Not that I know a great deal about it, but it seems to me that recovery from what you've been through doesn't happen overnight.'

'Aye, you're right about that, and some days it feels as if this body of mine isn't ever going to do what I want it to, but I'm getting there. And what Flora's done for us, well it's turned us right around. Never thought I could get that excited about flowers before, but it would seem I can…' He trailed off, smiling. 'Course I might feel differently once I'm properly back at it. I'm still on what the missus calls "light duties" at the moment, which means I don't get my hands dirty. But there's plenty still to be done.' He narrowed his eyes. 'Which I reckon is where you come into things… Funny, you just turning up like that…' He cleared his throat. 'I don't mean to sound ungrateful or nothing, but not sure I totally understand it, all the same.'

Amos didn't blame him. He'd probably be saying exactly the same things if he was in Fraser's position. He looked out across the garden, knowing that the man deserved some sort of an explanation.

'I had a regular life once,' Amos began, carefully. 'Same as most people. I went out to work, I paid my mortgage and my bills, went drinking with friends on the weekend. But then, like you, something just came along when I wasn't looking and changed all that. And then it seemed like the life I had before didn't belong to me any more... and it was time to find a new one. So, I left home. Rented my house out, and followed the sun, to see if I couldn't find something that made a difference.'

'Aye... and did you?' asked Fraser, taking a swig from his mug.

Amos turned to look at him. 'Yes,' he said clearly. 'I found plenty. It took a while, not surprisingly seeing as how I didn't know what I was looking for in the first place. But then, I learnt to trust my instincts, to follow what I knew to be right, and after that, well the rest just seemed to take care of itself. I found a reason to keep going, Fraser, just like you have. It may not be the same as what other people have, but it works for me.'

Fraser upended his mug, draining out the dregs of his tea into the flower pot that stood beside him. 'Sounds to me like there's a bit more to it than that,' he said. 'But as long as you promise to look after what we have here, I reckon you're entitled to keep that to yourself until you're ready to tell us.'

'You have my word,' replied Amos, solemnly.

'Fair enough then, lad.' Fraser coughed slightly, pushing himself away from the wall. 'Now then, Flora tells me you might be the man to fix up our cottage. And I can't deny that wouldn't be mighty useful.' He squinted into the sun. 'You'd best come with me. Have a spot of breakfast and then you can look at the plans, see what we have in mind. That sound any good?'

'It sounds perfect,' said Amos, smiling, as he followed Fraser into the house.

The kitchen was already humming in readiness for whatever the day might bring. Hannah was at the cooker, stirring a big pan of something, and Ned and Flora were already sitting at the table, a sheaf of papers spread out in front of them. The old dog gave a soft woof of greeting as Amos entered and slowly got to its feet.

'Well, someone has definitely made a friend,' remarked Flora. 'Would you look at that, out-and-out favouritism…'

Brodie crossed the room to stand by Amos's side, pushing his nose against Amos's hand as he ruffled his fur.

'Come and sit down,' added Flora. 'We're just about to have breakfast.'

Hannah turned from the cooker. 'Now, tell me, do you like porridge at all, Amos? Or there's eggs, or beans, and plenty of toast. What would you like?'

Amos smiled; the table was already heaped with fruit, and what looked like a dish of yoghurt beside an almost full jar of honey. 'Porridge would be perfect, thank you. I haven't eaten it in years, but I always liked it as a child. Every morning without fail.'

'It's very good for you,' said Hannah. 'Just the thing to set you up for the day.' She frowned slightly. 'So long as you don't smother it in cream and sugar, that is.'

Amos nodded towards the table. 'I'm rather partial to honey, I'm afraid,' he replied. 'Might I be permitted a little of that?'

Hannah nodded. 'Oh, we make allowances for honey.' She smiled. 'Under the circumstances it would be rather churlish to refuse a gift like that.'

Amos was about to ask her what she meant when he suddenly realised what she was referring to. 'Ah, the bees,' he said. 'Yes, I guess you do rather depend on each other.' He took a seat as Ned pushed a mug towards him.

'Would you like some tea, Amos?' he asked, gesturing at an enormous teapot. 'Please help yourself if you would.'

Ned watched while he did so, waiting until he was settled before continuing.

'Dad mentioned showing you the plans for the cottage this morning, cracking on and all that?'

Amos nodded politely. He was way ahead of Ned and wondered at what point he should speak himself; he didn't want to appear rude. But then Flora smiled across at her husband, a reassuring gesture, and Amos realised that Ned was rather nervous of what he was about to say. People invariably were and Amos had learnt that it was best to be as open as possible, right from the start – it saved no end of embarrassment. If he wasn't much mistaken, with Fraser's heart attack and subsequent recovery, Ned had either been given or assumed the mantle of head of the house whether he'd wanted it or not. Amos had no desire to make the role any more difficult for him than it already was.

He added milk to his mug, before looking back up. 'Yes, and I'd be very happy to help... once you've seen my references and are happy for me to go ahead.' He monitored Ned's expression, currently showing slight surprise. 'I don't think I'd be happy starting work before then. I mean, watering the plants is one thing, but working on a house is something else entirely. You need to be absolutely sure I know what I'm doing.'

Ned's expression changed to one of alarm. 'Oh, I didn't mean. It's not that we don't—'

'I wouldn't expect you to trust me, Ned, you scarcely know me, and the circumstances of my arrival were unusual to say the least. So,

I am neither offended nor embarrassed by your imminent request for information.' He sat back in his chair, grinning. 'In fact, I much prefer it this way.'

Ned's shoulders dropped by several inches.

'I appreciate your integrity, Amos,' he said. 'I wish everyone behaved that way.'

He exchanged a look with Flora that Amos noticed, but didn't comment on, simply smiling instead and dipping his head slightly in acknowledgement.

'Right, well, now you men have squared up and sorted yourselves out,' said Hannah, 'I'd appreciate it if we could eat breakfast before it all goes cold.'

She placed a huge dish of porridge down on the table, together with a toast rack stuffed with thick golden slices. Amos's mouth began to water.

He caught Ned's eye, smiling again, and felt himself begin to relax. This was a good place to be, of that there was no doubt in his mind.

'Besides,' added Hannah. 'This one here…' She pointed to Flora. 'Has a very well-developed sense of intuition, and if she didn't think you were okay, you wouldn't be eating my porridge, make no mistake.'

A bark of laughter shot from Fraser's mouth. 'Welcome to Hope Corner Farm, Amos,' he said. 'You're practically one of the family now.'

'Don't put words in my mouth, Fraser, but… well, carry on as you are, Amos, and I reckon you're welcome to stay.'

Flora picked up a bowl and began to ladle porridge into it. 'Say when,' she said, directing a look at Amos. 'And there's plenty so don't stint yourself.'

Amos didn't nod until the bowl was practically full. He reached for the jar of honey.

'So, what else would you like me to help with while I'm here?' he asked. 'I can take care of the hens too if you'd like. What time do they normally lay?'

Hannah spluttered through a mouthful of tea. 'About eleven at this time of year, but how did you…?'

'I introduced myself to them this morning after I heard the cockerel crowing,' replied Amos. 'I hope that was okay. Besides, anybody with that many eggs lined up in their kitchen has got to have a few hens about the place.'

Flora laughed. 'There's nothing much escapes you, is there?' she said. 'And actually, those eggs are destined for the village shop, but taking them down there always seems to be the one job that no one has time for any more. If you wouldn't mind, perhaps you could take them?'

'Of course,' replied Amos. 'I'd be happy to.'

Fraser's spoon was already scraping his bowl and Amos picked up his own pace a little. The porridge was good: thick and creamy, the honey strong and sweet. He finished it in moments.

'Delicious,' he announced. 'Thank you.' He looked expectantly at Fraser and Ned. 'I'll just go and fetch my papers, shall I? And then you can show me what you'd like doing.'

*

Several hours later Amos found himself back on the road again and heading towards the village, a wicker basket hooked over one arm, his head tilted to enjoy the sun on his skin. He'd spent the morning discussing the work to be done on the cottage; like most farmers, Fraser and Ned could turn their hands to most things of a practical nature and much of the preliminary work had already been done, but things had recently ground to a halt. Amos hadn't wanted to pry too much, but Fraser's illness had clearly forced them to reconsider the future of the farm, hence the major change in direction from dairy to flowers. It was unsurprising to Amos that he had arrived at a rather pivotal moment in the lives of everyone here but, try as he might, he still couldn't get a sense of what any of this might be leading to. Were it not, of course, for the angry voices that he had heard last night. Someone needed help and now he was on his way to meet the woman who kept bees in her garden.

Flora had scribbled Amos a note to explain to Grace who he was so that she wouldn't question why he just happened to be carrying a basket full of eggs from the farm. Not that she would, explained Flora, sure that Grace would take one look at him and welcome him with open arms, but just in case. Amos had smiled and nodded, intrigued by the thought of meeting her.

Somehow he had pictured Grace to be much older than she was, but her wavy grey hair couldn't disguise the smooth skin and confidence of someone much closer to his own age. Only the creases that lay at the corners of her eyes, brought on by half a lifetime of smiling, gave her away as being a little over fifty. They appeared now as she greeted him warmly.

'Good afternoon,' she said. 'Beautiful day—' She was about to say something else when she suddenly frowned. 'Oh,' she said. 'Stand still a minute.'

Amos did as he was asked, his face dropping in confusion as he watched her come around the counter, picking up a piece of paper on her way.

'You appear to have been accompanied into the shop,' she said, still smiling. 'Come on, little fella,' she added. 'Let's get you back out in the fresh air.'

She placed the sheet of paper against Amos's shoulder, and it was only then he noticed that a bee had settled there. Despite Grace's best efforts, however, it refused to be enticed onto the paper so he wriggled his shoulder, holding his head away at an awkward angle to get a better look.

'It isn't dead, is it?' he asked, when it didn't move.

'No, it's alive. Stunned perhaps…'

Amos handed her the basket of eggs. 'Could you hold these a moment?' he asked. 'I'll go outside. Perhaps the air will persuade him to move.'

Grace nodded and took the basket, placing it down on the counter before following him out.

'If he flies off inside, I'll have a devil of a time trying to catch him. They usually end up beating themselves to death against the window.' She shuddered. 'I can't bear it.'

The path to the shop, which passed through a small front garden, was flanked on either side by a low wall and Amos sat down on it, hoping that the flowers behind him might prove more interesting than he was. Grace sat down beside him and glanced at her watch.

'Good job we're not busy today,' she said. 'You weren't in a hurry, were you?'

'Not especially,' said Amos, squinting towards the sun.

'Well, thank you for not running off, screaming,' said Grace. 'Bees don't sting unless provoked but you'd be surprised at the number of people who become almost hysterical.'

'Ah,' said Amos. 'Well, I figured I'm in safe hands. If the beekeeper isn't worried, neither should I be.'

Grace turned, a perplexed expression on her face. 'How do you—?'

Amos laughed, and fished in his pocket for the note that Flora had given him. 'I'm staying up at Hope Corner,' he said. 'And I'm afraid I know *all* about you.'

Her eyes crinkled. 'I did wonder where the eggs had come from,' she replied as she quickly scanned the note. 'Well, Amos, I'm pleased to meet you,' she said, holding out her hand. 'And I'd already worked out that you're a friend; this little chap seems to have taken a remarkable liking to you.'

Amos shook her hand, instinctively knowing the moment before his hand touched hers what it would feel like. He saw the flicker of surprise cross her face too, but then he dropped her hand and, bending down, picked a forget-me-not from the side of the path. He held it out.

'Do you think this might help?' he suggested, smiling to himself as his purpose in Hope Corner suddenly became clear.

Grace took the flower and held it against Amos's shoulder, murmuring a stream of encouragement to the tiny creature. 'Aha! There you go, see, isn't that better?'

She turned and transported the bee from the forget-me-not onto the middle of a rose head that was poking over the top of the wall. They both watched it for a few moments as it explored its new home, cheering when it finally flew off.

Grace glanced at her watch again. 'Right, where were we?' She stood up, a troubled look crossing her face.

Amos followed her back inside the shop, sensing that the relaxed atmosphere that greeted him when he first arrived would be gone, replaced by something… He couldn't quite put his finger on it. Not hurried or fraught particularly, but changed somehow.

Back behind the counter, Grace pulled the basket of eggs towards her and began to remove the trays it contained.

'Three dozen?' she said.

Amos nodded.

'I have Hannah's money here from the last lot,' she added. 'Would you like to take it for her?'

Amos was torn. He wasn't sure whether Hannah would appreciate him dealing with the money on her behalf, and yet if he didn't take it, it would mean another trip to the shop for someone to collect it.

'We can leave it on the tab…' prompted Grace.

Or indeed Amos could be the one to return…

'I think I'll leave it,' he said, before his head had even fully considered the options. 'I can always pop back if necessary.' His own words surprised him.

Grace smiled. 'Right you are then.' She looked at him expectantly. 'Was there anything else?'

Their business was concluded but Amos was still staring at her, feeling a little like a rabbit caught in the headlights. He should say something, but he had no idea what. And then it came to him.

'I might just have a look around, if that's okay… in your other room. I didn't get the chance when I was here yesterday.'

Grace waved her hand. 'By all means. It's a bit of an Aladdin's cave; gifts, handmade crafts, local produce. There are some wonderful things and then some of it is… well, absolutely dreadful actually…'

She gave him another smile, but much tighter than the relaxed welcome of earlier. There was a new tension he just couldn't quite put his finger on.

The shop bell sounded and Amos backed out of the room, nodding gratefully at the customer who had just entered. It made his exit rather less awkward than it might otherwise have been. The shop, previously a house, was essentially two front rooms either side of a central hallway and as he crossed into the other room he was immediately struck by a series of botanical prints facing him on the top shelf of a display cabinet on the opposite wall. They were simple in design and beautifully composed, printed mainly in black and white, but here and there a flower head or two had been splashed with colour and accented with gold highlights. They were modern but nonetheless had a timeless quality to them which Amos greatly admired. He stood for a few moments considering each print individually before standing back and taking them in as a group. Amos didn't own much, but these he would be happy to take possession of.

He moved away, looking at the other items for sale, smiling when he reached those which Grace had quite correctly described as dreadful. Still, they were the results of someone's proud labours and Amos didn't doubt that one day, somewhere, they would find the perfect home. As he browsed, he kept one ear on the sounds of conversation drifting through from the other room; not because he wanted to eavesdrop but simply to garner when the customer might be about to leave. Hearing such a cue, he returned to stand in front of the prints and then carefully removed one from its shelf.

Pausing by the doorway into the main shop, he stood aside to let the customer pass by him. He was about to speak when he realised that Grace was staring out through the window of the shop, utterly lost in thought. At first, he assumed she must have been looking at something in the road until he realised that her look was vacant, seeing only the things inside her head and nothing of what the outside world had to offer. He hesitated, unwilling to break her reverie, but then, as he watched, she gave a sudden start, checked her watch again, and frowned.

'Is everything all right?' he asked, moving forward.

Grace looked up, startled, seemingly having forgotten that Amos was still in the shop, but then she recovered herself and the smile was back in place.

'Beautiful, aren't they?' She gestured towards the print in his hand.

'Only you've checked your watch at least three times in the last couple of minutes,' he added, ignoring her comment. 'And on none of those occasions have you looked particularly happy. Are you waiting for someone? Or something?'

Grace sighed and shook her head. 'I'm sorry, it's just that—' She broke off and made a noise that sounded almost like a growl. 'It's just so… frustrating!'

Amos waited to see if she would continue to explain, thinking that perhaps it wasn't something appropriate to share in public, or with a complete stranger like himself. He smiled, nodded encouragingly and waited some more while Grace chewed the corner of her lip.

'It's the not knowing, you see,' she said. 'Whether anyone is even going to turn up… And if they do turn up what they're going to say. I can't be there, obviously, because I'm here. If I'd have had more notice, I could have arranged with Bill to change my shifts. Which is of course *exactly* why Paul planned it for today.' She stared at Amos, as if waiting for his reaction. 'In fact, if it hadn't been for his secretary tipping me off, I still wouldn't be any the wiser.'

'No, quite…' murmured Amos. 'Is there anything… perhaps I can help?'

Grace was just about to reply when she suddenly stopped. 'Oh, God, listen to me. I'm so sorry, Amos,' she said, searching his face. 'I don't even know why I did that; blathering on about things which you know nothing about and which I had no right to trouble you over.

Goodness, I've only just met you...' She touched a hand to her hair as a slow flush spread up her neck.

But Amos smiled. 'Perhaps it's just that it's easier to talk to a complete stranger...' He rubbed a hand across the back of his neck. 'I've been told I'm a good listener...'

Grace cocked her head, thoughtfully. 'You are, aren't you,' she said. 'There's something about you. Something still... and calm.' She shook her head. 'No, it wouldn't be at all fair. I'm not going to move house whether an estate agent turns up today or not, and I absolutely meant what I said yesterday. If my husband thinks—' She broke off. 'I'm doing it again. Oh, for goodness' sake.' She turned away and moved back behind the counter.

Amos looked down at the print still in his hand, her words tumbling through his head, the memory of raised voices from her garden pricking at him.

'Grace?' He stood still, waiting for her to look up. 'Can I help?' he asked again. 'I could go to your house, not inside, but stay in the garden, and just see if anyone appears? At least then you'd know.'

'But you don't understand anything about this.'

'Do I need to?' Amos was thinking fast. 'I could just say I'm the gardener or something...'

Grace looked at her watch.

'When are they due?'

Her sigh was audible. 'In ten minutes... but you don't even know—'

'I know where your house is, Grace, I realised I was at the bottom of your garden last night when I went for a walk. Flora had mentioned it, you see, she talked about your bees... So I could just climb over the fence and, hey presto, I'm in the garden, just like I said.'

'I don't know, it doesn't seem right.'

Amos smiled. 'Look, you don't need to tell me anything. All you're interested in is whether an estate agent arrives to value your house today, is that right?'

Grace nodded. 'Yes, but I—'

'So, I can go and see if anyone turns up and report back to you. End of story. I don't need to know any more. And I won't talk to them, I'll just act like I'm a clueless gardener – which won't be hard under the circumstances.'

The clock was ticking and Amos could see how aware Grace was of this fact. She looked at him again, and then back down at the slip of paper on the counter, the note that Flora had given him. She picked it up, read through it once more, a small smile gathering at the corners of her lips.

'Right,' she said decisively. 'I must be *mad*, but yes, it would be great if you could go and see for me… please. Just observe though – if anyone comes, don't talk to them, okay…?'

Amos rushed forward, placing the print on the desk. 'I'll come back,' he said, already turning and heading for the door. He paused as he got to the doorway. 'What's your last name, Grace?' he asked.

'It's Maynard… why?'

But Amos had already gone.

Chapter Four

Amos was more than ten minutes away. It would take at least that length of time to walk back to the farm, and then he would have to cut through the yard, across the garden and through the flower field beyond before climbing the hill into Grace's garden. But perhaps the estate agent would be late? And they would need time to look around as well, they could well be at the house for half an hour or so…

He broke into a run. He had told Grace that he wouldn't say anything while he was there, but Amos had no intention of doing that. That wasn't the point at all.

Not owning a car and choosing to walk everywhere he went had made Amos pretty fit over the years. He wasn't used to moving quite this fast, but he didn't feel too bad at all as he turned through the gates of the farmyard, shot around the house, and into the garden. He was just about to vault the fence into the field when he met Flora coming through the gate. He raised a hand to wave.

'I'm sorry!' he shouted. 'On an errand for Grace! Got to run, I'll explain later!'

He didn't wait for a reply, smiling at Flora's astonished expression as he charged past her.

It was the slope up into Grace's garden that did for him. As he stood among the trees gasping for breath, he looked at his own watch.

It had taken him nearly twenty minutes to get there, but that should still give him enough time.

He dropped his head, sucking air into his lungs and trying to gather his thoughts at the same time. He was pretending to be Grace's gardener. It was a warm day and it would be okay for him to look a little hot and bothered, but he needed to aim for nonchalant as well; look as if he were comfortable in his surroundings, industrious but not manic. He looked around, searching for a task that would give his presence credibility. With any luck there would be a shed somewhere…

If Grace had designed this garden herself she had done an incredible job. It was beautiful. Every path, hedge, flower bed and area of lawn looked like it had evolved naturally, nothing forced, nothing contrived or overly perfect; cared for but still wild and carefree. Amos had spent a considerable amount of time looking after gardens for other people and he knew none of this was a happy accident. It would have taken careful planning, back-breaking work and a lot of patience to achieve. And, in the middle of it all, elegantly framed with roses and wisteria, was the most beautiful cottage Amos had ever seen. Amos felt the line of his jaw harden, suddenly understanding perfectly why Grace wouldn't ever want to be forced to move from such a place. He'd only just got here and he felt like he never wanted to leave. There must be some way he could help, and all he had to do was find out what that was. Keep your eyes and ears open, he thought to himself, it had always served him well in the past.

As he neared the cottage, he saw a large greenhouse sitting to one side with a shed beside it and he prayed neither would be locked. It wasn't until he got closer, however, that Amos realised there was already a car parked on the driveway. He picked up his pace, frowning when he saw the luxurious make and model of the agent's car; this wasn't some friendly local agent, this was someone from a swanky city office with an expense account to match. He paused for a moment, making sure there was no one in sight, and then he sauntered over to the greenhouse looking to slide the door open with the confidence of someone who did it every day.

Fortunately, it glided back with ease on well-used runners and, sitting inside on a bench, was exactly the prop Amos needed. Reaching for the pair of secateurs, he began to whistle, looking around for something in the front garden that needed deadheading. Making his way around the side of the house, he looked around him, and then peered back at the car with narrowed eyes. He approached it cautiously, circling it as if it were a wild animal, and then looked around him once more before moving forward to peer through one of the tinted windows. Then he went around to the rear of the car, leaned nonchalantly against the boot with one foot up on the bumper and pulled out his mobile phone from his pocket.

It took less than a minute for the muddy Doc Marten boot on the bumper to have the desired effect as the front door to the house swung open and an agitated, slim man in a crisp suit came out carrying a clipboard.

'Can I help you?' he asked.

Amos pointed to his chest. 'Me?' he mouthed, looking around. He removed his foot from the bumper and stood up. 'Not sure it's me that needs the help.' He peered past the man as if to see inside the house. 'Missus Maynard isn't home,' he said. 'Mister Maynard neither. So, what you doing here then?'

The man's eyes rolled in exasperation and then narrowed.

'And who might you be?' he asked.

'The gardener,' muttered Amos. 'What's that got to do with anything? I know where I am and what I'm doing. It's you I'm not sure about.'

'I'm Evan Porter, from Porter and Robinson, Estate Agents. I'm here to value the property.'

'But Missus Maynard didn't say nothing about there being any visitors today.' He frowned. 'For all I know you could be one of these scammer people you see on them TV programmes.'

'And they have keys, do they?' The agent dangled a brass keyring in front of Amos. 'I'm here because Mr Maynard instructed me.'

'Even so. I think Missus Maynard would have mentioned summat. I'd best check with her if it's all the same to you.'

Amos put the secateurs down on the boot of the car to get a better grip on his phone. The agent winced and shifted his weight from one leg to the other as he fished about in his inside jacket pocket. He pulled out a dark-blue, square business card and handed it to Amos.

'There, see.'

Amos studied it for a few moments. 'Looks genuine enough, but you could have had these done somewhere. Doesn't mean you are who you say you are.'

'Oh, for goodness' sake…' He pulled off a piece of paper from his clipboard. 'This is an email from Mr Maynard with his instruction to come here today. Or are you going to quibble about that and say the email could have been from anyone? And while we're on the subject, my client didn't mention that there would be a *gardener* here today. How do I know you're who you say you are?'

Amos bit back the sigh. And then screwed up his face and scratched his head. 'Well now,' he said, slowly. 'I don't have none of them fancy bits of paper, but see that there?' He pointed to a fragrant plant that was climbing up the front wall of the house. 'That's a *lonicera periclymenum* and, over there, that purple flower is a *passiflora caerulea*. Or, if you want it without the Latin, honeysuckle and passionflower. Will that do you?'

The agent nodded. Touché, thought Amos.

He looked again at the piece of paper in his hand and nodded his head, pretending to be mollified at last.

'I reckon that all looks to be okay, Mr Porter,' he said, handing it back. 'And I'm sorry for giving you a hard time. No offence or nothing, but I've worked for the lady of the house for many a year now, and a fine lady she is too. Just looking out for the place, you understand…?' Amos gave a wide smile, but then his face fell and he hesitated, looking a little embarrassed.

'I didn't know they was thinking of moving though,' he said. 'That's rather set me wondering, that has, about my own job. I'm getting on a bit, Mr Porter, not as young as you, that's for sure. Jobs aren't always that easy to come by.' He stared away into the distance.

The agent fidgeted with his papers. 'Look, Mrs Maynard doesn't actually know I'm here today, okay? Her husband is obviously thinking of selling the house or at least would like a current market value and, because he was concerned that his wife would be worried or upset about this, he arranged to have me visit on a day when she was at work. He asked me to deal only with him for the time being and I got the impression that this was so that he could pick the right moment to discuss the matter with his wife. Mr Maynard didn't mention that *you'd* be here today, so I think it wise if you could keep the matter to yourself, otherwise—'

Amos held up a hand. 'I'll not be saying anything, don't worry. I can see how it would look bad for you if I put my big foot in it…' He turned to stare back at the house. 'It makes sense, I suppose. It is a mighty big house and I always said to my missus how it must cost a bomb to heat in the winter, never mind anything else. Times are hard for us all, I guess. I'll be sad to see them go though; been here a long time, and the gardens… well, you can see for yourself. They didn't get like this overnight.'

He pushed his phone back in his pocket and picked up the secateurs, running a hand across the boot of the car. He then leaned down to rub at where his boot had rested on the bumper, polishing away the non-existent mark.

'Must be worth a bit though, a place like this?'

The agent nodded. 'It's a fine property in a very nice location.'

Amos would have liked to have asked exactly how much the property was worth but he thought that was probably pushing it a bit. He looked around him. 'Wouldn't mind it myself if I had the money. I reckon there'll be buyers queuing up from here to the other side of the hill…'

'Well, the market is more limited obviously, for properties above a certain value, but there are always people who will appreciate a house such as this.'

Amos scuffed at the gravel beneath his foot, his eyes downcast. 'So you think it will sell quickly then?'

'Difficult to say… The market's fair just now, but surprisingly not everyone wants such a large garden and, beautiful though this one is, it might actually make the property less desirable.'

'Oh, I see,' replied Amos, looking up. 'Sorry, I was just thinking about my job again, and Missus Maynard of course,' he added quickly. 'She'd be devastated to leave this place. Maybe she'll get to stay here a bit longer after all…' He trailed off, looking at his watch. 'So are you nearly done then?' he asked. 'Or will you be here for a while yet? I best get on, you see…'

The agent consulted his clipboard. 'Not too much longer…'

'And you will make sure you lock up properly, won't you?'

There was a nod.

'Righty-ho then. I'll be in the garden – if you need anything, just shout.'

'I will, thank you.'

Amos raised a hand in farewell and sauntered off, back the way he had come. Well, thank you, Mr Porter, he thought to himself. You've been very helpful, very helpful indeed. Things were beginning to become much, much clearer. When he'd first arrived he hadn't been able to understand why Grace would ever want to leave somewhere like this, but evidently the idea was her husband's, not hers. Now her behaviour in the shop earlier made perfect sense. Amos felt the back of his neck begin to tingle – he would just have to find some way he could help. It wouldn't get rid of the guilt he carried with him everywhere he went, but maybe one more good deed might lift it just a little.

Amos waited in among the flower beds, deadheading the roses and hoping that Grace wouldn't mind, until he heard the sound of car tyres sweeping across the gravel drive. Then he replaced the secateurs in the greenhouse and walked calmly down the slope of Grace's garden, nodding to the bees as he passed. Climbing the fence so that he was back in the field of flowers once more, he scanned the space in front of him, looking for Flora's bright figure; he had an apology to make.

*

That was the third time in a row Grace had jumped when the shop bell went and she was beginning to annoy herself. Worse still was that when she looked up, a hopeful smile on her face, it was to see Helen Bridgewater from the end of the lane, popping in for her bread just like she always did around this time.

'Brace yourself,' she quipped as Helen left to pick up her three energetic boys from school. It was a joke they shared whenever Grace was in the shop, knowing that the bread would provide an after-school 'snack' for the boys and be virtually demolished in no time.

Grace watched Helen walk back to her car, scanning the lane as she did so. Amos had been gone some time, surely he should have returned by now. Not that she knew what she was going to say to him when he did come back. *If* he came back at all. She had reread Flora's note a dozen times now and, despite Flora's admission that even though Amos had turned up out of the blue she felt she would trust him with her life, it didn't change the fact that Grace had just let a complete stranger visit her house. She would more than likely get home tonight to find that Amos had run off with the family silver. She tutted to herself and frowned, running a finger along the edge of a display shelf and heading to the cupboard to fetch a duster.

As she wiped invisible cobwebs from the shelves, she smiled at the memory of him standing in the shop in a white tee shirt under dark-blue dungarees, rolled up at the bottom to reveal bright red boots. His jet-black curly hair wasn't yet threaded with silver but Grace judged him to be around her own age; his deep brown eyes were surrounded by well-worn laughter lines, and the twinkle in them was indicative of his whole demeanour. And yet there was something else about him too, something Grace couldn't quite put her finger on, but which had nonetheless made her reveal things about her life that she would never usually dream of doing with someone she had just met. She was quite annoyed with herself. Whatever must Amos think? And then she shook her head, tutting again. She would apologise at the very least.

Grace put down the duster for a moment and went to make herself a cup of tea. Humming to distract herself while the kettle boiled, she thought about how the flowers in the window display could do with a freshen-up. At least if she kept busy there was a chance her thoughts might stop tormenting her. Deep in contemplation, she carried her tea and the cleaning materials back through to the counter. There, she jumped out of her skin so suddenly that half of her drink slopped out of the mug and spattered across the floor in biscuit-coloured splodges.

Amos was around the counter in seconds.

'Here, let me,' he said.

'No, don't worry, I... Gosh, you made me jump!' Grace hastily put down the mug and bent to mop up the liquid with the duster just as Amos fished a hanky from his pocket to do the same. Their heads crashed in the confined space.

Amos straightened first, catching Grace's arm as she rose, grinning and rubbing her head ruefully. 'Blimey, are you all right?'

'No damage done... Are *you* okay?'

'I think so. But if I start talking gibberish—'

'How will I know the difference?'

'Exactly!'

Grace stared at him for a minute, and then she burst out laughing, their shared amusement sparking across the space between them.

'Look, just stay where you are,' she said, still grinning, as she placed a hand on his chest to hold him at bay. 'Or we'll both be unconscious...'

She bent again and quickly mopped up the spillage with the duster, throwing it through the door of the small kitchenette so that it landed in the sink, then she turned back to Amos.

'I was just thinking about you,' she said. 'And then I turned around and there you were.' She frowned. 'In fact, I didn't hear the bell go, which is why you made me jump. Did you just materialise out of nowhere?' As soon as she said it, she felt foolish but there was something about Amos that made the impossible seem possible.

He grinned. 'Nothing so impressive, sadly. The door wasn't properly shut,' he replied.

'Anyway, I'm sorry,' they both chorused at the same time.

Grace spluttered. 'Go on, you first,' she said.

'No, you...'

They laughed again. 'What could you possibly be sorry about?' asked Amos.

'Just that I've made you go all the way over to my house which really wasn't fair,' said Grace, blushing. 'I had no right to drop my problems in your lap and I—'

'You didn't make me,' replied Amos, cutting in. 'In fact, I should apologise. I more or less twisted your arm to stick my nose into your business when I had no right to do that either. It's rather a habit of mine, I'm afraid.'

Grace studied him for a moment; his face was open and entirely honest. He was apologising, but she also got the sense that he had no intention of changing.

'So, what did you find out then?' she asked, teasing. 'Come on, tell me what happened.'

It was meant to be a light-hearted remark, but her face suddenly fell as she caught sight of Amos's sombre expression.

'Someone turned up, didn't they?' She turned slightly so that he wouldn't see the look in her eyes. She had tried to convince herself throughout the entire morning that Paul would never go ahead with the valuation, that he wouldn't dare after what she had threatened him with, and she had just about succeeded. But now she could see the truth of the matter written large across Amos's face. 'Bastard,' she muttered.

Amos held out a hand and nodded. 'I'm sorry, Grace,' he said. 'It was a chap called Evan Porter, from a company called Porter and...' He didn't need to finish, she was already shaking her head.

'Yes, I know of them.'

'He said that your husband was concerned you would be upset by the prospect of selling the house and that he'd been asked to deal only with him. I was pretending to be your gardener, you see, and the agent asked me not to mention anything to you either, saying that your husband wanted to pick the right moment to tell you.'

Grace pressed her lips together, her heart beginning to thud uncomfortably in her chest.

Amos cocked his head to one side. 'May I ask you a question?'

She nodded, just about managing to hold his look.

'You said earlier that your husband... Paul... had arranged to have an agent visit when you couldn't be there, and yet you weren't absolutely sure that anyone was going to turn up. You clearly aren't happy about the prospect of moving and – now that I've seen your house and its garden – I can see why. Forgive me for asking, Grace, but is everything okay?'

Grace opened her mouth to reply with a vague response about the length of time she had lived there and her fondness for the place, but instead, to her surprise, she burst into tears.

Chapter Five

'Grace?'

She glanced up a few minutes later, surprised to see Bill's concerned face hovering anxiously on the other side of the counter. She had completely forgotten the time.

'Is everything okay? Not bad news, I hope?'

Bill eyed Amos suspiciously as Grace gave her eyes one final wipe. She managed a weak smile, inhaling deeply.

'Sorry, Bill, I didn't mean to cry all over the place... Not bad news as such, just a bit of a shock, that's all. It's been quiet,' she added, explaining. 'I lost track of time...'

She rummaged under the counter for her handbag and, spotting it, pulled it out.

'It's time for me to go,' she said, sniffing.

'Oh, right,' Amos replied, looking rather uncomfortable. She smiled at him and then glanced back at Bill.

'This is my... friend, Amos. He was just...'

'Yes, we met last night, when Amos arrived.' Bill nodded. 'Did you get sorted, up at the farm?'

'I did, thank you. Flora and her husband have been great. So I'll be staying for a while and helping them out.'

Judging by the expression on Bill's face he had jumped to the entirely wrong conclusion. Grace cringed with embarrassment. Whatever must he think of her, or Amos for that matter…? Despite how he must have been feeling, Amos stood back politely so that Grace could pass, touching her arm to steady her as her legs wobbled slightly beneath her.

'Great, well, I'll get going then, Bill. Er…' She stopped to look around her. 'Not much to report, nothing out of the ordinary anyway. Although you might want to keep an eye on the cornflakes, not sure why but I've sold several boxes today. I'll see you next week as usual.'

'And you're sure everything is all right?'

'Yes, honestly. Just a bit of an upset, but I'll be fine.' She mustered a bright smile and moved out from behind the counter, straightening her hair.

'Erm…' It was Amos this time.

She turned back.

'I gave you a print earlier,' he said. 'Is it still here?'

'Oh, I put it back on display. I haven't sold it so it should still be there.'

Amos smiled at Bill. 'Then I'd like to buy it, please,' he said, fishing in his pocket and pulling out a twenty-pound note. 'That's right, isn't it?'

Grace nodded. 'It's a Daisy Doolittle,' she said to Bill. 'Do you want me to write it in the book?'

Bill rubbed a crease on his forehead. 'No, no, I'll sort it. You get off now, don't worry…'

Amos gestured for Grace to lead the way. 'I'll pick it up on my way out,' he said. 'No need to wrap it.'

'Right you are then. Well, bye, both of you…'

A minute later, to Grace's huge relief, they were back outside in the fresh air, walking quickly down the path from the shop and into the lane. Grace waited until she reached the slight bend in the road before stopping, knowing that they were now out of sight. She turned to look at Amos, a step behind her, the print tucked loosely under his arm. What did she say? She'd been trying out several opening statements in her head as they marched away from the shop, but all of them seemed somehow forced and rather pompous. And then she noticed the slight twitch at the corner of Amos's mouth and watched it grow until a sudden snort of laughter burst out from his lips.

The tension melted away and, before Grace could draw breath, she was gripped by an irresistible urge to join in.

'Oh my God, stop!' she managed, bent over, clutching at her sides in mirth. But she couldn't stop, and neither could Amos. It was a few moments before either of them could straighten and look at one another without being claimed by a fresh wave of laughter.

She wiped the tears away from under her eyes, the irony of the action not lost on her.

'Why are we even laughing?' she said. 'It's not funny!'

'It bloody is,' replied Amos.

She was about to contradict him, and then she grinned instead. 'You're right, it is.' She lifted her hair away from the back of her neck and let it fall back down around her shoulders. 'Poor Bill; he obviously thought there was something going on between us, and poor you…' she said. 'I probably should apologise, again… I seem to be incredibly good at putting you in awkward positions.'

Amos gave her a sideways glance. 'Would you believe I'm used to it?'

She thought for a moment. 'I would actually.' She began to walk again. 'But I am sorry, both for giving Bill quite possibly the wrong idea about you, and also for crying like that. I'm not entirely sure what came over me.'

'You shouldn't apologise for your tears, Grace,' replied Amos. 'Whether they are shed in sorrow or in happiness, they should be welcomed.'

'Really?' She stared at him. 'Only I have been led to believe that tears are only allowed out in the privacy of our own homes, and just as long as we touch up our makeup afterwards.'

Amos peered at her. 'But you're not wearing any makeup,' he said. 'Are you?'

Grace smiled and shook her head. 'And I can only imagine what I look like...' She sighed. 'Sorry, I wasn't fishing for compliments, but you've been very kind.'

'I simply sat with you while you expressed the depth of emotion you were feeling. And that tells me much more about the kind of person you are than the kind you are not...' He indicated the lane up ahead of them. 'You don't need to tell me anything more, Grace, not if you don't want to, and you certainly don't owe me an explanation. Whatever this is has affected you deeply and I just happened to be there at that particular moment. Some might say that's an opportunity, rather than a misfortune.'

Grace touched a hand to the little crescent-moon earrings she wore. Did Amos know that was how she felt too, or was it just a lucky guess? Either way, it would seem as if Amos *was* involved, however that had come about, and he certainly made her feel better, not worse.

'Do you watch much television, Amos?' she asked, hoping it wasn't a rude question under the circumstances.

'No, I can't say that I do.'

'So when you heard the name Paul Maynard, it didn't ring any bells with you?'

Amos raised his eyebrows.

'My husband is an anchor with the local television network, and host of umpteen programmes for them; entertainment shows, documentaries, Children in Need, you know the kind of thing… Over the years he has risen to become quite a valuable commodity.'

She plucked at a head of dead grass from the side of the road. 'But sadly, over the course of our marriage, some thirty-odd years or so, the value he has placed on himself has increased, while the value placed on our relationship has declined. And, well, after discovering his latest in a long line of affairs, I'm afraid that last night I asked him for a divorce.' She shuddered as a shiver ran down her back.

'Try as I might, I just really don't like my husband very much any more. Luckily, I don't think he really likes me, and he *certainly* doesn't like our house. And for that, I am truly thankful; for the last few years my home has been a haven for me, a place where I can mostly be alone and still try to be the person I have always been. If I truly still loved him, I would have been consumed by his rejection, and I would have lost even more of myself. Does that make any sense?'

Amos nodded. 'Perfectly.'

'And so, nothing has really changed recently except that I'm getting older, Amos. I no longer want to be laughed at by everyone around here who knows what's going on but never mentions it; the sympathetic looks, the shushed comments when I walk in the room. Nor do I want to feel like a stranger in my own home, having to watch what I do or say whenever he's around for fear of igniting his anger, having his nasty words sully the fresh air I'm breathing. But more than anything, I don't want to be with someone who considers me so worthless.' She swallowed, her voice dropping to almost a whisper. 'I think I'm worth more than that.'

It had taken Grace quite some time to admit that to herself, to sift through all the emotions that Paul provoked in her, and to understand that none of his behaviour was her fault. But years of believing herself worthless had left a mark that was not easy to erase. She turned to look again at Amos, who had almost stopped walking, trying to process her words. Had she shocked him?

'I see,' he said quietly. 'I may not know you very well, Grace, but what I can say, is that everyone is worth more than that. Even Paul. He treats himself badly by his actions too. The difference is that he hasn't been able to work that out, whereas you have.' He lifted his head to meet her eyes.

'Yes, I've realised that. Believe me, I've done a lot of soul-searching. But it's not my job to save him either.'

'No,' replied Amos. 'No, it isn't.' He squinted at the sun. 'So, I can understand you not *wanting* to sell the house, but if you divorce, you'll *need* to sell the house for financial reasons, is that it?'

Grace shook her head. 'Not at all. Which is what's so upsetting about all of this. The mortgage on the house was paid off years ago and Paul has pots of money stashed away in various places. He doesn't need whatever the house would raise, and that's not why he wants it sold. You see, the trouble with Paul is that he can't bear to be rejected, even by someone he doesn't want to be with anyway. His arrogance really is quite astounding! I always knew that when it came to leaving him that he would react badly and I would have to fight my corner. And my corner is my *home*, Amos. It's the one thing, the *only* thing that Paul can use against me to make me hurt. But I'm not prepared to let that go, under any circumstances, and he knows it.'

She stopped for a moment, wondering whether or not to go on.

'So, that's what today was all about; Paul deciding whether or not he was going to call my bluff and, thanks to you Amos, I now have the proof that he has.' She touched his arm. 'Which is really why I need to apologise to you. For involving you in this at all. This hateful "game" that Paul seems determined we should play, it's just too sordid for words.'

There was silence for a moment as they walked on. They were nearing Hope Corner and the turn in the lane which would take Amos down to the farm and Grace further on up to reach her house.

Amos frowned. 'I was supposed to be inviting you round for tea. I'm sorry,' he said. 'With all this I'd quite forgotten what Flora said before I left.' He smiled. 'It's such a beautiful afternoon and she said you'd be very welcome to call in after work and eat with them, have a drink, or whatever you prefer.'

Grace considered his words for no more than a millisecond. She really didn't think she could face going straight home today.

'Hope Corner Farm it is then,' she said. 'With any luck Flora will have made up a pitcher of Pimm's. She throws loads of fruit in it, mint too, and we usually have it with homemade lemonade so I can still walk home afterwards.'

She grinned, and brightened her expression. She didn't blame Amos for going all quiet on her, but she felt bad that she had caused it to happen. They would be at the farm in a few minutes, and enough was enough. No more talk about Paul or houses this evening. Tomorrow there would be quite enough time for all that.

*

Flora was crossing the yard as they approached the farmhouse, her arms full of flowers.

'Hello!' she called as she caught sight of them. 'Perfect timing. The kettle's on.'

By Amos's side, Grace laughed. 'When is it not?' she asked, moving forward to admire the blooms Flora had picked.

Amos hung back, happy to see the easy banter between the two women and to let their conversation go at its natural pace. There were tough times ahead for Grace and she would need the comfort and security of her friendship with Flora more than ever. Besides, Amos had work to do. His errand for Grace, worthwhile though it was, had taken up a large chunk of his time and he had hardly earned his keep for the day.

The two women fell into step, moving off towards the house. He stood for a moment to let them pass ahead of him and then made off in the other direction to continue on his way.

'Amos?'

He turned at the sound of Flora's voice.

'Aren't you coming in for a cuppa?' she said, and he could tell that she wasn't just being polite.

'I ought to get on,' he replied. 'But thank you. I'll get some water in the cottage. It's a little cooler now and perfect wall-building weather.'

Flora pulled a face. 'Are you really going to start that now?' she asked.

Amos nodded. 'There are plenty of daylight hours yet. It would be a shame to waste them.'

She frowned. 'Well, okay. But dinner will be at six. And I don't care what you're doing then, you'll stop and join us,' she said. 'No one is allowed to miss dinner. I don't have many rules, but that's one of them.'

Amos gave a small bow. 'Then I shall reappear just before, in case you need a hand with anything.' He started to move away.

'Oh, and just one more thing,' said Flora. 'What's the print?'

Amos had almost forgotten he still had it tucked under one arm. He pulled it out, looking at it for a few seconds before turning it to face Flora.

'One of yours,' he said, smiling.

'But how did you...?' Grace came forward, a quizzical look on her face. 'I don't remember telling you that Flora was the artist and, as far as I'm aware, they're signed *Daisy Doolittle*.' Then she turned back to look at Flora.

But Flora shook her head. 'No, I haven't told him either... and now I want to know too. Come on Sherlock, how did you know that's one of my paintings?'

Amos grinned. 'Isn't it obvious?' He studied the picture for a moment. 'It is signed Daisy Doolittle, but over in the other corner is a tiny set of initials – FJ – that's you, if I'm not very much mistaken,' he added, looking at Flora. 'And then there's the fact that you run a flower farm and, from what I've seen so far, many of your clothes are patterned with flowers too, so I'm guessing they're a real passion of yours. And then there's the painting itself, a bunch of daisies in a bucket, a simple enough subject, but it just looks like you, if I may say so. It looks like it was painted by someone with a smile on their face and a certain... lightness about them...'

Flora stared at Grace and then back at Amos. Her face was ever so slightly pink. 'But that still doesn't really explain it.' She touched a hand to her cheek. 'It's a lovely thing to say, but it still could have been painted by anyone.'

Amos laughed and placed his free hand over his heart. 'Okay,' he said. 'Guilty as charged. Every word of what I just said was true, but there is also the small matter of the pot of paintbrushes I noticed standing by your kitchen sink last night. Artist's paintbrushes...'

Grace tutted and rolled her eyes. 'And there's me thinking you were psychic,' she said.

Flora flapped at her friend's arm. 'Don't be so dismissive, Grace,' she said, turning back towards the house. 'I'm not so sure he isn't.'

Amos smiled as he watched them walk away. It wasn't the first time he had been called that. He held great store by his intuition, that much was true, but mostly he just went through life with his eyes and ears open. People told you pretty much everything you needed to know without even speaking.

He continued through the yard until he reached the cottage and let himself in, propping the print up against a bowl of fruit on the table. Not only had he noticed Flora's paintbrushes yesterday, but when he had visited Grace's garden that afternoon he had noticed a huge pot of daisies on a little patio area where he could imagine Grace sitting. If she had chosen to place those particular flowers so close to where she liked to sit and think or relax then they must be very special to her.

Moving to stand in front of a section of wall which faced the door, he surveyed the bare brick which had yet to be rendered and painted. As long as he was here it would be the perfect place for the print. He rubbed the back of his neck thoughtfully. He would see the painting whenever he came through the door and it would be a good reminder of why he was there.

Chapter Six

Dinner was lovely; taken around a table dragged out under the trees on a triangle of garden that lay on the other side of the yard a little distance from the house. The food was simple but tasty, the conversation easy, and the setting amid the fragrant tubs of flowers idyllic. But even so, Amos excused himself as soon as he judged it polite to do so.

He had work to be getting on with and, as he began to gather together the tools he needed, he noticed that Hannah left the gathering with Fraser and Ned shortly after he did. Perhaps they too had sensed that Flora and Grace might be better left alone. Grace had appeared relaxed throughout the meal but Amos had caught a distracted expression on her face once or twice when she thought that no one was looking.

The task in front of him wasn't difficult but Amos wanted to take his time. The cottage was essentially sound, but the brickwork badly needed repointing in places and the current warm spell of weather meant that now was the perfect time to do it. He took up his chisel and hammer and set to work.

He was some distance from where Grace and Flora were sitting but even though he was much too far away to hear what they were saying, he got the gist of it every now and again as he glanced across at them. He saw very clearly the moment when Grace revealed what had happened the evening before and earlier that day. Flora got to her feet and pulled Grace from her chair, wrapping her in a warm hug, before sitting her back down again and pouring her another drink. Amos looked away. He might not be able to hear what was being said, but they still deserved some privacy.

It was a good ten minutes or so before he glanced up again at the sound of someone walking towards him.

'I've been waving at you the last five minutes,' Flora said as she reached him, a wide smile on her face. 'But something tells me you've been determined not to look in our direction.'

Amos dipped his head slightly in acknowledgement. 'It would have been an intrusion,' he replied.

Flora smiled. 'Well, Grace wants to ask you a question. Would you mind coming over a moment?'

He hesitated, looking down at his clothes which were now covered in brick dust. 'Are you sure that's okay?'

'Amos, neither of us are going to be bothered by what you look like.'

He put down his tools and rubbed his hands together.

'Then I will be happy to oblige,' he replied, following Flora across the yard.

Grace still had a glass in her hand when he reached her, but she immediately placed it down on the table and patted the chair beside her. Her face was blotchy and her nose a little red. Amos looked at her with concern.

'I'm okay,' she said in reply to his unspoken question. 'It's just... just...' She threw up her hands, at a loss to find the words she needed.

'You don't need to explain,' said Amos. 'It's understood.'

Grace held his look and swallowed. 'I've obviously been telling Flora what's been happening, and I'm upset and cross and... well, I'll deal with all that later, but for now what's worrying me the most is what happens next. What I do in practical terms. There's so much to think about, and what's worse is that I don't want to think about it at all.'

'The house?' said Amos.

'Yes, the house,' she replied. 'And if there's a possibility that I am going to lose it, I want to know how long I've got. You spoke to the agent, Amos, did he say anything?'

Amos thought back to their conversation, wishing he had tried to probe a little harder. 'Not a great deal, I'm afraid. I didn't want to say too much myself, thinking it would make him suspicious, so all he really said was that he'd been asked to deal directly with your husband. He didn't give any indication of whether the house would be going on the market, just that he was there to provide a market valuation.'

Grace narrowed her eyes. 'I see. Well Paul would certainly instruct them if he was going to sell. Evan Porter has handled all Paul's other transactions; the ones he doesn't think I know about…'

'One thing he did mention though… I commented on the house being such a lovely place that folks would be queuing up to buy it… and he agreed, but a little cautiously, I thought. Apart from the size of the property, which would put it beyond the financial reach of a lot of folk, he said the extent of the gardens isn't to everyone's liking and it could take longer to sell as a result.'

'Well, that's hopeful at least,' said Flora. 'It could take ages.' She looked across at Grace. 'Still, better not to have to sell it at all… The pig, after all you've done for him, Grace, you'd think he'd have the common decency to leave you the house.'

'Paul wouldn't know the meaning of the word decency,' replied Grace. 'He has chased all my friends away over the years and made it difficult for me to have any kind of life outside of the house, and now he wants to take away the one thing that brings me any pleasure.'

Flora paused for a second. 'What will you do if he does decide to sell? Will you do what you threatened?'

Grace sighed, looking more resigned now than anything. 'Yes, I will...' She broke off, taking a deep breath. 'In fact, it's already done. If I wanted to stop it, I should have called my solicitor by five o'clock this afternoon, but I didn't, so...'

'Grace, you could have used the telephone if you needed to, you only had to ask!' Flora looked horrified.

'No, no. I had no intention of calling. Paul went ahead and sent the agent despite my threat, so now it's in the hands of my solicitor. Dominic, Paul's Head of Programming, will probably already have received an email by now, detailing some of his "activities" – what Dominic may or may not decide to do with that information is his business. And Paul will reap the consequences of his actions. I want nothing more to do with it.' She turned to look at Amos. 'You didn't know I was such a cow, did you?'

He stared at her, his pulse racing as a rush of fierce protectiveness swept over him.

'I don't think that at all! Grace, you...' He stopped himself. What he wanted to say would have been quite inappropriate, and his thought surprised him, sneaking up on him unannounced until that very second. 'None of this is black and white,' he said instead. 'But I don't think you should chastise yourself for what you've done; you've still been treated appallingly. Let's hope that Paul sees some sense and decides not to put the house on the market after all. At least that will be of some comfort to you.'

Grace's hands were clasped in her lap, one thumb rubbing across her knuckles. 'Except that that will be the point at which my fight really begins.'

Flora leaned forward. 'What do you mean?' she asked.

'Because, as I said to Amos earlier, Paul does not like to lose, especially to someone he considers beneath him. Even if I get to keep the house, he'll still find a way to make life difficult for me. I'm not foolish enough to think that he would openly offer me a generous settlement in a divorce – and actually I'd rather not have his money at all. He'll fight me financially every inch of the way. You said it yourself, Amos, it's a very fine house, and it costs a fortune to run. I have a small income from my job at the shop and some modest savings which I started scraping together once I'd begun to read the writing on the wall, but it won't last long. Even if I do get to keep the house, I really have no idea how I'm going to continue living there.'

Flora's mouth dropped open. 'Oh, Grace. I had no idea…'

Grace gave a weak smile. 'So you see, I'm rather going to have my work cut out for me…'

'But there must be something you can do. You've done nothing wrong, and it's just not right that Paul should win like this.'

'But I have no skills, Flora. My age is against me, and a lifetime of cooking, entertaining and keeping house so that Paul could impress all his showbizzy friends has left me qualified for absolutely nothing.'

Amos looked across at Flora. His thoughts had been whirling at ninety miles an hour for the last couple of minutes and he wondered whether Flora's had been heading in the same direction. They were sitting in the middle of a farm that had undergone a total transformation in a matter of months, and Flora herself had been its instigator. If anyone was capable of making something out of nothing, it was her. He would wait just a moment more to see if she would say anything. Her lips were currently pursed, and her brow furrowed in frustration; she was definitely thinking about something. She caught him looking at her and raised her eyebrows.

'Penny for them, Amos?'

He dipped his head. 'No, you go first. What was it you were going to say?'

'Me? I wasn't going to say anything. I was just thinking.'

'And?'

Flora raised her eyebrows even further. 'Well, if you must know, I was about to tick you off, Grace.'

Grace had just taken another sip of her drink and she coughed slightly.

'Because what you just said sounded like the kind of thing that would have come out of Hannah's mouth when I first got here,' she continued, frowning. 'That whole "a woman's place is in the kitchen" thing, and you are so much more than that, Grace.' She pulled a face. 'I've been in your house don't forget, on many occasions, and it's an absolute oasis of peace and serenity. It's beautifully decorated because you have an incredible eye for what works and what doesn't, and I've also eaten enough of your food to know that you're an amazing cook. You have plenty of skills, Grace, but you're in danger of lumping them under the "domestic trivia" heading and thinking them worthless.'

Amos sat back slightly and smiled.

'Go on…' said Grace. 'I *think* I want to hear this…'

Judging by the expression on her face, Flora was still marshalling her thoughts. She narrowed her eyes. 'So, I'm thinking off the top of my head here, but…' She broke off suddenly, looking across at Amos. 'Oh, that was clever,' she said. 'How did you know this is what I was going to say?'

Amos shrugged. 'I don't know what you mean…' he said, innocently. 'But now that you come to mention it, I believe my own thought processes *were* heading the same way as yours. But don't let me stop you, Flora, do carry on.'

She rolled her eyes. 'So, as I was saying, off the top of my head, it strikes me that instead of thinking about the battle ahead we need to look at this situation as an opportunity. And, far from lacking in skills, Grace, I'd say you have a huge range of talents, we just need to find a way that utilises them in a better fashion than as a prop for Paul's glittering career. You do need to be able to provide for yourself in the future, but the way I look at it you have two huge assets at your disposal.' She gave Grace a warm smile. 'And the first of those is *you*…'

There was a slight crinkling at the corners of Grace's mouth, but her eyes showed her indecision. She's pleased by the compliment, thought Amos. But she doesn't quite believe it, yet. He held Flora's look.

'And the second…' she continued. 'Well, perhaps you'd like to say what the other asset is, Amos.'

There was a teasing smile on her face, which Amos matched.

'Oh, that's easy,' he replied. 'Your house, Grace.'

'Exactly!' cried Flora, excitement brewing. 'Oh, Grace, think about it. There must be a million and one things you could do there, things that you would be absolutely brilliant at. A guest house, running courses… a cookery school? And your house would make a wonderful setting for all of those things. We could even tie it in with the farm somehow, make it into a joint venture. Oh I don't know, but it's just alive with possibility! Don't you see?'

For a moment Amos could see the light dawning across Grace's face as Flora's enthusiasm flowed between them, but then he saw the emotional weight of what she was going through gain the upper hand and the light died.

'But I don't have the money for any of that,' she said. 'Even if it were possible. Getting a business off the ground can cost a huge amount and I'd need income to be coming in pretty much straight away. I don't have the time to build a reputation, for word of mouth to spread. It's a lovely idea, Flora, as were your words, but I'm really not sure—'

'There must be a way around all of that, surely?' Flora was looking at Amos for guidance. 'We'd all help and, after all, you know what they say, necessity is the mother of invention...'

But Grace's face wore a closed expression. She had made up her mind, for now at least.

'Perhaps Grace needs a little time to have a think about all of this,' said Amos gently. 'I imagine today has been somewhat trying and maybe now isn't the best time to make decisions.'

Grace smiled gratefully. 'I confess, I'm suddenly feeling utterly drained. But I will think about what you've said, Flora, I promise. I have to do *something*.'

Flora gave a rueful smile. 'I'm sorry, Grace. I do tend to go off on one when I get the bit between my teeth.'

Grace patted her hand. 'And we all love you for it,' she replied, and then she got to her feet and gave Flora a hug. 'I'm going to go home now, have a bath, and hopefully fall into a deep refreshing sleep. And on the way I shall ask the bees what they think. No doubt tomorrow I will wake up with the answer in my head, clear as a bell.'

She smiled at Amos. 'And thank you for all your help today too.' She cocked her head to one side. 'It's so odd,' she added, 'because I feel as if I've known you my whole life...' And then she paused. 'I obviously have had far too much to drink. Please say goodnight to everyone for me, Flora, and thank you for a lovely meal.'

'Oh, Grace, you're always welcome. I'll see you tomorrow.'

Grace dipped her head and began to move away from the circle of chairs. Flora was looking helpless.

'I'll walk you home,' said Amos, stepping forward. 'I usually go for a wander around this time of night. The air is so lovely, don't you think?' He picked up Grace's bag and handed it to her, before raising a hand in farewell to Flora. He wasn't about to give her a reason to refuse.

It seemed to take only a matter of minutes before they were at the bottom of Grace's garden. The air was beautiful, cool now, but still fragrant from the flowers and filled with birdsong. He stopped to listen for a moment.

'Did you hear that?' he said to Grace. 'Nightingales.'

She lifted her head. 'Beautiful, aren't they? I come down here sometimes just to listen to them.'

The words hung in the air between them, a poignant reminder of the earlier conversation.

'What do I do, Amos?' she asked.

The question itself didn't surprise him, but the fact that she had asked him did. She was still looking up into the canopy of trees, the last golden rays of the sun casting a soft glow on her face. He had a sudden urge to hold her hand.

'You do whatever you want to do,' he replied, waiting until she lowered her gaze to look at him before continuing. 'But only you can really know what that is, Grace. You've taken the first, hardest step in the right direction and I think you already know that, as a result, things cannot stay the same.' He smiled softly. 'I like to think, however, that the universe rewards bravery by lending a helping hand where it can.

So, if whatever you decide is the right thing for you to do, and you honestly believe that with all your heart, then I don't see how you can fail. Take the opportunity you've given yourself, Grace, make something of it and forge the life you want for your future.'

'But what if I don't get to keep the house?'

'Then you will have a slightly different opportunity to forge the life you want. The path it leads to may be different but the opportunity is still there. Don't let it slip through your fingers.'

Grace nodded and indicated that they should continue walking, turning her face away. Amos would have liked to have said more but he could sense that Grace was struggling with her emotions and needed a few minutes to collect herself. He let her walk slightly ahead, following as they made their way up the hill towards the beehives. It seemed as if an age had passed since Amos had taken that very same route earlier in the day.

Attuned as his ears were to the sounds around him, they had gone only a matter of a few yards up the slope when Amos suddenly stopped. He could hear something vibrating, almost like a hum but deeper in tone although it was hard to decipher just where it was coming from as the trees deflected the sound. He walked forwards, concentrating, overtaking Grace as he quickened his pace.

'You have very good hearing,' came the voice from behind him. 'Most people don't even notice.'

'What is it?'

Grace came to stand beside him. 'The bees...'

'But it sounds like it's coming out of the bowels of the earth. Like some huge machine coming to life.' Now that he knew where the sound originated from, he moved a little closer to one of the hives.

'What are they *doing*?' he whispered. 'Holding mass or something?'

She smiled. 'No, they're cooling the hive… The noise you can hear is thousands of tiny wings all beating at once. Clever, isn't it?'

Amos's mouth had fallen open. 'I had no idea they even did such a thing.'

'They are their own air-conditioning system. It's their busiest time of year and honey production is at its height just now. They have to remove most of the water from the nectar they've gathered in order to make honey and this raises the temperature and humidity levels inside the hive. By beating their wings en masse they set up currents of air and it helps to regulate it.'

And now something else was literally buzzing around Amos's head because his thoughts were coming thick and fast.

'How long have you been a beekeeper, Grace?' he asked.

'Too long… It makes me remember how old I am.'

'And have you ever thought about passing on your skills to anyone else?'

'Like who? Who'd be interested? Most folk just pick a jar of honey off the shelf and like it that way. They don't want to know how it gets there.'

'Well I would…' He broke off, thinking some more. 'Grace, can I make a deal with you?' he said.

She narrowed her eyes. 'Go on,' she said. 'What am I about to let myself in for now?'

The more Amos thought about it, the more it seemed like the perfect solution. And it certainly answered the questions he had about why he was there. He rubbed the back of his neck.

'Are you going to think about Flora's suggestion? Seriously, I mean.'

Grace sighed. 'I admit, right now, I just want to curl up somewhere and not have to think about anything much, but, yes, I will. I have to,

Amos, I have no choice. And I am not giving up this house.' A hint of steel had crept into her tone.

'Then, as you said earlier, there will be things that need doing. Only you can decide what those need to be, but I can pretty much turn my hand to anything of a practical nature and I'm going to be around for a bit working on the cottage at the farm. If I promise to help with whatever you need, would you teach me about the miracle of your bees, Grace?'

She was so still, he thought for a moment that he might have offended her, that he had pressed her too hard to think about things she wasn't ready for yet. But then he saw a ghost of a smile flicker across her face.

'Thank you for accompanying me home, Amos,' she said. 'But I think I'd like to go the rest of the way alone now.'

It wasn't a rebuke, her voice was soft.

'Of course.' He took a step backwards. 'Goodnight, Grace.'

'Goodnight.' She turned to go. 'Oh, and Amos?'

He stood among the birdsong and the humming of the bees. His eyes met hers.

'I'll give you your answer tomorrow.'

Chapter Seven

Grace hadn't imagined for one moment that she would sleep but, to her amazement, she had drifted off almost immediately and woken feeling a little stiff but otherwise none the worse for wear.

Her soothing bath and good book had undoubtedly helped, but more than that was the feeling of utmost peace which had stolen over her as she had stood at her bedroom window for a few moments before climbing into bed. The garden lay shrouded in shadow, but it wasn't at all threatening, more the caress of a light blanket. She had climbed beneath her own covers with thoughts of her garden sleeping peacefully through the night beside her.

Now, the mid-morning light was harsh by comparison, but it was energising too; the bees had been up and about for hours. Several had already buzzed around her cup of tea before going on their way and something about them brought Amos to mind. She smiled at the thought of his offer the night before.

She picked up her mug from the table beside her on the patio and swallowed the last of its contents. It was hard to decide exactly what she thought about Amos. On the one hand, she felt as if she had known him for most of her life. He was kind, considerate and had an uncanny ability to see exactly what she was thinking. She had never met anyone who seemed so in tune with his surroundings before. But on the other hand, there was something about him that seemed... dangerous. Not in the traditional sense, but that he was more than capable of pushing her far outside her comfort zone. If she let him, that was.

Walking into the kitchen, she put down her mug beside the sink and was about to go upstairs to collect some washing when there was an unexpected ring of the front doorbell. Still deep in thought, she opened it without thinking, and was shocked to see who was standing on the other side.

'Dominic!'

The tall figure stepped forward, his arms full of flowers.

'Grace, it's so lovely to see you.' He kissed both of her cheeks, oblivious to any damage the blooms might incur as they sandwiched between them.

'I do hope you bought those at the farm next door,' she said, opening the door wider.

His brow creased in confusion. No, of course he hadn't. Don't be silly, Grace, his secretary had bought them.

'Our neighbours have opened a flower farm,' she explained, stepping backwards as Dominic's spicy aftershave enveloped her. Some things never changed.

She smiled as she took the bouquet from him. 'These are beautiful though, thank you. Come in.'

She led the way down the wide hallway to the kitchen.

'I must say you're the last person I expected to see,' she said, opening a cupboard to take down a vase. She turned around to look at her husband's boss, assessing what damage the last few years had done to him. But he looked to have hardly changed at all since she had last seen him. Still impossibly handsome. Slender-hipped, broad-shouldered, tall, and with floppy dark hair shot through with grey, Dominic struck an imposing presence in her kitchen. His sharp suit was softened by his relaxed pose and his round tortoiseshell glasses which gave him a rather owlish appearance; one he certainly knew how to use to maximum effect. He did it now, peering at her in that innocent way of his that had all the women queuing up to mother him.

'Grace… how could I not?' He fished inside the inner pocket of his suit jacket, drawing out a sheet of paper. 'I came as soon as I got this.'

Straight down to business then.

'I'm so sorry. I had no idea that things had got so bad.'

'Would you like a coffee?' she asked. 'It's a beautiful morning, we could sit outside if you like.'

He nodded and she reached for the cafetière, knowing Dominic wouldn't tolerate instant. She busied herself running water into the vase, filling the kettle and spooning out the coffee, all the while aware that, behind her, Dominic would be watching.

'It's been a couple of years,' he said, after a moment, coming to stand beside her. 'And I don't know how, but you've managed to make this place look even more gorgeous than before.'

He looked around at the lovely light airy space that was Grace's kitchen. When she had first met Dominic, it had been two rooms, but now, opened up and with only a wall of glass separating it from the garden, it was a stylish but welcoming centre of the house.

'Yes, well, over the years, as my husband's interest in it has declined, I've been able to add a few things about the place that are more to my liking.'

Dominic gave her an amused smile. 'Grace, let's not kid ourselves, all that entertaining, the parties, the weekends away, the charity events you organised, we always knew that the creation of the seemingly effortless stage on which Paul could shine was down to you, all of it. Things don't become as effortless as you made them seem without an awful lot of hard work.'

She nodded, but bit her tongue. She had no wish to score points. What was done was done and it was time to move on from that. She took a jug of milk from the fridge and placed it on a tray, which she began to load with everything else they would need. Dominic, she noticed, had crossed to the double doors at the far end of the room which opened out onto the patio.

He inhaled an exaggerated deep breath. 'Ahhh... I always did love your garden, Grace. The house's crowning glory, and still the same, I see. It has this air of... I don't know... tranquillity? Serenity?'

She rolled her eyes behind his back.

There was silence for a moment.

'Listen, Grace, what happened before, well I—'

'You apologised before, Dominic, and I accepted your apology then, there's no need to go over old ground.' She really wished he wouldn't, she had no desire to revisit that particular episode in her life.

'No, quite. It's just that... well, I wish we hadn't parted on such bad terms.'

'We didn't. You made an arse of yourself by making a pass at me. I called you out and you took offence at being rejected. You apologised because you didn't want to lose face, and I accepted that apology because I could see that you were acting completely out of character.'

The shriek of the kettle coming to the boil invaded the silence between them.

Dominic gave a wry chuckle. 'Well, that told me, didn't it? But you know I only did it because I could see how unhappy you were.'

'And that makes you the perfect gent, does it?' Grace squared up to him. 'Dominic, when my husband made me a laughing stock in front of a house full of guests, the thing to do would have been to offer me support. As his boss, you could have taken him to one side and told him to shut up. But what did you do…? Corner me in the kitchen and make a clumsy pass at me. How in the world did you think that was going to make me feel any better?'

He hung his head. 'I wasn't thinking straight, I know. We'd all had a lot to drink.'

'I hadn't, Dominic. I was stone cold sober, especially after several hours of trying to fend off my husband's drunken advances in front of a bunch of people I scarcely knew and then suffering the indignity of him snogging one of the guests right in front of me. Do you remember how everyone teased me for not finding it funny? There was nothing funny about the whole thing and you made it ten times worse!' She glared at him, trying to push the memories back where they belonged.

'I know, and I am sorry, Grace. I only did it because I wanted to make you feel better… I've always thought the world of you, you know that, but that doesn't excuse what I did. It was entirely inappropriate.'

Grace sighed. 'So you said at the time, Dominic.' She gave a slight smile. 'Look, why are we even going over this again?'

'Perhaps because I'm still an idiot and I brought it up again?'

She smiled properly then. 'So what do you see now, Dominic? Do you still see someone who looks unhappy?'

'No…'

'Then a woman scorned perhaps?'

He rubbed at a mark on the back of his hand.

Grace laughed. 'Go and take a seat outside, and I'll bring our drinks through.'

She joined him moments later, placing the tray on the table and taking a seat.

'Dominic, let's just be clear about all of this before we begin. What happened before is all in the past and I'm really not interested in it any more. Neither am I interested in making things difficult for you. I didn't expect to see you today, but I am appreciative of the fact that you've bothered to come.'

Dominic cleared his throat, pushing his glasses up his nose. 'Well, I won't insult your intelligence by saying that coming here has been easy. Your letter has put me in a very difficult position.'

'Yes, I'm sure… Do you still take sugar?'

'Just the one please… So, as we're being open and honest about these things, what is it you'd like me to do, Grace?'

'I don't want you to do anything, Dominic. I'm under no illusion that anything I have said to you about my husband's disgraceful behaviour will spur you into action, but I told Paul that I would be giving you a letter detailing his activities unless he withdrew the threat of selling this place. He didn't, so that's exactly what I've done.'

Dominic sighed. 'It isn't that I don't want to do anything about it, Grace, but it's not as easy as that. Whether you like it or not, Paul is a very vital part of what we offer as a station. He's also very good at what he does, as the countless messages from fans will testify.'

'So, you're loath to do anything which is going to affect the status quo. I understand completely, Dominic. At the end of the day it's about ratings and revenue. I'm well aware of that.'

'All I'm saying…' He broke off. 'I will admit that some of what you've detailed in your letter I found… surprising, shall we say, even for Paul. And I've no doubt that it's true,' he added quickly. 'But I have known about Paul's proclivities for years and the fact of the matter is that he is still outperforming pretty much all our other talent and...'

'That's the price you have to pay for genius?' she suggested.

Dominic took a sip of his coffee and smiled appreciatively. 'I wouldn't have put it quite like that, but, for some people, I can see that the behaviour fits the stereotype.'

'And, of course, you don't condone it for a minute...'

'Stop giving me a hard time, Grace. I'm sorry, okay? I'm sorry I made a pass at you, I'm sorry your husband's a bastard, and I'm sorry that I can't do anything about it.'

She regarded him with an amused expression on her face. 'Fair enough,' she said, picking up her coffee cup. 'So how are the boys?' she asked. 'Both at uni now, I expect?'

Dominic nodded. 'Yes, not doing a whole lot of work by the sounds of things but Will is in his third year at Reading, studying politics and international relations, and Luke is in Norwich doing photography.'

'Is he now... And how do you feel about that?' she asked, knowing that photography had been Dominic's field before the lure of showbiz took him away from all that.

He grinned. 'We'll see. As long as he doesn't end up an old reprobate like me.'

'Well, I'm sure Karen will make certain that never happens.' Grace smiled. 'Do you see much of them?'

'More now, funnily enough. I think as they've got older they've realised that Dad isn't all bad. It's Luke's first year so I think he'll probably spend the summer with his mum, but Will has already said he plans on coming over to me, at least for some of the time, work permitting.'

Grace nodded. It was an accepted form of small talk, to ask about someone's children, but as Grace didn't have any that was pretty much it. She settled her cup back in its saucer.

'So, why exactly *are* you here, Dominic?' She held his look.

He was doing his best to look relaxed, the suave sophisticate he liked to think he was, but she could see he was uncomfortable.

He wrestled with his words for a moment longer before asking her what she knew he had wanted to all along.

'Believe me, Grace, I understand your position very clearly. If I lived here I couldn't bear to leave either and there is also the obvious desire to call Paul to account. But I was just wondering whether you were planning to take your "information" to anyone else... *outside* of the network.'

She could, she knew that. If she wanted to she could probably ruin Paul's career, or at least make a very nasty dent in it. But while she wasn't happy being thought of as the poor rejected wife in private, she had even less desire to see that scenario played out in public.

'Aha... Yes, of course, protecting your interests, I see, Dominic.' She fell silent and let her words hang in the air between them. At least he didn't try to deny it.

'Grace, that's not fair. Did you really expect me to do otherwise?'

She smiled. 'No, I didn't expect you would.' She regarded him for a moment. 'I'd be lying if I didn't say I'd hoped so, but I know the world doesn't really work like that, that's just for fairy tales.'

She smoothed out the fabric of her skirt and took a deep breath. 'I'm not interested in taking this any further, Dominic. You have my word. I want Paul out of my life in the quickest and easiest way possible. By defying him over the house, I've already given him enough ammunition to justify making my life a misery. I don't want to give him any more. If I make an issue out of this in the hope that it will give me even more leverage, he will retaliate with everything he's got and annihilate me.' She smiled weakly. 'I'm not really cut out for that, am I?'

Dominic was quick to defend her. 'Oh, come on Grace, do you really think that after all you've done for him he would…' And then he stopped because they both knew the truth. 'I really am sorry. For what it's worth.'

Grace cleared her throat. 'Have you spoken to him yet?'

'No, I wanted to come and see you first.'

'Well of course, otherwise how on earth would you know what type of conversation you need to have?'

'The bottom line is that the conversation will let him know in no uncertain terms how his actions could have brought the network into disrepute. And I will obviously strenuously advise him not to do that again…' He smiled nervously. 'I will also mention that he has you to thank for the fact that he still has a job.'

'I gave you my word, Dominic. *I* will not be taking things further, nor do I engage in blackmail. You have my letter and should *you* wish to use its contents to bring Paul into line at any point in the future, be my guest, but it will have nothing to do with me.'

Paul sat back in his chair and looked around the garden. 'I'm glad I came, Grace. You're looking really well… Better than ever in fact.' He held up his hands. 'And that's just a compliment, don't read anything into it, okay?'

And just like that their business was concluded.

'I'd like if we could keep in touch though,' he added. 'We've known each other for twenty-odd years, it would seem strange if this were our last meeting.'

She thought about his words. Did she want to keep in touch with this man? Her last link with Paul…

'You've been a good friend over the years,' she said. 'And some of it was good fun too, in the early days at least. I'm not sure what we would ever find to talk about now, but, yes, it would seem petty to dismiss all of that just because my husband doesn't know how to behave.' She raised her eyebrows. 'Just make sure that *you* behave,' she added.

'I will,' he said, laughing. 'Thanks, Grace.'

'What for? Giving you such an easy time of it?' She couldn't resist one last dig.

But he held her look. 'Yes, actually. I know I have you to thank for where we are today. You're a remarkable woman.'

She scrutinised his face for the teasing expression she expected to see there, but his face was open and sincere. He actually meant what he said, with no agenda. That was a first.

He got to his feet. 'Lovely coffee,' he said. And Grace got to her feet with him ready to show him out. He got as far as the kitchen doorway before turning back. 'And I promise I will do everything I can as far as the house is concerned. After all you've done, I think it's the least I can offer in return.'

She followed him down the hallway and closed the front door behind him as he left. Yes, after all that she had done. She'd given her life to make Paul the success he was, thinking that his happiness would bring her own with it. It had been the biggest mistake of her life.

She returned to the garden to collect the coffee cups and assess her plans for the rest of the day. Dominic's visit had been unexpected, although she had known she would hear from him one way or another, but now it was just another thing that she could cross off her list. Your move, Paul, she thought.

It wasn't one of her days for manning the village shop and so a little gentle gardening felt like a good way of passing the time. It would help her to regain her equilibrium after the trials of the last couple of days. Solutions to the problems that Grace was troubled by often found their way to her when she pottered in the fresh air.

The telephone rang just as she was rinsing the cups. She dried her hands, glancing at the time as she did so. Perhaps it was that which made her anxious, or some sixth sense, but by the time she picked up the receiver she was already expecting bad news.

It wasn't a long conversation, but it left Grace trembling. She thought she would have more time than this. She recognised the name of the caller from the information that Amos had given her yesterday and although Evan Porter sounded apologetic, nothing could alter the fact that he had been instructed to put the house on the market and would need to visit in order to take more detailed information. They made an arrangement for later that day.

There was still a little coffee left in the cafetière but it had already gone cold. Grace would have liked one more cup, but she didn't have the energy to make another pot. Instead, she made a quick cup of tea and, collecting her notepad and pen from a drawer, took them back out to the same spot where she and Dominic had sat. The gardening would have to wait, she had plans to make.

Chapter Eight

Amos was accustomed to rising early and it was his favourite time of the day, particularly in the summer. While the temperature was still cool, the air had a languid feel to it, which would disappear once the heat began to build and it began to vibrate with an almost restless energy. But it was the expectation Amos enjoyed the most, the feeling of promise that each new day brought. He rolled over and sat up. A glass of water was what he needed first, then a walk would be just the thing to make the most of the early hour. The cottage didn't have much in the way of plumbing; the single tap in the corner of the kitchen area was the sole source of water and cold water at that. There were no washing facilities at all and although he had been told he was very welcome to visit the main house whenever he needed, as far as he was concerned water was wet wherever the location of the tap.

After drinking his fill, he quickly stripped and washed, relishing the feel of the cold water against his overheated skin. Judging by the clearness of the sky outside the day would warm up rapidly and he pulled his clothes onto his still-damp body. Taking an apple from the bowl on the table he let himself out and in moments was out of the farm gate and into the lane beyond. To the right lay the village, but in the other direction lay undiscovered territory. Naturally, Amos turned left.

At some point today Grace would give him the answer to the question he had posed the night before, and he prayed the answer would be yes. Amos rarely accepted money for the work he did, usually he laboured in exchange for board and lodging or lessons in a new skill. Over the years he had amassed a wide knowledge in this way, but never about beekeeping. It was a subject that intrigued him for many reasons and, he realised, if the answer from Grace was no, he would be very disappointed. He trailed his fingers along the hedgerows as he walked, letting the peace and calm of the early morning settle his thoughts.

The sun was beginning to climb when Amos judged it was time to return to the farm. His walk had done the trick and set him up ready for a full day's work.

'Amos!' The urgency in Flora's call surprised him as he walked across the yard.

'Is everything all right?' He picked up his pace, fearing something had happened.

But then she laughed, wild black curls shaking in the sunlight. 'Oh God, I thought you'd gone.'

'I went for a walk,' he said, shaking his head. 'Although I suppose I should be flattered.'

She turned her head up to face the sky. 'You should definitely be flattered. How is it that you've been here only a matter of days and yet it feels like forever? I've just been over to the cottage and, honestly, my heart was in my mouth.'

Amos bowed slightly. 'Then I apologise for alarming you.'

Flora stopped, her eyes widening. 'No, that was a horrible thing to say,' she said. 'I'm sorry. Assuming you'd just take off like that without even saying goodbye was incredibly rude.' Her hand went to her mouth. 'I don't even know what made me say it.'

Amos's smile was easy. 'You meant no offence,' he said. 'And my absence startled you.'

'No,' insisted Flora. 'Don't make it easy for me. Treating you like that is inexcusable. Please tell me that other people don't do that, just because…'

She didn't finish her sentence.

'It happens sometimes,' replied Amos, shrugging. More often than he cared to remember. 'Except that when it's meant, folks never apologise.' His smile widened. 'I shall take from your comment the compliment it so obviously bestowed and also make a promise that I will never up sticks and leave without saying goodbye. We'll both know when it's time for me to go.'

Flora rushed forward and pulled Amos into an impulsive hug, before pulling away, laughing.

'Now I'm just making it worse,' she said. 'But earlier this year, you know, we nearly lost Fraser and, well… No good telling people how you feel after they've gone, is there? These days I wear my heart well and truly on my sleeve.'

'And it suits you,' replied Amos, smiling. 'Anyway, what did you want me for?'

She broke into a grin. 'Breakfast,' she said. 'Very important.'

'It is indeed. And I should have hated to miss it.'

'I also wanted to ask your opinion about something. Only, it's a bit hush-hush at the moment.' There was a quizzical expression on her face.

'I can do discretion,' he replied, leaning in towards her. 'Who is it I'm not supposed to tell?'

'Fraser,' she shot back. 'And, believe me, that man has ears like a bat, so…'

'Fingers on lips,' said Amos. 'Understood.'

Flora lifted her face to the sun again. 'Do you want to do this before, or after breakfast?' she asked. 'It shouldn't take long.'

Amos's stomach rumbled into life.

'After it is then,' said Flora, grinning. 'Come on.'

*

Amos had eaten far more than he should have, but Hannah was such a good cook his willpower dissolved in an instant. He would pay for it mid-morning when he had a few hours' work under his belt and all he wanted to do was sleep in the sunshine, but for now he followed Flora across the yard, intrigued by her query.

They were headed further down the yard than he had explored before, towards a series of low-lying buildings at the far end. As they got closer, he recognised them immediately.

'Of course!' he exclaimed. 'The milking sheds.' He'd had one or two stints in similar places over the last couple of years.

Flora glanced over her shoulder. 'Sorry, I'm paranoid,' she said. 'But if Fraser knows I've come down here with you, he'll put two and two together quicker than I can say it.'

Amos remained silent until they had rounded a slight bend which took them out of view from the main yard. He could see Flora visibly relax.

'Don't worry, we're not doing anything wrong,' she said straight away. 'Both Hannah and Ned know we're here, it's just that... Look, come with me, and I'll explain.'

She led the way along a concrete path to the closest of the sheds and pulled open the door. Her face looked pale in the dim light.

'This is where Fraser had his heart attack,' she explained, pressing a switch on the wall to her left. After a flickering hesitation, two banks of fluorescent lights sprang into life and the shed was filled with harsh light. 'Even I don't like coming in here, so you can imagine how Fraser feels.'

'I see,' said Amos slowly. The shed was empty of machinery, just a concrete shell, but he could feel the emptiness inside it deep within him.

'We had all the equipment removed. Well we had to, we needed to sell it, but since then, well, as you can see it's not been touched.' She gave an involuntary shiver. 'Sorry, do you mind if we go back outside to chat?'

Amos stood aside to let her pass, grateful himself to be headed back out into the warm summer air.

'It's so weird,' added Flora. 'I mean, Fraser's fine. He's recovering beautifully from his operation, just gone five months now. I won't deny it's been tough but we're in a much better position than we've been for a long while.'

'But?'

Flora smiled. 'But... Fraser won't set foot in here.'

Amos thought for a moment. 'No, I can understand that. It's his *what if*,' he said. 'We all have them.'

'I'm sorry?'

'His *what if*. You know... *what if* this had happened. If he had died... Too many memories locked in there. Sometimes we almost need to keep them, as a reminder that we're okay, that the worst didn't happen. But for some, it's too much.'

Flora stared at him. 'You're exactly right!' she exclaimed. 'But short of knocking the sheds down, I haven't been sure how to improve the situation. What I do know, however, is that these buildings are a valuable resource, and it seems criminal not to use them. So, I've been thinking...' She turned back to look at the shed again. 'In fact, I can't stop thinking – about Grace.'

Amos smiled. 'You too?'

'Really? I just hope she's okay… Grace is the loveliest person you could ever wish to meet and she helped me a lot when I first came here. I think she understood what it felt like to be so lacking in confidence…' She looked up at Amos. 'She wasn't always like that apparently, and she puts a brave face on it, making light of things, but apart from coming here or going to work in the shop, Grace hardly ever goes out. I can't bear to think of her being treated so badly, or losing the house, her garden…'

'The bees…'

'Exactly! And then I got to thinking about our conversation last night and what she might do, what we might be able to do to help her, and that's when I began to think about the sheds.'

'Go on…'

'Well, I've always had a mind to expand what we do here in time. At the moment it's all we can do to keep up with the planting, but I would love to have a shop here in due course, or run workshops, something anyway…'

Amos could see she was buzzing with excitement.

'But what I don't know is how easy it would be to make something of the buildings here, what our options might be. And, more to the point, what it might cost.'

'Which is where I come in…'

'Would you mind?' asked Flora. 'In my head these ideas were originally way off, something we might get to at some point, but now I'm thinking that Fraser needs to move on from all of this, and whatever happens with Grace is going to have to happen pretty damned quickly.'

Amos nodded. 'Let me take a look,' he said, thinking rapidly. He pulled open the door once more and strode first of all to the far end of the shed, looking up to the roof where a false ceiling had been added at some point. He was pretty sure that above it would be the building's original wooden rafters. The walls were bare but looked in good condition, and the windows were sound. A central concrete pathway split the shed down the middle, with a raised walkway on either side, flanked by metal railings. It was on these that the cows would have stood to be milked.

Flora walked up the path towards him. 'When it was in operation as a milking shed it was hard to see beyond the machinery and you couldn't think with the incessant clanking.' She shuddered. 'And then after Fraser got ill I spent as little time in here as possible.'

Amos was staring at the windows. 'It's an old building though,' he said. 'Which in many ways makes it far more adaptable than if it were a modern shell.' He frowned. 'Hang on a minute,' he said, ducking back outside and walking the length of the building. Now that *was* interesting...

Ten minutes or so later when they were both back outside, Amos delivered his verdict. 'The only real issue I can see is that the raised walkways are made of concrete. They could be removed but it would be messy and expensive and so if you could come up with a use where they could be an asset or made into a feature then so much the better. I would also suggest you remove the ceiling and leave the interior open to the rafters.' He pointed to rows of windows along the side of the shed. 'See, two rows of windows... and the bottom set are nice and clean while the top set...'

Flora had a puzzled expression on her face. 'Two rows of windows?' she queried. She looked at Amos. 'But inside...' She peered back through the door of the shed before turning back to look at Amos. 'Inside there's only one row,' she continued.

'Indeed… Because the second set is above the false ceiling,' supplied Amos. He grinned at her. 'Just imagine what the space would look like with the ceiling removed. Rising to the vaulted roof, exposed beams, flooded with masses of natural light…'

'Of course! Oh, God, it could look stunning, Amos.'

He could see her mind beginning to explore the possibilities, the smile on her face getting bigger and bigger.

'Did that answer your question?' he said. 'I think there are all sorts of possibilities here, and to convert the basic space wouldn't take much, both in terms of time and in cost. How much longer it takes and how much more it costs would obviously depend on what you ultimately want to use the building for.'

He studied her face, now lost in thought. 'So, are you still thinking about Grace?'

She turned to look in the direction of Grace's house. 'Very much so. I guess we'll just have to wait and see what happens. I do hope she's okay.'

Amos followed her line of sight. He hoped so too.

*

The sun had reached the highest point in the sky when Amos stopped for a break, stretching his back and wriggling his shoulders to relax them. He had nearly finished taking out the loose mortar from one whole section of wall and was just about to go and get some water when he saw Hannah coming towards him from the direction of the farmhouse, carrying a tray. He raised his hand in greeting.

'Goodness it's warm,' she said as she reached him. 'We shouldn't complain, it's bringing on the flowers beautifully, but not so much fun when you're out in it all day with no shade.' She lifted the tray, indicating that he should take a drink. There were three glasses, already full, and a tall jug of what looked like homemade lemonade. Amos took one and downed the contents in one go.

He grinned. 'Absolutely delicious,' he said. 'And very welcome, thank you.'

Hannah beamed with pleasure. 'It's thirsty work,' she said. 'And you've been at it non-stop.'

'Are the other drinks for Flora and Ned?' he asked, knowing that they were out in the field. 'Would you like me to take them down for you?'

'Oh, could you? I can get on with lunch then.' She passed the tray across to Amos. 'And when it's ready you must all stop and have a proper break. From what Flora was saying earlier there might be lots to discuss. It's so exciting, and that's not something I ever thought I'd hear myself say.'

Amos watched as Hannah walked back to the house, a warm smile on his face. Now there was someone who had been through the wringer and was revelling in the joy to be found on the other side. He adjusted his grip on the tray and set off through the garden.

Reaching the field, he carried the drinks to the small shed that sat a little way from the gate, setting the tray down on a table before scanning the rows of flowers. Even among the blooms, Flora was easy to spot with her bright-orange leggings and blue smock. Ned, in khaki shorts, tee shirt and matching hat, wasn't quite so obvious. Eventually Amos spied him, right at the far end of the field. Sticking two fingers in his mouth, he gave a piercing whistle. An arm was raised to signify that Amos's signal had been heard and the two bent heads lifted, bodies straightening.

He had a glass in each hand ready for when Flora and Ned finally reached him, picking their way through the rows of flowers; hot, tired and sweaty from a morning's back-breaking work.

Flora pressed her glass against the side of her face, relishing the coolness, and then, like him, she drank the contents in one go. Beside her Ned grinned, his face pink from the sun.

'Well, it's official. We are completely bonkers.'

'Indeed,' replied Amos. 'Mad dogs and Englishmen…'

Flora giggled. 'Even your freckles have freckles,' she said, laying an affectionate hand on Ned's cheek. 'Whatever you do, don't take off your hat.' She peered at him. 'You are a bit rosy,' she said. 'When I had my idiot idea for transforming the farm to grow flowers, I didn't factor in that half of the workforce were redheads!'

Ned rubbed the back of his neck. 'Well at least the sunburn detracts from the pain in my back and shoulders,' he said, but he was grinning. 'We're getting there though. We've almost finished the last bit of planting out and then we're done until the autumn—'

'When we start all over again with the bulbs,' finished Flora. 'We missed out on these this year, but it will extend our growing season no end.' She looked out across the field, smiling with pride at their accomplishment.

Amos doubled back to the shed to collect the jug and his own glass, refilling them all. 'To Hope Blooms,' he said, raising his glass. He was about to clink it with Flora's when she suddenly waved.

'Grace!' she shouted. 'Come and join us.' She handed her glass back to Amos, walking forward.

Amos turned slightly to see Grace picking her way along the edge of the field. Her slender form was elegant as always, unhurried and seemingly relaxed, but Amos knew instinctively that he was about to find out whether he was to become a trainee beekeeper. He took Ned's glass as well, replacing them all on the tray.

'Oh, I do hope it's good news,' Flora added.

'Don't bank on it,' muttered Ned. 'You know what Paul's like.'

By the time Grace reached them, an air of expectancy had risen, so much so that Grace laughed. 'Goodness, you all look as if you're waiting to find out whether it's a boy or a girl.'

But her face immediately fell as she turned to look at Amos; there was a tightness behind her eyes that he took for unshed tears. He was struck by the way she held herself – even though he could see that what she was going to say next was difficult for her.

'To bee, or not to bee?' he murmured softly.

'Yes indeed… that is the question,' she replied with a sad smile. 'To which the answer is a resounding yes,' she added. 'I *am* going to need your help Amos, if you're still willing. I'm going to need everyone's help. I don't think I can do this on my own.'

'Oh, Grace.' Flora pulled the older woman into a warm hug, the strength of their friendship removing the years between them. 'I'm so sorry.'

Grace held her tight before pulling away, drawing herself up straight. 'No, no tears. I won't let Paul have the satisfaction. Besides, I need a clear head, not one muddled by emotion.'

'Do you want to come up to the house?' asked Ned. 'We've just stopped for a bit of a break as it happens and, you know Mum, the kettle's always boiling. Come and have a cup of tea.'

'I don't want to hold any of you up, I know how busy you are.'

'Grace,' said Ned firmly. 'I am beginning to feel and look like a boiled lobster. You will be doing me a very great favour if you give me any kind of excuse to get out of the sun.'

'Oh yes, please come up, Grace,' urged Flora. 'Hannah and Fraser will want to hear what's happened, and we've been having a think too. There's so much to talk about.'

Grace checked her watch. 'I have to be back by two o'clock,' she said. 'The estate agent is coming.'

'The same one as yesterday?' asked Amos, thoughts beginning to swirl around his head.

She nodded. 'Altogether far too keen.'

Hmm, well, we'll see about that, thought Amos. 'Then we've no time to lose,' he said, standing back and ushering Grace onto the path ahead of him. Ned took her arm as Flora fell back to walk with Amos.

She let them walk on ahead a little way. 'What are you up to?' she whispered.

Amos put his hand over his heart. 'Me?' he said innocently. 'I don't know what you mean.'

'Yes, you do. I can see it written all over your face. You're plotting something.'

But Amos simply smiled. 'As if I would,' he said.

Chapter Nine

Hannah rushed over as soon as they walked through the kitchen door.

'Come and sit down, Grace,' she said. 'You'll be needing a cup of tea.'

Ned shot Flora an amused 'I told you so' glance, and then to Amos's surprise Grace groaned.

'I'll sit down, but dear God, no more tea. I'm sick of the sight of the stuff. Actually, what I could do with is a massive slab of chocolate, or a big thick scone, laden with jam and clotted cream.'

'Oh dear,' said Flora.

'I know,' said Grace sighing. 'And I don't usually eat chocolate, but right now I could eat my entire body weight in the stuff.' She took a seat at the table.

'I can cut you a slab of fruit cake. Would that do?' asked Hannah.

'Fruit cake?' asked Fraser, coming into the room. 'Where have you hidden that? I never get cake…' he grumbled.

'Oh, go on with you,' she replied, smiling fondly. 'Anyway, lunch is almost ready and the cake is for dessert, so come and sit down everyone.'

'May I help?' asked Amos, reluctant to take a seat before anyone else.

'Thank you. If you pop into the pantry through there, you'll find a fresh loaf and a dish of strawberries, I'll get the rest from the fridge. Perhaps you could see to the cutlery, Flora dear?'

Moments later when they were all settled, Hannah cleared her throat. 'Now then, Grace. You must tell us all what's happened.'

'Mum!' admonished Ned. 'Grace might not even want to talk about it just now.'

'Don't be silly, dear, of course she does; we're her oldest friends. Besides, if we don't know what's going on, how can we possibly help?'

Amos looked up from his seat beside Fraser at the end of the table but Grace was smiling, no doubt used to Hannah's forthright manner.

'There's not much to tell, actually,' replied Grace. 'As I've already told the others, an estate agent is coming this afternoon to take further details of the house and it will be going on the market. I haven't heard from Paul since he left, but I assume that if he had wanted to cancel the agent's visit he could have done.'

'But what about the information you were sending to his boss?' asked Flora. 'Doesn't Paul realise what that could do to his career?'

'Actually, I've already had a visit from Paul's boss. He arrived about ten this morning and must have driven like a maniac to get here so early. But Dominic was only checking on his investment, seeing how far I was prepared to push things or whether I had sent the information to anyone outside of the network. Paul is the proverbial goose that lays the golden egg and Dominic is not about to do anything which will damage that, not unless there's a real threat to the organisation.'

'So, Paul's going to get off scot-free?' argued Ned. 'I don't believe it, that's insane. It's criminal. It's—'

'Only what I expected,' replied Grace evenly. 'I won't take the information any further because I have no wish to sully myself with it. But, I have left it with Dominic. He is now its gatekeeper and I have made it very clear that I don't want to lose the house.'

Ned frowned. 'But Grace, that's giving him carte blanche to ignore it.'

'That's one way of looking at it, but I like to think that what I'm doing is giving Dominic the opportunity to be the better person. To do what's right given what happened, even to try and make amends...' She stopped and thought for a few seconds. 'Your mum and dad both know this, but Dominic made a pass at me a couple of years ago. He'd had far too much to drink and I sent him packing with his tail between his legs. This morning was the first time I've seen him since that night, but before that he and I always got on well and I think, underneath his brash and somewhat vain exterior, there is a good man trying to get out from under the spell that showbiz has cast on him. I'd like to give him the chance to find out.'

'And if he doesn't?' said Ned. 'You could lose the house, Grace.'

'I could lose it anyway.'

'Grace and decorum,' said Amos quietly.

Grace stared at him. 'Say that again?'

Amos looked up, startled at her tone, and repeated the phrase.

'That's what my mother used to say,' Grace replied. 'All the time.' She laid an absent-minded hand across her heart. 'Goodness, I haven't heard that in years. Grace and decorum in all things.'

'Wise words,' said Amos, a soft smile spreading over his face at the wistful note to her voice.

'Yes,' said Grace slowly. 'Yes they are...' Her brown eyes held his until he was aware of only the sound of his heart beating.

The clatter of a knife broke the moment and Grace laughed. 'Crikey, that was a bit of a trip down memory lane. Sorry...' She looked around as if to orientate herself. 'What was I saying?'

'About the house... and Dominic,' prompted Flora.

'Oh yes. Well he could choose to do absolutely nothing, but he did say he would do what he could to get Paul to change his mind about selling, and I do believe he will. Whether Paul takes any notice of course is another matter.' She brightened her expression. 'But, it's done now, and I will simply have to wait and see, and in the meantime...'

Flora leaned forward.

'Provided I do get to keep the house of course... I think I would like to open a guest house. I used to enjoy looking after everyone when I hosted the weekends for Paul, but his hateful behaviour ruined it. With him gone, I thought I might just manage it again.'

Flora clasped her hands together in excitement. 'Oh, I knew it,' she exclaimed. 'I think that's a wonderful idea, Grace, and you'll be absolutely brilliant at it.'

Grace beamed at her response. 'Thank you. It's what you said about the house that helped me make up my mind,' she said. 'I know how living there makes *me* feel and so I thought that if it does that for me it might be the same for other people too. How lovely to be able to offer that feeling to anyone who wants it.' She broke off to pull a face. 'They'd have to pay for it of course, I'm not that altruistic... But I also tried to think of things that might make what I'm offering a bit different from everyone else and so I wondered whether offering guests the chance to learn about beekeeping might work, or gardening.' She looked directly at Flora. 'Even floristry...'

Flora could barely contain herself. 'And if we had somewhere here on the farm that we could turn into a practical space for people to learn those things, practise them as well, in a relaxed setting, offering refreshments maybe...'

She was thinking as she spoke, but Amos could see that much of it was a description of a dream she'd already had. There was a low chuckle from beside him.

'Shame we don't have anywhere like that.'

Amos turned to see a teasing grin on Fraser's face. 'Good lord, lass, did you really think I hadn't noticed you sneaking off to the milking sheds every spare minute of the day?'

Flora rolled her eyes and looked at Amos. 'What did I tell you? Bat ears... and bionic eyes too.' Then she grinned at Fraser.

'But what do you think, Dad?' asked Ned. 'Amos took a look at the shed this morning and it wouldn't take much to convert them and—'

Fraser held up his hand. 'As if I could even try and stop you,' he said. 'When that girl there gets the bit between her teeth, there's no stopping her.' He winked at Flora. 'But I think it's a splendid idea,' he added. 'And there's no one more deserving of a little help than you, Grace. I reckon we might have a bit of a battle on our hands, but you'll not lose your house, not if we have anything to do with it.'

'It's so exciting!' exclaimed Flora, squirming.

'I'm frankly terrified,' replied Grace, but a little light had come back to her eyes and Amos nodded.

'Nothing wrong with fear,' he said. 'It's the place where courage is born.'

*

Amos met Evan Porter at the top of the drive, stepping to one side to make way for the huge car to pass him and then following as it swept around in front of the house to park. Amos was at the vehicle's side before the agent was even ready to open the door.

'Good afternoon, Mr Porter, Sir. A fine day, is it not?' Amos pulled the car door open and stood with a deferential stoop, waiting until the agent had collected his things together and climbed out.

Evan frowned as he straightened. 'Indeed, Mr... er...?'

'Fry, Sir,' replied Amos. 'Or Amos if you prefers.' He stood back. 'Mrs Maynard said I was to keep a look out for you around two, so I thought to myself best not make a start on the mowing just yet or I might miss you. Wouldn't be able to hear the car, see, on account of the noise the mower makes. Big thing it is.' He scratched his head. 'Anyway, I promised I'd take good care of you… Would you like to come with me, Sir, that's it, right this way…'

Amos took a couple of paces backwards, indicating that Evan should walk on ahead of him. The agent glanced up at the house and then back at Amos.

'Mrs Maynard is inside, is she?'

'Ooooh, no, she couldn't bear it, could she? That's why I'm here,' replied Amos, pointing at his chest. 'I've got the keys here, some-where…' He made a show of fishing in his pockets.

Evan looked down at his clipboard. 'I see,' he said. 'It's just that I spoke to Mrs Maynard on the telephone this morning, and I was led to believe that she would be here.'

'Aye, well, yes she would say that, wouldn't she? 'Cause she's far too polite to say anything else, but getting herself in a right state she was 'cause she don't want to go. In the end I had to say to her, "*Missus Maynard, it's not right to be getting yourself all ruffled up, not when there's really no need.*" There's only one person knows this place as well as she does and that's me. No disrespect or nothing, but Mr Maynard, well, he's never really here and he doesn't take a right lot of interest when he is.' Amos flashed a huge smile. 'So, I said I'd be very happy to show you round.'

'There's really no need…' Evan's smile was cool. 'I'm familiar with the layout of the house obviously and today I just need to take measurements and so on. I'm sure you have things you need to be getting on with.'

'Aye, I do…' Amos appeared to think about his words for a few seconds, but then he screwed up his face. 'No, it wouldn't be right. A promise is a promise, so I reckon we'd best get on with it. Where would you like to start?'

At best Amos had ten minutes to familiarise himself with the layout of the house before the estate agent had arrived, but it had been enough for him to understand even more keenly why Grace couldn't bear to let it go. He could see her warm-hearted personality everywhere he looked; every small touch that brought comfort to the airy rooms, a friendliness and homely feel to what might otherwise have appeared stark. The furnishings, like Grace, were elegant, simple and stylish, and there were flowers everywhere. He strode confidently down the hallway.

'Come along to the kitchen then,' he said, beckoning. 'Everyone always heads for the kitchen first, don't they? And right fancy it is too.'

Evan paused, a Dictaphone now held in his left hand. 'I'll start at the front door if you don't mind.'

Amos looked around him. 'Oh, right you are… so the hallway… and then the kitchen.'

Evan ignored him.

'And don't forget to make a note of that there,' said Amos, pointing to a large botanical wall-hanging. 'Only Missus Maynard made that. Right proud she is of it too, and who can blame her? Properly gorgeous, I reckon.' He smiled.

There was a curt nod. 'Yes, it's very stylish. But I don't need to make a note of it Mr… er, Fry, because it's not actually included in the sale. Not a fixture or fitting.' He exhaled loudly. 'What I'm here to do is to describe the accommodation, and take measurements and photographs.'

'I see…'

'So I don't really need to know details like that, even though I'm sure Mrs Maynard is very proud of it.'

Amos did his best crestfallen impression. 'Oh… but then perhaps you could make sure you get it in the photograph? I think she'd like that, show it off, like…?'

Another gadget was removed from Evan's pocket.

'Perhaps if you could just stand to one side so I can record the width here?'

Amos moved a foot to his right. 'About here okay?'

There was a loud sigh.

'Mr Fry—'

'Amos… I reckon it's okay to call me that.'

'Mr *Fry*,' Evan insisted. 'I think it's best if perhaps you could just let me get on. That way we'll get this done a lot quicker and easier. I'll ask if I have a question…'

Amos frowned. 'Right you are then,' he replied. He planted his feet and took up a stance a little distance away with his hands held behind his back. Then he picked a spot on the opposite wall and stared at it. He didn't move for about a minute but then he turned his head to stare at Evan, following his every move. The moment the agent looked up and caught his eye, Amos snapped his gaze away, back to the spot on the wall. He couldn't remember the last time he had enjoyed himself so much.

After perhaps another ten minutes, which included taking the details of the cloakroom, Evan moved off down the hallway. Amos practically galloped past him.

'Right, the kitchen now, is it?' he panted, taking up an almost identical stance in the middle of the room. 'Now don't forget—' he began.

Evan held up his hand.

'Or, the—'

A glare this time.

Amos could keep this up all day.

'Mr Fry… As I really don't wish to capture the essence of this beautiful room with you standing in the middle of the photograph, please could you move?'

Amos moved as if to stand by the wall.

'Over here… *behind* me.' There was an exasperated sigh.

By the time Evan had finished taking the details of the ground floor, he looked fit to burst. Amos, on the other hand, was finding it harder and harder to keep from laughing and had to cough on a couple of occasions to hide his mirth. It was too cruel, Amos knew that, but there was something much bigger at stake here and Grace needed all the help she could get.

He eased off the act a little as they toured the upstairs, but only because Amos wanted Evan to feel relatively comfortable again. After all, he was saving his pièce de résistance for the garden…

They had been in the garage block, looked at the storage sheds and greenhouse, and toured the patio area and flower beds around the area of garden closest to the house. Amos was sure that Evan had taken some beautiful photos of the garden and its sumptuous lawns. He also knew, however, that the best view was from the area of garden where it began to slope away, down to the flower field, past the bees…

They had just got to the top, in among the apple trees, when Amos suddenly ran in front of Evan, and raised his hand in the air. He stood waiting patiently, a hopeful look on his face. The agent was doing his best to ignore Amos, fiddling with the settings on his camera, and so Amos stretched his hand higher and waggled it, looking for all the world like he was about to burst.

'Yes, Amos… what is it?' came the weary voice.

'Sorry, Mr Porter, Sir. I know you said to be quiet, but I can't stand by and let you just carry on. I'd hate for anything to happen to you, that wouldn't be right at all… and, oh dear…' He cocked his head to the side as if listening for something. 'Can you hear that?'

Evan gave a tentative glance down the garden and then, with a dismissive shake of his head, began to walk forwards. Amos ran in front of him again, arm raised high. Evan stopped dead.

'What?' he snapped, his irritation starting to show.

Amos looked hurt. 'It's just that the bees…' He rubbed his neck.

'Bees…?'

'Aye… In a right proper temper they were this morning, and by the sounds of things they don't sound much happier now. Trouble is, you need to go right down by 'em to get the best photos of the view…'

Evan swallowed.

'I tell you what though,' offered Amos. 'I could go down first and see what I can do. They're used to me, see, and I might be able to calm them down a bit…'

'But no one mentioned anything about bees.'

'Didn't they?' asked Amos, scratching his head. 'Oh… well, yes, there's bees all right, hundreds of 'em, thousands probably. Three huge hives… they're normally all right, but it's a busy time of year for 'em and tempers get a bit frayed, plus of course they're due to swarm any day now.'

Evan took a step backwards.

'I'll go,' said Amos. 'I'm sure it will be fine… You best wait here.' Amos moved off cautiously. 'It's all right, ladies,' he said softly. 'It's only old Amos… Just passing through, no need to get your knickers in a twist.'

He waited until he knew he was out of sight and then leaned up against a tree trunk for a moment, his shoulders silently heaving with laughter. He turned his face to the sky and listened to the birdsong, aware that there *was* a gentle hum in the background, but if anything it sounded even happier than it had the day before. A good five minutes passed before he even contemplated returning to where they had been standing before.

He approached Evan, wiping imaginary sweat from his brow. 'Lord, that was a mite scary for a minute,' he said. 'But it's okay... I think we'll be safe to go down now. We had a good chat, and I explained what you was here for and that they weren't to have a problem with you. They usually do listen.'

Evan stared at him. 'You talked to the bees? Really?'

Amos stared right back. 'Aye, well what else do you do?' He paused, looking Evan up and down. 'Oh, I get it,' he said. 'You think I'm just some old country bumpkin who's a bit soft in the head, don't you? Well, I might be, but I know a thing or two about bees, Mr Porter, and one thing I do know is that you tread very carefully around angry bees. I've seen what they can do...' He left his sentence unfinished and stood his ground.

Evan shuffled his feet. 'Perhaps if I show you how the camera works you could take one or two shots for me. It's really quite simple.'

Amos sniffed and peered at the instrument as if it were on fire. 'No, I don't reckon so,' he replied. 'I'm not good with things like that.' And then he softened his expression. 'Come on, lad, I'll take you down,' he said in resigned fashion. 'It'll be all right, I'm sure.' He took a couple of paces forward. 'Just stay on my right-hand side until I tell you,' he added.

And in that fashion, with arms held wide to the sides forming a 'protective' barrier, Amos shepherded Evan down the slope and past the bees, stopping every now and again to listen before waving him on. After they were well clear of the hives, Amos cautiously lowered his arms and gestured at the view.

'Right, best take your pictures, and then we'll get back,' he said, letting Evan know in no uncertain terms that the bees could only be held at bay for so long.

With one ear cocked for the sound of an approaching swarm, Evan did just that, firing off several photos before practically running back up the slope.

Amos walked across the lawns with him.

'There now, that weren't so bad, was it?' He smiled. 'And worth it for the view, I reckon. There's not a finer spot around here.' He shielded his eyes from the sun and gazed around the garden. 'Well, I dunno about Missus Maynard, but it's going to fair break my heart leaving this place an' all...'

Evan fiddled with his camera, trying to replace the lens cap.

'Indeed... Well, I think that's all I need for now. I had best get back and make a start on the details. The sooner they're done the sooner we can offer this beautiful house for sale.'

Just like that, thought Amos. He knew that Evan had a job to do, but if Amos had felt any remorse for the show he had just put on over the last half hour or so, it departed pretty quickly. The agent clearly felt no compassion for Grace's circumstances. Too busy thinking about his commission most likely.

Amos nodded sadly. 'Aye, I suppose you must,' he replied. 'I'll see you off.'

'There's really no need, I can find my own way.'

'I'm sure you can but, like I said before, a promise is a promise. I promised Missus Maynard that I'd be here for when you came, and in

my book that means both greeting you *and* seeing you off the premises.'
He held the agent's look and they walked back to Evan's car in silence.

Just before climbing in, Evan consulted his clipboard once more, checking the detail on the page.

'Just one more thing before I go, Mr Fry... I don't seem to have a note of who will be showing prospective purchasers around. I'm not really at liberty to discuss it with you, but perhaps you could pass on a message to Mrs Maynard and tell her that with properties such as these we recommend that someone from our office attends.' He plucked a business card from the top of the clipboard and handed it to Amos. 'If Mrs Maynard could call me to discuss it, I'd be very appreciative.'

Amos stared at the card. 'Well, I'll tell her... but I can't rightly see her wanting to show folks around, can you? Probably best if I do it for her, I reckon, save her from fretting, but I'll certainly pass on your message, Mr Porter.' Amos gave him his best cooperative smile.

Evan got in the car and drove off without saying another word.

Chapter Ten

'You said *what*?' said Grace, waving her hand. 'Oh no, don't tell me, don't make me laugh any more, it *hurts*…'

They were sitting on the patio just beyond Grace's kitchen, enjoying a cup of coffee in the evening sun. Grace had spent most of the last ten minutes bent double with laughter as she listened to Amos regale her with the events of the afternoon.

'Oh, Amos, you're a genius,' she said, wiping the moisture from underneath her eyes. 'I just wish I had been there to see it in person. I can't get the image of the estate agent out of my head, creeping gingerly past the beehives with you trying to shepherd the bees out of his way. As if you could.'

'His face was a picture,' agreed Amos. 'I'm really not sure what he thought was going to happen, but his imagination was certainly working overtime.' He reached forward to pick up his coffee cup and took a sip. 'Whether any of it will have made any difference, I have no idea, but it was worth a try.'

'I can't thank you enough,' replied Grace. 'Just the fact that you did it makes me feel less helpless, like I have some control over what's happening. That's not a feeling I'm all that familiar with, at least not where my husband is concerned anyway.'

She was about to continue but then closed her mouth again. Amos didn't need to hear any more.

'And I also need to thank for you all of this,' she added, indicating the pile of chocolate bars on the table, one of which had already been eaten. 'It was such a lovely thought.'

'I have a terribly sweet tooth, I'm afraid,' admitted Amos. 'Delivering these here without having eaten any first showed considerable restraint on my part...' He picked up another bar. 'Fruit and Nut, or Galaxy?' he asked.

Grace pursed her lips. 'Oh, Galaxy please...'

Since lunchtime when Amos had first put forward his suggestion of showing around the estate agent, Grace had spent an inordinate amount of time thinking about this man. It had seemed a perfectly sensible suggestion to start with and yet the moment she had watched him leave to go back to the house without her she had begun to question herself. So much so that, by the time they had arranged to meet up afterwards for a 'debrief' as Amos put it, she had convinced herself that she needed to politely withdraw from his offer of help. And then he had appeared, arms loaded with half a dozen different chocolate bars, laughing that, while it was not quite her body weight, it was the best he could come up with at short notice. It was such a thoughtful gesture that she hadn't been able to say a word. Since then, they had shared a simple meal, a coffee and made a pretty good start on the chocolate. Sitting, laughing in the sun, had been the perfect end to the day. It had been effortless, in fact, and now Grace was beginning to wonder why that was.

She turned to look at Amos, his dark curls glinting in the golden light, his eyes closed with pleasure as he allowed a chunk of chocolate to dissolve in his mouth, exactly the same way she always did, and she smiled at his obvious enjoyment. Tomorrow she would have to start thinking seriously about what she was going to do, but, for tonight at least, she was happy to just let things drift.

'Would you really do that for me?' she asked after a moment.

'Do what?' Amos's voice was thick with chocolate.

'Do the viewings on this place?'

'I would, if you wanted me to. You'd be surprised how little it takes to put someone off something. Most people are entirely suggestible, once you've worked out what their susceptibility is. Play up to that and it's not that difficult at all.'

Grace tipped her head to one side. 'That sounds like you might be speaking from past experience?'

'Well, I hope it won't be necessary,' he replied. 'The house isn't on the market yet, Grace. There's still time for a halt to be put on proceedings.'

'And you didn't answer my question,' she said, teasing him gently. 'You don't give much away, do you?'

Amos gave a small smile. 'I meet a lot of people,' he said. 'And mostly what I've learnt is that folks like to talk. But, more than that, they like it when someone listens. If you do that, you'd be surprised at the things people will tell you.'

Grace smiled and popped another piece of chocolate in her mouth. Hadn't she done just that herself? 'And who listens to you, Amos?' she asked.

He grinned at her. 'Would you be fishing for information now, Missus Maynard?' he asked, adopting his country-bumpkin voice from earlier. 'Because I'm just a simple gardener, don't reckon there's anything much to tell, truth be told.'

'I don't believe that for a minute,' Grace volleyed back gently. Then she sighed. 'So, what do I do, Amos?' she asked, changing the subject.

She would leave Amos to his secrets, for now anyway. 'I guess it will be a few days before the details on the house are ready, but do I wait and see what happens, or do I press ahead with things? I haven't heard a thing from Paul yet.'

'You forge ahead,' said Amos, without even a flicker of hesitation. 'You've made the hardest decision, Grace, and now that you have, believe that you're going to be able to keep the house and act accordingly. The only reason to delay in carving out the future you want is if there's any doubt in your mind about what you want to do.' He looked over at her.

'No,' she said, quickly. 'There's no doubt.'

'Then there's no point in waiting. I can look at the house with you tomorrow if you like, through your eyes this time, and decide what things need to be done to turn you into a guest house extraordinaire.' He broke off and grinned at her. 'And my minimum payment for doing so is one beekeeping lesson.'

She gave him a wry smile. 'You have a deal,' she said, and then grew more serious. 'And I need to phone my solicitor too,' she added.

'Yes,' said Amos gently. 'You do.'

The exchange signalled the end of their conversation, but it was well over half an hour before either of them stirred.

*

Despite the relaxed few hours she had spent in Amos's company, Grace's head filled with anxiety the moment she laid her head on the pillow. It was one thing to talk about what she was going to do, but another entirely to make it happen. Even if everything turned out exactly the way she planned, there would be massive change accompanied by huge emotional turmoil; she would be foolish to think otherwise. And that was if things went well, there were any number of points along the way where it all could go wrong...

Given the nature of her thoughts it was no surprise that by two in the morning, Grace was once again wide awake. She had fallen asleep relatively quickly, the tiredness and stress of the day catching up with her, but even if she was not consciously thinking about her problems, her unconscious was doing a marvellous job all by itself. She threw back the covers, feeling stifled by the warmth of the bedroom, and turned over her pillow seeking to find a cool spot.

Another hour of tossing and turning had Grace heading for the kitchen to get a glass of water. She wasn't especially prone to insomnia, but there had been times in her life before when it had plagued her for nights on end. She had always found that writing down her worries helped to take the weight of anxiety from her head enough to allow her to sleep again. She collected a notepad and pencil from a drawer in the kitchen and took them to the table with her drink.

With the moon approaching fullness, she found she could still see well enough to write without turning on any lights, and, angling the paper towards the glow from the moon, she allowed the pencil to trace line after line of silvery thoughts.

After a while she realised that her attention was drifting from the paper to trace the outline of the pots of daisies that stood outside on the patio. She got up and slid open one of the glass doors, feeling the silky coolness of the night air rush in. It enticed her outside in a moment.

Grace was never scared being alone at night. Paul's work often meant that he was away from home, even when she had considered their marriage happy. Nowadays of course he was more likely to be away due to an illicit liaison rather than any work commitment but, despite the size of the house and its grounds, Grace had never felt uncomfortable.

She wandered out past the seating area and onto the lawn, feeling the softness of the grass beneath her feet. Far in the distance an owl hooted, answered seconds later by another, while closer to home the air rustled with tiny creatures scurrying through the undergrowth. Grace walked on, picking her way down the path that led through the apple trees and out onto the rougher grass. She had no real thought as to where she was headed, until she arrived at the top of the slope where the beehives lay. She smiled at the thought of Amos's antics that afternoon, picturing the scene being played out as Amos had described it. She doubted that Amos's intervention would have had any real effect on the agent, but even if it meant that the house details were not quite up to their usual standard, that at least was something. She might not have much choice in the house going on the market in the first place, but she didn't have to let Paul have everything his own way.

She walked on carefully to the point on the slope where the cover from the trees grew thinner and she was able to look out across the fields planted with flowers. They looked as if they were sleeping under their silvery blanket. She took a couple more steps but then stopped suddenly, her heart leaping into her mouth at the sight in front of her. On the slope below lay Amos, not injured as she had first thought, but instead, fast asleep. A blanket had been spread on the ground and Amos lay flat on his back, one hand resting on his chest with the other held loosely by his side. His head was turned slightly to one side, allowing moonlight to play across one cheek.

Crouching down where she stood, a feeling of enormous calm stole over her and Grace touched a hand to her heart without even knowing that she had done so. It felt as if she had never seen a man asleep before, but she must have. There would have been nights, surely, when she and Paul were first together, when she would have gazed at his face as he slept, but for the life of her she couldn't remember doing so. In fact, Amos looked more peaceful than she could ever remember seeing anyone look before and the more she tried to tell herself that it was wrong to be watching him without his knowledge, the harder she found it to tear herself away.

A faint golden glow began to breach the horizon and within minutes it seemed the first glint of the sun's glowing orb became visible, streaking the sky with bright orange and fading to a delicate pearlescent pink. She watched the shadow lift from Amos's face, saw the slight flicker of his eyelids as perhaps, subconsciously, he registered the first stirrings of the dawn. And still she sat, quiet as a mouse, listening to the swelling excitement of birdsong around her.

She had no idea who this man was, nor where he had come from. They had spoken about all the things that Amos might help with, both in her house and across at the farm, but that still didn't explain the mystery of why he was there in the first place. The thought should have filled her with anxiety, but strangely it didn't seem to matter at all. And even though she knew that it was an odd thing to find a man lying asleep in her garden, and that sitting watching him was equally weird, what was just as bizarre was that instead of making her feel like Amos was an intruder, what she felt was that she was no longer alone.

As the sun continued to bring light to the day, Grace got slowly to her feet and crept from the garden, walking through her house with feet damp from the dew and utterly at peace; something she hadn't felt in a long time. She was asleep the moment her head hit the pillow.

*

Just below her, on the gentle slope of the hill, Amos shifted slightly in his sleep and smiled.

Chapter Eleven

Grace awoke to the jarring sound of the telephone ringing. She lifted her head from the pillow but it felt so heavy that she immediately let it rest back down again, snuggling into the dent she had already made. She felt languid, deeply relaxed and incredibly comfortable and, given the choice, would happily have stayed in bed. Most unlike her.

The telephone stopped ringing and she closed her eyes, thankful for an end to the awful noise, but no sooner had she drifted off to sleep again than it rang for the second time. And kept ringing. She dragged herself into a semi-upright position and tried to focus, eventually managing to lift the phone from the receiver beside the bed.

'What the *hell* do you think you're doing?' said the voice from the other end.

There was only one person who would speak to her like that.

'Paul,' she said, closing her eyes in resignation. 'Do you mind not yelling at me down the phone? If you've got something to say perhaps you could say it politely.'

'When you tell me what game you think you're playing with the estate agent, I might consider it. Don't try and be clever, Grace, it doesn't suit you.'

Grace pulled herself up into a sitting position, glancing with horror at the clock as she did so. She switched the receiver to the other hand and tried to concentrate.

'I really have no idea what you're talking about, Paul.' She sighed.

There was a huff of indignation from the other end. 'Evan Porter?' he intoned. 'The estate agent, who made an appointment with you yesterday to take down the house particulars and was given the run-around by some idiot gardener.'

'Oh, Amos you mean.' She gritted her teeth. 'Well, firstly, he's not an idiot, and second, he did me a favour by standing in for me, actually. I got called away at the last minute. He was trying to be helpful, that's all.'

'What utter rubbish, Grace. I don't know what you think you're going to achieve but it won't make any difference. The house is going to be sold no matter how many silly games you play.' He paused for a moment to speak to someone in the background. 'Besides, we don't even have a gardener, and I better not be bloody paying for him.'

'Actually, Amos is working for free, which is just as well given the amount of time it takes to keep the grounds of this place looking at their best.'

'Payment in kind, is it?' he sneered. 'Very creative, Grace... or should I call you Lady Chatterley?'

Grace could feel her pulse begin to quicken and was about to bite back when she stopped herself. She'd had enough of her husband's insults and jibes and it was about time she refused to let them affect her.

'I've always known in which direction your moral compass points, Paul, you don't need to remind me. But as far as the garden goes, perhaps you'd prefer me not to bother with it... see how those prospective purchasers like the house when the garden looks a complete mess... It's peak growing season just now, Paul, and it really wouldn't take long for it to look completely overgrown.' She let her words sit with him before adding, 'Was there anything else you wanted? Only I'm rather busy.' She stretched out her legs languorously.

'Just get it sorted out. And next time the agent needs to call, make sure you're there.'

'Yes, of course, darling,' she replied. 'Anything you say.' And then she dropped the receiver back on its stand and scrambled from the bed.

She stood in the middle of the room full of indecision. There were so many things she would normally have done by this time in the morning she didn't know where to start. But then, out of nowhere, came a burst of laughter as Grace realised that she didn't care. She felt free for the first time in years.

Looking back towards the telephone she made a rude gesture at it, quickly covering her mouth as if someone might see her naughtiness. That was so unlike her as well. She stared at herself in the tall mirror on the other side of the room, gave a nod of satisfaction and went downstairs to make a coffee.

There was a text waiting for her on her mobile.

Morning! it said, followed by a sunny-face emoji. *We're drawing up battle plans for the milking shed at lunchtime, come over if you fancy it... and bring your notebook. About one. Flora xxx*

Grace looked at the clock again: 10 a.m. That was perfect. She texted back a reply to say that she would be there and crossed the room to throw open the patio doors. She stood there for a moment, half expecting to see Amos's curly head of hair bobbing about some-where, but knowing that he would have woken hours ago and would certainly no longer be in her garden. The image of him sleeping under the stars last night still made her smile. Pouring hot water into the cafetière, she picked up her mobile phone again, only this time she rang her solicitor.

*

It didn't matter how many times she saw it, Grace always thought the table and chairs laid out under the trees at the farm was like a 1950s' advert for the quintessential family day out. The table was covered in a red-checked cloth, a huge vase of flowers stood on top, and dish after dish of lovingly prepared food was laid out ready. Add to this a big pitcher of lemonade, several happy people and a backdrop of lush greenery and it was nigh on perfect.

Flora waved the moment she saw Grace walking towards them.

'Can you go and fish Amos out for me please?' she asked, as soon as Grace was close enough to speak to. 'He's round the back of the cottage. I've tried to get him to stop working and come and have some lunch but he's said he'll only be five minutes about twenty times now.'

Grace grinned and nodded, walking further on down the yard past the table and chairs on the triangle of green. She could hear the rhythmic tapping of a hammer as she drew nearer. Disappearing around to the rear of the low building, she found Amos hard at work, easing out the mortar from between the old brick joints.

She waved her hands. 'Lunch!' she shouted.

He pulled down the mask that was partially covering his face. 'Hello, Grace.' He smiled. 'Just give me five minutes.'

'Uh oh, no you won't,' replied Grace. 'I've been told to fetch you now.' She could see the desire on his face to finish the bit he was working on, but he shrugged easily enough.

'In that case, I'll pop and have a quick wash. Food doesn't taste so good when it's covered in a layer of brick dust. I've discovered that the hard way.' He put his tools down and followed Grace back around to the front of the building.

'And how are you today?' he asked. 'Did you sleep well?'

The question surprised her, but then she realised that Amos didn't actually know the answer to his question, it was just her that felt as if he had somehow been with her the whole time she had slept. The thought brought an immediate blush to her cheeks and she kept her head turned away slightly so that he wouldn't see.

'I was very lazy,' she replied. 'I'm normally up with the lark, but this morning I slept in until almost ten. I don't think I've done that since I was a teenager.'

'Well, other than missing an exceptionally beautiful dawn, I don't think it will have done you any harm at all,' he replied. 'You must have a lot on your mind just now. Sleep doesn't always come easily at such times.'

'No,' replied Grace, thinking of his peaceful face as *he* slept. 'Well, I think plans are afoot,' she added, drawing them away from what felt like a strangely intimate discussion. 'I can see you're very busy, but I hadn't forgotten I promised you a beekeeping lesson, so perhaps when we've heard what Flora has to say, we could fix up a time?'

They were standing by the cottage door. 'I'd like that,' said Amos simply, indicating that he should go inside. 'I'll catch you up, Grace,' he added. 'I won't be a minute.'

Grace made her way back to the others, taking a seat next to Hannah who was busy passing around dishes of salad amid a hubbub of conversation.

'Amos is on his way,' she reported.

'Good,' said Ned. 'Because if you've seen the number of things to do that Flora has on her list, he'll need feeding up – the poor man is going to be busy for the next seven years…'

'Oi!' replied Flora indignantly, slapping his arm playfully. She turned towards Grace. 'I've been trying to come up with some ideas for the best way to utilise the milking shed, which is why I'm really keen to hear what you might have in mind for your place. It strikes me that there could be a lot of crossover between what we'd like to accomplish here and what you might like to develop for your own business.'

Grace laid her notebook on the table. 'A joint venture?' she asked.

'Possibly,' replied Flora. 'Joint use of the space, almost certainly.'

'I phoned my solicitor this morning,' said Grace. 'And I'll know more when I meet with him on Tuesday but, as the house is in Paul's name, I have no automatic right to stay there. To do so may well be down to his "generosity" because otherwise any settlement I receive will be based on the value of his assets, which may mean they have to be liquified...'

'Oh, Grace...' Flora's face fell.

'However... what he did say is that if I could show I had the means to support myself and could therefore refuse ongoing maintenance, this would put me in a better position.' Grace lifted her chin. 'So, as far as I'm concerned, that's what we're going to do.' She opened her notebook. 'I've made a list too,' she added.

'I'll pour us some drinks,' said Hannah. 'All this thinking is thirsty work.'

Amos joined them minutes later and, once they were settled, Ned cleared his throat.

'So we already know that you want to open a guest house, Grace, with the potential for those staying to also learn some skills, perhaps in beekeeping, gardening, cookery and the like. And Flora can add floristry to that list obviously. So I guess the question is whether you have the space and facilities to do that from your house or whether some of it can take place here, alongside what Flora has in mind. The latter would certainly be more cost-effective.'

Grace pulled a face. 'My worry with all of this is that although I like the idea of running courses, I really don't think I'd be any good at it; working out the structure of what to teach, how to deliver it, that kind of thing. So I'm wondering whether it should be much more of a retreat-based experience rather than a learning environment. A bit more easy come, easy go. I don't think I'm cut out for lecturing.'

Flora giggled. 'You and me both. Can you imagine *me* trying to talk to a room full of people? It would disintegrate into a farce within a matter of minutes. What I would like to do, however, is open up this place to the public. I said from the start that I'd love if people could come and choose their own flowers for their events, be it weddings or otherwise. And to have a pick-your-own section too, where people could just buy what they want, when they want.' She shot a glance at Ned. 'On top of that, I'd really like to run a few short courses; like making seasonal flower garlands for example, or some ideas for table decorations. But nothing longer than a few hours and with no more than just a handful of people.'

Amos nodded. 'You could even replicate some of your interior-design ideas, Grace. Like the wall-hanging you have at home or some of the smaller ones you've used to decorate the shop.'

Grace turned to look at Amos. 'I didn't think you knew about those. How did you know I'd made them?' she asked.

Amos merely grinned. 'You did, didn't you?'

'And then there's all your artwork, Flora,' added Ned. 'I would love to see those on display, here in the very setting that provides most of the inspiration.'

Flora rolled her eyes. 'Oh God, there aren't enough hours in the day.'

'And we're rapidly running out of pairs of hands,' said Hannah. 'It isn't just the space to run these things from, but you need people to help out too.'

'So ideally it should all be located, if not in the same place, then at least close together so that you can man it all simply and efficiently. Otherwise you'll be looking at employing a whole army of people just to keep folks happy and attended to.'

Fraser held up his hand. 'I'm your man for the shop,' he said. 'I'm feeling better as each week goes by, but let's not kid ourselves. It's going to be a long time, if ever, before I can do a day's work in the field. But I can man a shop.' He grinned at Flora. 'Turn on the charm, you know I'm good at that.'

Flora snorted, and Grace smiled at the easy-going relationship the young woman now shared with her father-in-law. It hadn't always been that way, but Fraser's heart attack had brought them all closer together.

'Well, pardon me, who said anything about a shop?' asked Flora, but she grinned as all eyes turned on her. 'Okay, so we need a shop,' she said. 'And that would be the place where people could buy artwork from, ready-made bouquets, pay for flowers they've picked… and then we would also need another space where we could do demonstrations, or hold small workshops.'

Amos plucked a cherry tomato from a bowl on the table and threw it into his mouth like a sweet, grinning as he sought to contain a burst of juice from his mouth. 'Grace,' he managed, after a moment. 'What kinds of people do you reckon will come and stay with you? Or let me put it another way – what kinds of people do you *want* to come and stay with you? Who is your advertising going to be aimed at?'

She handed him a napkin. 'Go on,' she said. 'Explain. I know there's a reason why you've asked that question… What are you thinking?'

'Only that when I first came here, Flora nearly bit my arm off because the students she had thought were coming to help on the farm had just stood her up…'

Hannah drew in a breath, rather sharply.

'Now I'm not suggesting we have students staying here,' continued Amos, giving Hannah an easy smile. 'Because, lovely though young people are, they sometimes have a bit of working out their place in the world to go through. I think what we need here are folks who know exactly what they're about, want to indulge it, and... are more than happy to pay for it.'

'So?'

'So, working on the basis that you like the idea of a retreat-based holiday, why not give folks the choice? They either could opt for a completely relaxing and pampering break to do with as they please, where they pay for any workshops, et cetera, they like. Or they could choose a "get away from the rat race working holiday", one where, in return for putting in a few hours' help on the farm, they get the workshops, courses or whatever free as part of the package, all in a very relaxed and informal setting. Either way they pay for sumptuous accommodation and gorgeous food, so Grace gets an income, and then the farm gets either some free labour or some paying punters for its courses... or very probably both.'

'And then Fraser hits them with his winning smile and cheeky patter and gets them to part with even more dosh in the shop,' suggested Flora.

There was stunned silence for a moment as everyone digested what Amos had said. Fraser was blushing a little, Flora was beaming from ear to ear and Ned and Hannah were exchanging looks. And Grace? She wasn't sure what she was feeling, except that sitting here, under the shade of the trees, with a balmy breeze ruffling the tablecloth, it felt like a little slice of heaven. And if she could feel like this, perhaps other people would too.

'What do you think, Grace?' asked Amos.

He was leaning towards her, his voice hinting at the excitement she knew he was feeling, but it was his eyes that made Grace feel as if there were only the two of them sitting there. They held a softness that was wholly unnerving; Grace wasn't used to that at all.

'Could we really do all this?' she whispered, hardly daring to voice it out loud.

Flora laid a hand on the table. 'Amos?'

'We could,' he agreed. 'The milking shed could be split quite easily to give you the space you need… and the design, with its raised walkways, would lend itself to becoming areas for display, or to facilitate demonstrations. Reinstate its original ceiling as well and you'd have a wonderfully light and airy building.'

Grace grinned at Flora. 'Then I think it's absolutely the best idea I've ever heard. I can't quite believe it.'

Ned reached forward to take both Grace and Flora's hands.

'And are you still feeling frightened?' he asked, looking at Grace.

She shook her head decisively. 'Not any more,' she said. 'I've never been more certain of anything.'

Chapter Twelve

'I just hope the bees didn't spot my antics the other day,' said Amos, following Grace out of the house. 'Otherwise I think I'm in for a rather hard time. I don't suppose they take too kindly to strangers trying to give them a bad name.'

'Oh, I'm sure you'll have been forgiven. I like to think my bees are very good judges of character.' She smiled, the golden afternoon sun catching her eyes as she did so. 'And make no mistake, they'll have spotted you, it's their busiest time of year.'

'So how often do you check the hives then?' asked Amos.

'In winter, not at all, and at other times of the year it varies depending on what I find when I open them. It's incredibly tempting to keep checking on them, especially when you're new to beekeeping and can see all the changes beginning to take place. But make no mistake, I need the bees much more than they need me, so the minimum necessary is what's required. You'll see when we open it how much it disrupts them, it's almost like a shudder passes through the hive.' She looked up to the sky. 'This time of year, about once a week is a good idea, and on a day when it's warm and still is best. Never when it's raining, and I prefer to visit them early afternoon. Most of them will be out foraging then.'

Amos nodded. 'And do they really have bad moods, or is that just an old wives' tale?'

'No, not at all,' replied Grace. 'They don't like stormy weather, but there are also days when, for no reason that I can deduce, they just seem "off". Before I knew any better, I've opened the hive on days like that and immediately regretted it. A bee loses its life when it stings, so to do so is a very last resort. It's a salutary and very humbling lesson to learn that your inattentiveness or arrogance has caused their deaths.'

Amos almost stumbled as Grace's words reached him. He had not expected such a stark reminder of his past on a day like today, with so much beauty around him, and it was all he could do to keep walking; grateful at least that he was following behind. Most people didn't notice the tremor of emotion that ran through Amos at times, but Grace would, and he had no wish to cause her any more anguish; she'd had enough of that over recent days. He tried to concentrate on the task at hand, knowing that he needed to approach the bees with a calm stillness that right now was distinctly at odds with how he was feeling.

'I like the way you talk about your bees,' he said, hoping that Grace would be able to pick up the conversation again.

'Well, I like the way you like the way I talk about my bees,' she replied. He couldn't see her face, but he could hear the smile in her voice. 'Not everyone gets it, or, worse, they make no attempt to understand it. Anyone who takes even just a few moments to consider what bees do for us would realise how much they deserve our respect.'

She suddenly stopped and Amos almost crashed into her back.

'In fact,' she continued, obviously having paused for thought. 'That's true for most things, isn't it? I like to think I'm a great respecter of all living beings. Every life has value whether we consider it to be big or small, important or irrelevant. It's certainly not for us to choose which one of those it is, they should all have equal merit.'

She turned around to face him, frowning. 'Well, I try at least. I'm not sure I always succeed,' she added. 'There have been quite a few occasions when I could cheerfully have murdered my husband.'

Amos stared at her, his heart beginning to beat uncomfortably fast in his chest. He knew that her comment about Paul was a flippant one, but the conversation was becoming increasingly dangerous, straying onto subjects that he had no wish to discuss, not in Grace's company anyway. He visited them often enough in his dreams.

He cleared his throat to try and dislodge the tight ball of anxiety there, but he really had no idea what he was going to say.

'Amos... are you all right? You've gone very pale all of a sudden.' Grace was searching his face and her scrutiny was hard to bear. She touched the back of her hand to his forehead gently. 'And you're boiling hot...'

He swallowed, nodding as best he could, but Grace's words had struck at his very heart. 'Sorry... I'm fine, just a little light-headed. I suffer from low blood pressure from time to time. It'll pass.' He took a few deep breaths. He hadn't intended to lie, but his need for self-preservation overrode everything.

'So you probably feel dizzy then? Amos, you should have said instead of letting me ramble on. We can look at the bees another time, it's no problem. But you ought to sit down or something...'

He smiled gratefully. He'd had no idea that the conversation was going to take this turn, but did he carry on and hope that they could return to discussing safer subjects? Or put some distance between him and Grace? Although that hardly seemed fair, it wasn't her fault he'd reacted badly. But then he thought back to the very start of their conversation.

'Sorry, would you mind?' he replied. 'I'm conscious that my head isn't in the right place to greet the bees at all, and the last thing I want is to keel over while we're at the hive. I think another time might be better, but I was really looking forward to it. This doesn't happen very often, don't worry…'

She took hold of his arm gently. 'Come on, come back inside and I'll get you a drink.' She gave him another appraising glance. 'Look, there's no easy way of saying this, so I'm just going to come out with it, okay? But, given your… circumstances… do you ever even get to see a doctor? What do you do about medication?'

Amos could have kicked himself. Given Grace's nature he should have known she would react this way. He plastered a reassuring smile onto his face.

'This is nothing, really. And I could go and see a doctor if I needed to, don't worry. But, like I said, I don't get it very often and it isn't something I've ever needed to see anyone about.' He pulled a face. 'More self-diagnosed actually… but usually I am in extraordinarily good health.' He pulled himself up tall and grinned.

'And you're not going to let on otherwise,' added Grace, peering at him shrewdly. 'Okay, I'm backing off… but we're still going to have that drink.'

So Amos began to follow her again, but in the other direction. And by the time they made it back to the house he made damn sure that he was 'feeling' better.

'Oh God, I feel such an idiot,' he said, taking a seat in the kitchen as directed. 'I feel absolutely fine now.'

Grace handed him a packet of biscuits. 'Right, well the kettle's on. Get a couple of those down you as well for good measure, just in case. They won't hurt.' She gave him another once-over. 'You do look better actually, but the bees can wait until another day. Apart from the fact that it's always a good idea to get in the right frame of mind whenever you approach them, I want you to enjoy the experience, not be worried about how you might be feeling. You won't get half as much out of it if you don't, and surely that's why we're doing it in the first place?'

Amos nodded, struggling to speak through a mouthful of biscuit crumbs. 'Which brings me neatly to the other part of the equation,' he said. 'In that the beekeeping lessons were supposed to be in exchange for work that might need doing on the house, and I'm conscious of the fact that we haven't even talked about that yet. Perhaps we could have a look at that today, instead. Flora isn't expecting me back for a couple of hours, so we've got plenty of time.'

He chased a speck of biscuit from the corner of his mouth with his tongue. 'In fact, it would probably help me to know what work there is to do here so that I can factor it in along with everything else.' He grinned. 'There's rather more to do now than when I first arrived.'

Grace rolled her eyes. 'Yes…' She let the word slide out on the back of a long breath, but although it was tinged with a slight reticence, there was excitement there too. 'My main problem would have been where to run workshops or courses from, and I was thinking I would have had to convert a space somewhere, but seeing as that problem has been neatly solved it's now more a case of some cosmetic tidying up. I don't think there's masses to do.'

'I can't think how there would be, Grace. You have a beautiful home.'

Aware that there was a poignancy surrounding his words, Amos got to his feet. 'I tell you what, why don't we have a walk round now?'

It didn't take long; there were six bedrooms in total, but Amos had already been in five of them when the estate agent had visited. He hadn't entered Grace's room, preferring not to intrude on what was a very private space when she herself wasn't present. But it was beautiful, as he had known it would be.

'And this is my dilemma,' said Grace. 'I love this room, but looking at it from a purely business point of view, so will my guests. And given that it's twice as big as the other rooms I could charge more for it as well. It makes much more sense for me to relocate to one of the other bedrooms.'

'Which are lovely, but nowhere near as nice,' added Amos. 'I also think you need to bear in mind that you'll need somewhere of your own to go to once your house is full of people. And that somewhere should be a haven, a respite from the busyness of the rest of the house. Don't underestimate how that will make you feel – you've been used to being on your own, or with just the two of you, for quite some time, and having other people around is going to take a little getting used to.'

'But I have to be practical,' reasoned Grace. 'And the room on the end is fine. It still has an en-suite and with a few adjustments I could make it more like what I've been used to.'

'Then that's what we'll do,' said Amos, firmly. 'I think that Flora would like the alterations to the milking sheds underway as soon as possible. It's still early in the season and the earlier they capitalise on the extra space the better, but I'm sure I can fit what needs doing here around all that. We should aim to have things ready to go as soon as possible. That way when you hear that the house is safe we can swing into action.'

Grace gave a wry smile. 'I like your optimism,' she said. 'Thank you for not saying *if* you hear…'

'It's going to be fine,' replied Amos. 'I can feel it.'

They were walking back down the landing to head downstairs when Grace suddenly stopped. She turned to face him.

'Amos, why are you doing all this?' she asked. Her eyes were on his, and he had a horrible feeling she could see inside his very soul.

'What do you mean?' he replied, hoping to sidestep her question.

'Why are you helping me?'

He shrugged. 'Because you need help,' he said simply, beginning to move off again.

She caught his arm. 'No, I'm serious. Why would you even do this? I'm a virtual stranger but I feel you'd be happy moving heaven and earth if I asked you to. I don't get it.'

'But this all fits,' he replied. 'You're friends with everyone at the farm next door and you each have need of the other. I'm helping them, why on earth wouldn't I help you too?'

Grace looked at him quizzically. 'That's rather what I meant,' she said. 'Forgive me, Amos, and I don't mean this the way it's possibly going to sound. But aware as I am that I don't actually know any homeless people, you don't exactly fit the stereotype.'

'And what would that be?' He raised his eyebrows.

She sighed. 'You know what I mean, stop evading the question. You're articulate, obviously educated, wise… and very astute.'

'People from all walks of life lose their homes, Grace. That doesn't mean anything.'

'Yes, and I'm well aware that makes me sound like a horribly judgemental snob, but there's something about you… something I can't quite put my finger on. I find it curious, that's all.'

Amos simply smiled, not wishing to invite further questions.

'And you have a house, I know that. But yet you choose to travel around from one place to the next, sleeping outdoors and working for your board and lodging. It's not what most people choose to do.'

'Perhaps not. But there's a freedom that comes with that way of life too, Grace. I'm not tethered by belongings or responsibility. I've met some amazing people and had the opportunity to do things I would never have done otherwise.'

Grace paused, one hand on the bannister. 'So, going back to my original question then,' she said. '*Why* are you doing this? I can understand the appeal of what you've just described, up to a point, but I still don't quite understand why you would choose to do it in the first place. Don't get me wrong, I'm incredibly grateful that you are, but given that I'm fighting to keep my home, I'm wondering why you were so keen to give up yours.' She fixed him with a look that Amos could not evade. 'Were you looking for freedom? Or an escape...? Or perhaps, in your case, they're both the same thing.'

Chapter Thirteen

Grace was still thinking about their conversation two days later, even when she should have had her mind very firmly on other things. Amos had been very polite – she couldn't imagine him being anything else – but he had obviously been affected by her words and now she only wished that she could take them back. He had shown her nothing but kindness and consideration and she had no right to go prying in things that were none of her business and making him feel uncomfortable by doing so. Worse, she'd had no opportunity since to apologise, having spent yesterday in the shop and then this morning visiting her solicitor. Amos had been busy too, so it wasn't unusual that she hadn't seen him, but the thoughts still weighed heavily on her mind.

The visit to her solicitor had thrown up no surprises. He had been at school with Grace, later on a guest at her and Paul's wedding, and had looked after her affairs for more years than she cared to remember. There was, however, something reassuring about talking to a man with whom she had also discussed maths homework many years ago. He had been married, divorced, remarried and a solicitor for over twenty-five years; there wasn't anything he hadn't seen or heard before and he listened to what she had to say as a friend might. He took her instructions and promised to contact her once he had established a dialogue with Paul's solicitor. She had left feeling relieved that the meeting was over and, to some degree, her marriage.

Driving home, she was surprised to realise that her mind was not on the events of the last couple of hours but on the fact that she hadn't seen Amos for almost two days now. Distracted, she scarcely noticed the flash of silver through the trees as she turned off the road onto the sweep of her long drive. Emerging from the shadowed canopy onto the final stretch in front of the house, she almost collided with a sleek Mercedes driving at speed towards her. She slammed on her brakes.

The other driver was out of the car much quicker than she was.

'Grace!'

She raised her head from her hands and turned towards the sound of the voice just beyond the driver's side window. She groaned.

The door was pulled open and a concerned face loomed into view.

'Grace… Are you okay? Sorry, I…'

'Dominic,' she said slowly. 'Why is it that you constantly feel the need to drive everywhere at ninety miles an hour? No one is *that* busy, ever.'

He had the decency to look ashamed.

'I didn't think you were home,' he replied, pulling the door wider and offering a hand.

'No, I wasn't. Which, considering this is my driveway, is the reason *I* didn't expect to see you come careering towards me.' Her heart rate was beginning to slow slightly, enough for her brain to start processing information. 'What are you doing here anyway?'

He looked at her, bemused.

'Well, I came to see you.'

She clambered from the car. 'Yes, obviously… but what for?'

He didn't answer but gestured back towards the house. 'Could we go inside?' he asked. 'I feel I should make you a cup of tea, or something…'

'Dominic, I'm fine. I'm more worried about the potential for damage to your very expensive car than about any I may suffer myself. But you'd better come in.'

It was the last thing she needed given the mood she was in but there could be only one reason why Dominic was here. She collected her handbag from the car and walked on ahead to open the front door.

'I hope you've got some good news for me,' she said as she turned the key in the lock.

There was no reply but then Dominic was never the type to discuss anything without a cup of coffee in his hand. She could do with one herself, but she also had no real desire to waste any more of her day on conversations about things she really didn't want to talk about.

Walking into the kitchen, she dumped her bag on the countertop and threw open the double doors into the garden, flooding the room with the sound of birdsong.

'So…' she said. 'Have you come all this way to see me without even checking if I was in, or had you some other reason to be out this way? You're lucky you caught me at all.'

Dominic smiled. 'Nothing much gets past you, does it?' he replied.

'Just that a busy man like you wouldn't waste several hours on a fruitless journey.'

He crossed the room to stand by the threshold to the garden. 'I've been to see my mother,' he explained. 'A slight emergency late last night; a fall which resulted in a trip to the hospital and a broken wrist, but my sister is with her now so all is well. She's back at home, giving out orders left, right and centre, so obviously not feeling too diminished.'

'Oh, Dominic, I am sorry. But you know I've always said that Nancy will probably outlive us all.'

'You may well be right. The circumstances of the fall worried me slightly until I found out that she'd been waltzing around the living room and tripped over the cat.'

Grace laughed, she couldn't help herself. 'Well then I'm glad to see that some things never change.'

Dominic turned around to focus directly on her. 'However, I was going to come over to see you this week anyway…' He trailed off, running a hand through his hair. It was a gesture that Grace knew of old.

'What's the matter, Dominic?' She sighed. 'Go on, sit down. I'll put the kettle on.'

He took a seat as directed but, she noticed, with his back slightly to her so that he could look out into the garden. His supposedly relaxed pose was undermined only by the tell-tale jiggling of his foot as he crossed his legs.

As soon as they were settled she wasted no further time.

'I would imagine you need to talk to me about Paul,' she said, handing him a cup of coffee.

He put it straight down on the table. 'There have been some further developments, yes, and, under the circumstances, we felt it was probably best if I talk to you.'

'*We* felt?' queried Grace.

Dominic's eyes flickered to his lap. '*I* felt… Because I really don't want to make this any harder than it already is, and I don't believe that Paul would handle it particularly well.'

'So you've come to smooth the way, have you? Because whatever it is you know I'm not going to like it one little bit—'

'Grace, I've done what I can for you. I actually have, you have to believe me.' There was a pained expression on his face. 'Despite what you think about me, you probably ought to know that I think very highly of you, I always have and I—' He stopped himself, picking up his coffee and gulping at the hot liquid. 'Look, let me just explain,' he said, changing the subject. 'I obviously spoke to Paul after we last met and, much to my surprise, he was considerably more contrite than I thought he was going to be. I think he's genuinely sorry for the distress he has caused you.'

Grace gave a bitter laugh. 'Dominic, if you've come here to effect a reconciliation, don't waste your breath. You really don't know Paul at all well if you think that was a genuine reaction. On the contrary, I would say that what you saw was a very measured response to Paul's assumption that his neck was on the block with the network. I think you've been played.'

'Which would have been my first thought,' admitted Dominic. 'And I went into that meeting expecting just that but, as things progressed, I saw what I honestly do believe were the defences coming down. We had a far more honest conversation than I thought possible and I don't think Paul realised how unhappy you were. A sad testament to the shallowness of his character, but there you are. Sure, he was aware you knew about his affairs, and his other... misdemeanours, but I think he thought, or rather he assumed, that you were happy in your own life and had accepted that his actions didn't really affect you.'

Grace couldn't believe what she was hearing. 'That's absolute rubbish, Dominic. Paul doesn't like being rejected, that's all. He wasn't surprised by my asking for a divorce, he was just furious because he didn't get there first.' She took a deep breath to calm herself. 'How can anyone think that what we had was an acceptable basis for a marriage, I—'

'Grace,' said Dominic gently, holding a hand out towards her. 'I didn't say I agree with him. I don't, on any level. Why on earth would I want to see the two of you reconciled? I hate the way you've been treated and, as far as I'm concerned, Paul is a spineless, shallow, thoughtless and incredibly stupid excuse for a man in doing that to you, but...' He winced. 'But, he is still the guy who pulls in our highest viewing figures. And for that reason, and that reason only, I listen to what he has to say. Otherwise I would have punched his lights out years ago.'

Dominic's voice had risen as he spoke, falling abruptly at his final words. And now he sat quietly, looking at his hands in his lap. There were implications contained in what he had just said that Grace probably needed time to think about but, for now, she was only interested in one thing.

'So, is Paul going to let me keep the house, or not? That's what this all boils down to. I've been to see my solicitor this morning, Dominic. I've renounced my claim on everything else I'm entitled to, save for the house.'

'He's not in as good a position as you think, Grace,' replied Dominic.

'Oh, my heart bleeds for him.' Grace picked up her cup and finally took a drink of her coffee, pinning Dominic with her stare.

He dipped his head in acknowledgement. 'Financially, there are no worries, and obviously, as you know, there are other properties that he has acquired over the years and so accommodation is not a problem either, but emotionally... Stupid as it may sound, I don't think Paul ever thought you would ask him for a divorce. And now that you have, it's genuinely hurt him and selling this place is his reaction to that. A spoilt child throwing his toys out of the pram perhaps, but there you have it.'

Grace opened her mouth in stunned disbelief. 'Then he should have thought about that before he... did all those things he did.' She couldn't bring herself to say the words. 'That's the most ridiculous thing I've ever heard.'

'I know. I'm not excusing him, Grace, far from it. I'm just telling you what I understand from what he told me.'

'So I *am* going to lose the house then?'

Dominic exhaled a slow breath. 'I tried my best to persuade him to let you keep it, Grace. Pointed out the way he'd behaved, what you've done for him, all of that, but all I could do was leave it with him and hope that he would see sense, or be man enough to do the right thing.'

Grace nodded. Dominic had done what she had asked of him and perhaps it wasn't fair of her to ask him to do any more, or worse take advantage of the way that he felt about her for her own gain. That would make her almost as bad as Paul. But then something else occurred to her. Her eyes narrowed.

'Wait a minute... You said before that there had been some further developments and that *you* wanted to be the one to tell me about them. What's happened, Dominic?'

He gestured at the coffee pot. 'May I?' he asked.

She nodded as he refilled his cup, aware that her heart was beginning to beat slightly faster. Dominic was used to having difficult conversations, it was part of his job. The fact that he was stalling for time now was worrying.

He waited until he had taken a sip before continuing. 'We've been courting a certain production company for months. I can't give you the details because it's all incredibly hush-hush, but they have a series they're launching next year which is going to blow everything else off the top spot. Everyone's talking about it. And everyone is vying for the contract. I don't need to tell you how much these things are worth, Grace.'

He offered a sheepish smile and she braced herself.

'Yesterday, I had an incredible meeting with them, and we're almost there,' he went on. 'We're so close. They love Paul and the rest of the team, and next month the main man is coming over from the States. One final push and we should have a deal, but you know how it is, nothing's ever over until it's over. We're not the only network in the running and, although I think we're a nose ahead, we need everything to be perfect. In short, we need you, Grace, one last time.'

She stared at him, a surge of heat rising rapidly up her neck. Whatever she'd thought he was going to say, it wasn't this.

'You need me?' she clarified, shaking her head. 'I don't believe I'm hearing this… From Paul, maybe, but not you, Dominic. I actually thought you were better than that…' She stopped, thinking. 'No, wait, you even told me, didn't you? How you were going to break the news to me rather than my husband because you thought you'd do a better job of it, because you didn't want to make this any harder for me than it already is. A commendable sentiment, Dominic, but not really true, is it? It's not about that at all, it's about making sure that you succeed in your mission to get your glittering contract.'

She broke off, glaring at him. 'Go on,' she added. 'Admit it. Was there anything about what I've just said that isn't true…?'

Dominic hung his head.

'I should throw you out.' She got up from her chair. 'How dare you?' She towered over him, collecting the coffee pot from the table and placing it by the sink. Then she doubled back and snatched the cup from Dominic's hand and moved that too. 'And you even had the audacity to sit in my kitchen a couple of days ago and tell me you were sorry for what happened that last time, and now you want me to do it *again*?'

'Grace, please… just listen a minute. I know it sounds dreadful, and I'm not going to insult your intelligence and deny this contract isn't important to me. I'm Head of Programming, it's my job, for God's sake, what do you expect me to do?'

'Oh, I don't know, act like a decent human being?' She marched back over to the table. 'I'd like you to leave now, please,' she said, hating herself for even being polite.

Reluctantly he got to his feet. 'This is a shock, I know. It wasn't what you wanted to hear. And I wasn't expecting this either, Grace, you have to believe me. I had left things for Paul to mull over. I had made it quite clear what I thought he should do about the house. I even made one or two veiled threats about his position at the network, but then this meeting yesterday hurled everything forward at a rapid rate. I had no idea they were so close to making a decision, and...' He made a low groaning noise, before inhaling sharply and reaching out to touch her arm. 'Grace, if you do this, Paul will give you the house.'

His statement hovered in the air like a fat balloon waiting to be popped.

Seconds clicked by.

'It's one weekend, Grace. Just like the old times. One weekend, three guests, your amazing hospitality and you get to keep the house. It's as simple as that.'

She swallowed hard. 'So what you're saying is that thirty-odd years of marriage, love, faith, and loyalty, don't amount to anything. None of those things we shared would make Paul change his mind about the house, but a bloody new starring role would. Well, that's quite a sobering thought, isn't it?'

She sat down heavily. 'Do you know what's really sad is that I don't actually believe you, Dominic. I only have your word over the house, and past events have given me no reason to trust my husband. I'm not sure why I should even consider doing so now.'

Dominic's jaw clenched. 'If you do this, Grace, I will guarantee it. I'll get a legal document drawn up, anything.'

She couldn't believe he was actually waiting for her answer.

'Get out of my house,' she said quietly.

'Please, just think about it. I'm not making any excuses, I know what this sounds like and you're absolutely right, it's blackmail by any other name. But, I can also see how it could work, Grace; how we could all win from this situation, turn it into something good. Just think about it. They don't come until next month so you have a little time and—'

'Get out of my house!' she shouted, lurching to her feet again. She took a step towards Dominic. 'I mean it...'

He backed away, pushing his glasses up his nose. 'I'm sorry, Grace, I never wanted...'

'Get out!'

She was shaking with fury as she watched him turn and walk from the room and she stood, rooted to the spot, until she heard the front door close. She walked to the sink, picking up the cups and placing them in the bowl, picking up the dishcloth and putting it down again, clenching and unclenching her fists. A sudden shadow fell across the room and she looked up, startled. Then, before she even knew what she was doing, she had crossed the room and hurled herself at the figure that stood on the threshold to the garden, bursting into noisy choking sobs.

Chapter Fourteen

Amos wasn't one for fighting but when he'd heard the shouts from halfway down Grace's garden he had raced across the lawn fully prepared to do battle. His heart was pounding by the time he reached the patio just in time to see a tall figure leaving the kitchen. He hadn't stopped to think about how his own presence might be construed and so he was quite relieved to see the man walking away as he neared the house, avoiding any confrontation.

Preoccupied by this thought, he was completely unprepared for finding Grace in his arms and, surprised, he instinctively pulled her close. His emotions reeled. Her hair smelled of apples, her skin was warm and soft, her body firm and yet yielding to his as her head rested snugly against the dip of his shoulder. Amos had spent a lot time away from home, but in this moment he had never felt more like he *was* home. Every fibre of his being wanted to stay the way they were forever, just as much as every fibre of his reason told him he had to move. But Grace was upset. Whatever had just occurred had left her stricken and her need for comfort from him was as instinctive as his desire to give it. To withdraw that now, just when she was feeling at her most vulnerable, would surely only compound her pain, and Amos really didn't think he could do that to her.

Just at the point when he thought he couldn't wrestle with his emotions any longer, something shifted within Grace and she tore herself from him, gasping as she pushed herself away, her eyes wild, staring. Her hand went to her mouth. She made no move to wipe away her tears, but instead stared at him as if seeing him for the first time.

'I'm so sorry,' she stammered. 'I've never…' And then she trailed off, peering at him. To his immense relief, she suddenly started to laugh. 'Oh, my God, the look on your face.' Her hand moved to her cheek. 'Is that what I look like? Oh, that's *bad*… No, it must be worse because I've been crying…' She rubbed her palms across her face, catching the drips on the end of her chin and then wiping her hands down her jeans. She sneaked another glance at him and giggled. 'I'm such a mess.'

She wasn't. She looked beautiful.

'And even though I *am* sorry, I'm going to make you take some of the blame. That was spectacularly bad timing on your part, Amos.'

'Some would argue my timing was no less than exemplary.'

She wrinkled her nose. 'Well I suppose you did save me from smashing every piece of crockery I possess. That, or hurling a chair through the window…' She smiled. 'So perhaps it *was* good that you turned up when you did. I don't think I've ever been that angry. And I don't know why I'm laughing, it's really not funny at all.' She sniffed and Amos fished in his pocket and pulled out a tissue. It had seen better days but was clean.

'Here,' he said. 'Have a good blow. And before you apologise again, can I just say that I'm sorry too, for barging in. I didn't mean to intrude. I was on my way up here, as it happens, but I heard shouting and I'm afraid my damsel-in-distress mode came on all of its own accord. I'm usually far too much of a wuss for that to happen, and given that your husband is at least a foot taller than me, I'm glad I just missed him.'

'My husband?'

'Yes, the man who just left.'

'Oh, that wasn't my husband, that was Dominic – he's my husband's boss. Although, given the way he's just behaved, if he was, I'd be divorcing him too.' She frowned at him. 'Tell me, Amos, is there something about me that brings out the worst in the men in my life? Because I'm beginning to wonder. A tattoo on my forehead perhaps that says *use and abuse…*'

Amos smiled. He couldn't speak for the two idiots Grace was describing, but as far as he was concerned, nothing could be further from the truth. *Love and adore* perhaps… He peered at her.

'Nope, nothing there…'

'Well, that's a relief at least.' She sat down at the table and blew her nose loudly. 'Very elegant,' she commented.

Amos joined her. 'Can I get you anything?' he asked.

She rolled her eyes. 'I'm tempted to say the number of a good hitman, but there's a packet of ginger nuts in the cupboard which will do nicely.' She smiled a thank you as Amos got to his feet. 'Just above the mugs.'

He fetched the biscuits and flicked the switch on the kettle to boil the water. He wasn't sure whether Grace was a dunker of biscuits, but he certainly was.

She smiled at him nervously as he sat back down again. 'I ought to say, that despite evidence to the contrary, I'm not in the habit of bursting into tears and throwing myself at strange men.'

'Men you don't know very well, or strange men? Be careful how you answer that, I could be very offended.' Amos looked up at her and smiled. 'Although in my case, I'm probably both those things.'

'And that's twice now I've embarrassed you.'

'Grace, it's not embarrassment I'm feeling.' He saw no reason to hide his feelings.

'No,' she said quietly.

He pulled open the packet of biscuits. 'So, am I allowed to ask what Dominic has done that's so heinous? Although of course, if you'd rather not I—'

'No, I want to tell you. If I don't I think I'll go mad. But before I do, can I just ask you something first? It's been on my mind and I feel I owe you an apology.'

He raised his eyebrows.

'Did I offend you the other day by asking you questions about your past? And if not offend, then upset slightly, irked a little?'

'Not in the slightest. In fact, it's natural that you might want to know.'

'Then the comment I made about giving up your home. You went awfully quiet after.'

'Did I?'

Grace gave him a look that made him realise he would never get away with denying it. He gave a rueful smile because that was precisely why he had been on his way over, to apologise to Grace. He knew he had reacted badly and he hated that even after all this time the odd comment could still trigger feelings that were utterly out of his control.

'Because it's none of my business why you chose to do that. Not everything in life conforms to our set way of looking at the world, does it? But I hope you know that I wasn't being judgemental in the slightest, just interested, that's all.'

But Amos was prepared this time. 'Then ask me anything you like,' he replied. 'And I will answer.'

Grace shook her head. 'No, that's backing you into a corner and I have no intention of doing that either.'

Amos studied his biscuit before biting it in half and chewing slowly, but then he couldn't help himself and, catching Grace's eye, broke into a grin. 'Would now be a good time to tell you that I actually came over here to apologise myself for my reaction the other day... and to offer an explanation?'

She rolled her eyes, but there was amusement in them.

'And given that I have just asked *you* to share with me the reason why you're upset and you agreed, I feel it's only fair that I should support your spirit of openness by going first.' He paused as the kettle switched off with a click, then gave Grace a meaningful look. She tutted, but got to her feet and went to make their drinks.

'You asked me the other day why I was helping you. Why I left my home and whether that was because I was seeking freedom or an escape...'

Grace groaned from across the room. 'Thanks for reminding me how awful that sounds,' she said. 'I am sorry.'

'But you have no need to be,' countered Amos. 'They're reasonable questions, and the answers aren't very exciting, I'm afraid. More just a good old-fashioned midlife crisis. I'd reached a point in my life where everything just seemed so...' he broke off searching for the right word '... *stultifying*. Does that make sense? I've never married, and wasn't in a relationship, my work was steady but unfulfilling, and I realised that I was barely able to remember what it felt like to be alive. I had already decided that travelling might be a way to reenergise my life when, purely by chance, I met a young woman in difficult circumstances who had need of somewhere to live. The solution seemed obvious, if a little crazy, but then I was ready for that and – this is where it gets a bit clichéd, I'm afraid – her reaction to what she termed my random act of kindness made me feel better about myself than I had in a long time. Deciding to combine travel with a certain hopefulness about people seemed like a good course of action. And the rest, as they say, is history.'

Grace had been watching him intently but, with a slight narrowing of her eyes as he finished his speech, she turned away to finish making the tea. It seemed to take an interminable amount of time, but eventually she carried two mugs back to the table.

'How much history, Amos?' she asked. 'How long have you been away from home?'

'Coming up five years,' he replied.

'Five *years*?' She looked incredulous. 'And you've never been home in all that time?'

Amos took the opportunity to reach for another biscuit now that he had a brew to dunk it in. 'A few times. A couple of years ago when we had a really hard winter… I enjoy a challenge, Grace, but I'm not a complete idiot.' He grinned. 'But apart from that, yes, pretty much continuously, although, as it happens I'm working my way back there now.'

'Are you?' Grace looked surprised.

'In a roundabout way, yes. I keep in touch with Maria, that's the woman who looks after my house for me, and so every now and again I just make sure that I head in the right direction. I'll get there eventually.'

'So, are we close?'

'Not close as such, but my house is in a tiny village just across the Worcestershire border.'

'Oh.'

Amos took in her expression. 'But, as I've already told Flora, I won't just up sticks and leave. We'll all know when it's time for me to go, and that will be when the time is right. I don't stay a set amount of time anywhere. In fact, I don't ever know how long I'm going to be in a place, I wait for circumstance to tell me and time just passes of its own accord.'

'But when you travel, you help people along the way?'

He nodded. 'We help each other.' He touched a finger to the corner of his mouth. 'I know I can tell you this without having you laugh at me,' he said. 'But I have a view of the way the world works, or how it likes to work given the chance. All I do is encourage that process by looking for the openings, the little chances; the opportunity to help and be helped is always there if you keep yourself open to it.'

He pulled a face. 'And over time I've kind of developed a sixth sense for knowing where I need to be. Plus, every once in a while you meet people who think the same way and then, whoosh, pretty much anything seems possible.'

'A wise observation,' commented Grace. 'You wouldn't be talking about Hope Corner, would you, by any chance?'

Amos grinned. 'Now who's being wise?' he asked. 'You already know that there's a massive buzz about this place and I'm not just talking about your bees. I felt it as soon as I arrived and now, in answer to your very first question, the reason I am helping you is very simple – I look for the places where I can push what's already going on even higher. Or does that all sound a bit new age, hippy, woo woo…?' He dunked his biscuit and then popped it, whole, into his mouth.

Grace laughed, and he was pleased to see her finally beginning to relax. 'Probably,' she agreed. 'But I also happen to think it's true. It does take the right kind of people to make it happen though. There are certain people who wear blinkers their entire lives and never even notice what's happening around them. I love your ideals, Amos, but surely your hopefulness about the way people behave isn't always borne out?'

'No, of course it isn't. Some people are just morons whatever help you try to give them, mentioning no names, obviously...'

Grace caught the inflection in his voice. 'Isn't that the truth,' she said. 'I had high hopes for Dominic once. Despite some very silly behaviour in the past, I always thought he was basically a good soul and all it would take was a little nudge for him to shine. It seems I was wrong.'

'You never know, he might surprise you yet.'

'Oh, he's certainly done that.' Grace picked up a biscuit and jabbed it viciously in her tea. 'Although I suppose I shouldn't be surprised really; anyone who hangs around Paul for long enough seems to become tainted with the same low moral standard that he has.'

'Everyone except you, Grace,' Amos reminded her.

She smiled, but it was a tight, brief affair and went nowhere near her eyes.

'So you mentioned that Dominic is Paul's boss. Does that mean that he's the person to whom you sent the information about your husband's various dalliances? And presumably therefore the one who might hold some sway over Paul's actions as a result? It would seem that he's holding rather a lot of cards.'

Grace nodded. 'Yes, and when you're holding all the cards, it's pretty easy to use blackmail as a means to your own ends.'

'Blackmail?' He sat up a little straighter. 'Grace, that's serious.'

She waved her hand. 'Sorry, I don't mean it in the traditional monetary sense, but in a way I might as well have. Right now, if I do what they say, I get to keep the house, that's what it boils down to.'

Amos's mug was on the way to his mouth and he paused, holding the rim against his lips, holding her look for a moment before taking a swallow. 'I think you'd better tell me what's been said.'

Grace settled herself. 'When Paul's career first began to take off there was a lot more money in the industry than there is now,' she explained. 'And everyone was wined and dined, it was the only way deals were done. And I'm not just talking a dinner party, I'm talking full-blown house parties which went on for the whole weekend, usually three or four people, sometimes as many as six or seven. Over the years, I got quite adept at putting on a good show.'

She gave a soft smile and blushed slightly. 'Actually, it was a bit more than that. The three of us were quite a team,' she added wistfully. 'Dominic would hook in the business, I would set the stage and provide the setting, and Paul would reel them in. For quite a time it felt like we could do no wrong. Paul's career was in the ascendant and it seemed as if everything he touched turned to gold.' She shook her head as if to clear it.

Amos could see how hard it was for her. She had played such an important role in her husband's career, only to be cast aside like last year's out-of-date clothes. How anyone could do such a thing to someone like Grace was beyond him.

'Of course, after a while, as entertaining budgets became less and less, the weekends stopped, shrank into dinner parties, then drinks, then trickled away to nothing. Deals still got done, just not the way they had happened before. Except that now, Dominic has found a very big fish that he wants to land and he wants my help to do it.'

'Dominic wants your help?' he queried.

'Both of them do. Except that Dominic knew that Paul would never be able to talk me into doing what they wanted so Dominic came to do the dirty work instead. Dominic has his hook well and truly planted in some bigwig hotshot from America who's launching a brand new programme that all the networks are vying for. Paul is the bait of course and, although it seems that they like the taste of him already, Dominic needs something to set themselves above the competition.'

'And that something would be you, would it?' supplied Amos.

Two spots of colour were appearing on Grace's cheeks as her words brought back her feelings from earlier. 'I still can't quite believe he had the nerve to even ask me, but it would appear that in the cut-throat world of television, anything goes. I am to turn the clock back and provide the kind of weekend that I have done in the past for three guests, despite the fact that I can barely stand to be in the same room as my husband. If all goes well and the network gets the show, with Paul as host, then I get to keep the house. Dominic has even said he'll go so far as to get something drawn up legally so that Paul can't back out of it.'

Amos held her look. He could hear the anxiety in her voice and see the pain in her eyes and his own anger was beginning to rise as a result. How could anyone think it was acceptable to trade for something over which there should not even be any question? The trouble was that, as with all things negative, there was always a positive side to be found, and Amos had become adept at finding it over the years.

'You could look on it as a massive compliment,' he remarked.

Grace's withering look suggested otherwise.

Amos held up a hand. 'I'm playing devil's advocate here for a minute, but just hear me out. Aside from being supremely insensitive, and some would argue tantamount to blackmail, there is also one way of looking at this situation so that it works in your favour.'

'Yes, I know, I get to keep the house.'

'No, I don't mean that. When is this house party supposed to take place?'

'Sometime next month, I don't know exactly. Why?'

'Because, as you yourself said, what you used to do all those years ago is very similar in nature to what you're proposing to do in the future. We'd already agreed that there are areas of the house that you'd like to spruce up ready to receive guests, so let's do that anyway. It won't hurt the cause, and you could treat the whole house party thing as a dry run for when your business is up and running. You haven't done anything like this for a while, so it could throw up some other problems which you might not otherwise have thought of.'

'Yes, and I'd be giving Paul exactly what he wants. I've done that for too many years, Amos. And that's aside from the fact that after I caught Paul kissing one of the guests at the last weekend we hosted, I swore I would never, ever, do it again.'

'And that was when Dominic made a pass at you?'

'Yep, right after Paul made a laughing stock of me in front of everyone because I refused to find his actions funny. They all jeered at me, Amos... I've never been more humiliated in my life.'

Anger quickened Amos's heartbeat as he clenched his jaw. Who could even do that to someone as lovely as Grace? But anger wasn't the way forward, and he thought quickly.

'Does Paul know what you're planning to do with the house?'

'No... And I don't want him to; he'd hate the idea.'

'Then that's even more reason to do it! Take all the anger, humiliation and hurt that Paul has made you feel and channel it into a determination to succeed, Grace – that's the only way you'll win. You think you're giving him what he wants, but only if you view it in that way. Worse, by doing so you risk losing the very thing you want yourself. This is just one more step along the path that *you* have chosen, you and nobody else, and that's the only way to look at it. And if you do, you'll see that it's actually incredibly good timing.'

Grace sat up, staring at him. 'How did you do that?' she asked.

'Do what?'

'Suddenly turn what I'd thought of as the worst kind of insult into the best idea there's ever been?'

Amos merely smiled. 'What do you think?' he said. 'Could you make it work? Forget who these people are and why they're coming, and treat them as guests, just as you would any other?'

Grace was studying his face, listening to him but drawing in what he was saying deeper and deeper, thinking of the possibilities, what it would all mean. And as he watched her, taking it all in, he could see the moment when she decided that she could. Her face broke into a smile and she reached forward. Her hand slipped into his, taking his breath with it.

'Will you help me?' she asked.

'Of course,' Amos replied. 'I already am.'

'I know, but I meant...' She trailed off. 'Amos, I can't do this by myself.'

'Then I'll be here,' was all he said in reply.

Chapter Fifteen

Grace wasn't sure who was the more surprised, Dominic or her. She suspected that having practically thrown him out of her house he'd thought he would never hear from her again, save for the obligatory Christmas card, if he was lucky. And yet here she was, agreeing to his proposal and asking that he send her more details as soon as he could so that she could prepare for her guests in the best possible way. Likes, dislikes, she wanted to know it all.

It wasn't a long phone call and Grace kept it as business-like as possible. She could hear the intrigue in Dominic's voice – he was dying to ask her why she had changed her mind but that was a conversation she had no wish to hold with him.

She put down the phone and smiled at Hannah. 'There now, that's done,' she said. 'There's no going back.'

'I think you're incredibly brave.'

'Or incredibly stupid,' replied Grace. 'I know it makes sense, but it's not having the guests here that bothers me, it's having to pretend that I'm still part of a couple, that this is the home I share with Paul. He's hardly been here over the last few months anyway, and since I asked him for a divorce he hasn't set foot in the place, but I'm ashamed at how much I like it that way.'

Hannah smiled sympathetically. 'Grace, don't you dare feel bad about that, not given what you've had to put up with. Goodness, even in the last week or so there's been a change in you that's as obvious as the nose on my face.'

'Has there?' Grace's hand wandered to her hair. 'What kind of change?'

'A good one,' said Hannah. 'The kind that a certain dark handsome stranger has wrought.'

Grace swallowed. She feared as much.

'And don't you go looking like that either. If there's one thing I've learnt over the past six months it's that if there's something you need to say or something you need to do, then do it or say it. Don't wait, Grace, because you may never get the opportunity. The same goes for happiness. Life can turn on a sixpence, so don't waste the time you have now worrying about the rights or wrongs of a situation, or what other people might think about it. If it makes you happy, clasp it to you and never let it go. It took almost losing Fraser to make me realise that.'

Grace touched a hand to her friend's arm. 'Oh, Hannah. I can't imagine how it must feel to love someone so much that you can't bear to be without them. I just know I never had it with Paul.'

'No, but none of us have a crystal ball either. You didn't know what was going to happen all those years ago when you married Paul, and no one can accuse you of not giving it your best shot.' She gave Grace a coy glance. 'You've had a lightness about you recently, as if something bright and shiny, deep inside, is bubbling closer and closer to the surface. All I'm saying is if it's Amos that has done that for you, then that's a good thing. Don't let the opportunity to be happy pass you by just because Paul has only just gone. The reality is he left years ago.'

Grace sighed. 'I hadn't realised it was that obvious.'

'It isn't. But I've known you for a very long time, don't forget. Besides, I can recognise it in you only because I now recognise it in myself, Grace. I've come to life again these last few months, we all have, and seeing the same happen to you now makes me very happy.'

'I don't even know what it is about Amos,' Grace confided. 'And it's not as if anything has happened between us – I cried all over him and I held his hand, or he held mine, that's all. He's like someone I've known all my life and a total stranger at the same time. Let's face it, none of us know very much about him.'

She could see Hannah thinking about her words, trying to summon all the information she had about Amos and, like her, finding it lacking.

'That doesn't worry you, does it? I just think perhaps he's a very private person. I don't think there's anything sinister in it.'

'No, neither do I. In fact, given the way he lives I would imagine it's something he's very keen to protect. When you don't have much, perhaps the last thing you want to give away is your identity, it's the only thing left that's sacred to you.'

'So ask him, Grace. I don't think he'd be offended.'

Grace chewed the corner of her lip. 'That's just it, I did ask him. I was probably a bit heavy-handed but something I said really seemed to spook him and, although he tried to hide how he was feeling, it was pretty obvious I'd upset him.'

She paused, trying to recall what had happened on the day they opened the beehives. Amos had paled, claiming that his blood pressure fell every now and again, but Grace wasn't altogether convinced that had been the truth. At the time they'd only been talking about the bees though – it hadn't been until much later that she'd asked him why he had left his home. So why the strange reaction? She couldn't understand it. She looked back up at Hannah.

'I tried to apologise on the day when Dominic came around and, after I'd finished crying all over Amos, he claimed he had been on his way to see me too, saying he felt he owed me an explanation about his past. But although he opened up a little, somehow I knew I wasn't getting the whole story.'

'Then perhaps all you can do is carry on as you are. You need Amos's help, we all do, and he's prepared to give it, whatever the reasons. He's not going to be around forever, Grace, so whatever you're feeling now, just enjoy it while you can.'

Which was exactly part of the problem, thought Grace. From what he had said, Amos would be moving on as soon as he finished work at the farm, but the thought of him leaving wasn't something she wanted to dwell on at all. She didn't know quite what it was about him, but she did know that things felt better when he was around.

'So, what do you think then, Hannah?' she said, changing the subject. 'I really need your help here; I haven't cooked for a dinner party in years. What on earth am I going to feed these people for an entire weekend?'

Hannah's notebook was still tucked underneath her arm – it went pretty much everywhere with her these days – and she took it out now, pulling out the pen that was clipped to the spine. 'Run it by me again,' she said. 'When are they arriving?'

'Dominic is going to send over full details by the end of the day, but they fly in on the Friday, getting to us late-ish evening, so a light supper is all they'll need. Then a full breakfast the next morning, after which they'll be taken out and about by Paul and Dominic for the day, returning here for an all-singing, all-dancing dinner. Sunday will be breakfast and lunch, or possibly brunch if they want a slightly lazier morning. Then they leave mid-afternoon.'

Hannah tapped the end of the pen against her lips. 'You know, if the weather holds it might be nice to have at least one meal in among the trees so that they can take in the wonderful view across the field of flowers. It would show them a slice of our wonderful British countryside.'

'I was thinking that,' replied Grace. 'But what with my bees and the number of wasps which are starting to appear, it could be an unmitigated disaster. I had visions of everyone running around screaming.' She pulled a face.

'Hmm, you may have a point. But wouldn't it be glorious though? I'm sure we could think of some way to make it work.'

'I'll ask Amos, he's bound to know.' Grace stopped then, realising what she'd just said, and groaned. 'Oh, for goodness' sake,' she muttered, catching the smile on Hannah's face. 'And you can stop that as well.'

*

Amos was struggling to concentrate, and realised he had missed what Ned had said again. Halfway up a ladder was not a good time to have your mind on something other than the job in hand, but ever since he had found himself unaccountably holding Grace's hand, Amos had thought of little else.

'Sorry, Ned. What did you say?'

'I wondered if you'd seen the pig flying past, that was all.'

It took a moment for Amos to process what was being said.

'Oh, haha, very funny… Sorry,' he added. 'I was miles away.'

'So I see,' replied Ned, grinning from his own ladder. 'Although as the crow flies, not that far away as it happens.' He nodded in the direction of Grace's house.

Amos declined to answer.

'Actually, what I was wondering was how long you reckon this place is going to take to sort. I know Flora is already beginning to think about how to market everything and now that we know Grace will more than likely get to keep the house, it makes everything a little more real, doesn't it?'

Over the last couple of days they had already removed half of the false ceiling in the milking parlour, and another day would probably see it finished. In many ways, though, this was the easiest part.

'I think we've got another week at least to see the ceiling down and all the batons removed. After that the original beams will all need checking, as will the windows. Then there's the electrics to sort, the walls to paint, floor to finish and any dividers to add. About six weeks all told if we're lucky.'

'So the end of the summer then?'

Amos nodded, turning his attention back to the tile above his head. He just hoped that Ned wouldn't ask him what his plans were, because he really didn't want to have to answer that question.

'But what about the work that Grace needs doing?' Ned asked. 'Shouldn't that take priority at the moment?'

'I'm going around this evening to make a start,' replied Amos, evenly. 'Fortunately, the light nights mean I can keep working for longer, and it won't take much to spruce up the few rooms that need attention.' He was about to add that the last time he had seen Grace she was up to her neck in curtain fabric, when the door at the end of the room clanged open. He held up an arm to alert Ned and stop him from what he was doing.

Flora stood in the doorway, cautiously peering inside. Amos had made it very clear that the milking shed was now effectively a building site and should be respected as such. He waved to attract her attention once he was certain that Ned was not about to send another ceiling tile crashing to the floor. She walked forward, picking her way over the debris until she was standing close enough that they would hear her. Both men began to climb from their ladders.

'That looks amazing,' she said, gazing up, right to the top of the building where the original rafters could just be seen. 'I can't believe we didn't know all that was there. It seems criminal to have hidden it away.'

'But it made the building more cost-effective,' said Amos. 'Easier to heat, light and keep clean; but I agree, now that there are going to be people in here and not cows, this is a much better option.'

She smiled at Ned who, like Amos, was covered in dust. 'Although, I bet you'd have argued that the cows would have much preferred the building the way it's going to be rather than the old one.'

Ned grinned back. 'Cows like nice things too,' he said.

Flora rolled her eyes. 'Anyway, I popped over because I've just noticed there's a message on the pad in the kitchen for you, Amos, and I wasn't sure how urgent it was. A lady has rung called Maria, and she asked if you could call her back.'

Amos had been expecting her to get in touch. He turned to Ned. 'It's not urgent, but would you mind if I took care of this now?'

'You don't even need to ask, Amos. Of course it's all right.'

Amos added his thanks and followed Flora back across to the main house.

'Is everything okay?' she asked when they were halfway across the yard.

It was natural that everyone was curious, Amos knew that. It was always the same, the longer he stayed, the better people got to know him and the more they wanted to know. It was one of the reasons he moved on, better to be safe than sorry. He had already mentioned Maria to

Grace and had thought that would be the end of any explanation he'd need to give, but then he'd been really careless and broken his phone and he'd had no other alternative but to call Maria and let her know.

'It's fine, thanks, but I hope you don't mind my giving Maria the farm's number? Hannah said it was okay for me to call her.'

Flora shook her head. 'Of course not. Amos, you can use the phone any time you need.'

'I don't normally need to but Maria's a friend from back home who just checks in with me every now and again, or if there's a problem. She normally rings my mobile but I'm afraid that came a cropper under a brick so, until I get a new one, it would be reassuring if I knew she could call here if she needed to.'

They had reached the back door and Flora waved Amos inside. 'The phone is in the hallway, just help yourself. I came in to make some drinks actually, would you like one?'

'A glass of water would be lovely, thank you.'

He would have preferred to make his call in private, or perhaps even to have shut the kitchen door, but he didn't wish to draw attention to his conversation. Besides, he didn't suppose that Flora would listen in for one minute. He dialled the number and waited for it to connect.

'And how's my favourite keeper of the flame?'

'Amos!' He could hear the smile in Maria's voice from the other end of the line, but knew it would almost immediately be replaced by anxiety. 'Is everything okay?'

He was quick to reassure her. 'Nothing to worry about, I'm just checking in. But I went and dropped a brick on my mobile phone so it's rather useless at the moment.'

'Ah, I did wonder when I saw you'd called me from a landline. Not like you at all.' The line went quiet for a moment and Amos knew exactly what she was going to say next. Maria didn't miss a thing. 'And in Shropshire too…'

Amos smiled. 'Maria, don't pretend. We both know you've googled the address, or the phone number, or both, and that therefore you know exactly where I am.'

'Oh, but you're so close, Amos. When are you coming home? It will be so good to see you.'

'Well, I'm on my way back, Maria, this was going to be my last stop before home.'

'But?'

'Things have altered a little from when I first got here and I think I could be a bit longer now.'

Another pause. 'And?'

Amos wasn't quite sure what to say. 'And I'm not sure that's a good thing…' He almost whispered it, hoping that Flora was far enough away in the kitchen so that she wouldn't hear him.

'Why would it not be a good thing? Besides… Since when have you ever given me any indication of how long you were going to be in one place or another… What's going on, Amos?'

He swallowed, knowing that Maria would jump on his next words with excitement and he would have to explain himself. 'That thing you said would happen to me one day which would change my life forever. I think it might have happened.'

'Oh…' There was a soft sigh. 'Well in that case it won't be good to see you at all. Don't you dare come home.' He could almost hear her thinking and then: 'Oh no, no, no you don't, Amos, don't you dare run. Amos, this is a *good* thing. People have got to find out one day. And you know I'm only saying this because… well, probably because I'm the only one who can, but you've kept this inside for long enough.

It's time for you to realise that you're the only one who thinks the way you do. It's time to give someone else a chance to understand, someone that isn't me. And I know you're terrified there won't be anyone else, but do yourself a favour and find out.' Her voice rose as she spoke. 'Amos?' she prompted into the silence that followed.

Now it was his turn to sigh. 'You're not supposed to say things like that. You're supposed to say, "Yes of course, I understand, come home as soon as you can."'

'No, I'm not. I'm your friend and what kind of a friend would I be if I told you to ignore the one thing that could bring you happiness?'

'So, anyway,' said Amos lightly, and slightly louder. 'I was just ringing to let you know where I am and that if you need me for anything, to ring the farm.'

There was an exasperated laugh from the other end. 'No you didn't. You rang because you want me to invent some plausible excuse for why you need to leave, I know you too well. So, save your breath, Amos, because I'm not going to, not this time. But what I will be doing is rooting for you, because I believe in you and I want to see you truly happy.'

Amos smiled. 'Well, that told me then.'

'Yes, it did,' replied Maria. 'Come home, but only when you've done what you need to do... Oh, and bring her with you. I'd like to meet the woman who's finally mending your heart. Does she have a name?'

'She does...' He paused, wondering whether to share this information. 'It's Grace...'

Her name felt soft upon his lips and he smiled as he hung up. He could go for months without speaking to Maria, but it was always the same when he did; she had him sussed in seconds.

He moved away from the phone, heading back towards the kitchen to claim his drink. But he had only taken a couple of steps when he realised that the door to the dining room was partially open. On his way to make his phone call he hadn't been able to see into the room because of the direction the door opened, but now, walking back on himself, he was able to look directly in to where Fraser was sitting at the table, poring over some paperwork. For a moment he thought he might have got away without being noticed, but then Fraser raised a hand in greeting as he passed.

Amos could have kicked himself, but it never occurred to him that anyone else might have been in earshot. He tried to recall his conversation with Maria, focusing on the things *he* had said rather than her words, which Fraser would never have been able to hear. He'd said Grace's name, that was all. He had probably got away with it.

Chapter Sixteen

Grace hadn't been able to shake the feeling all morning and now, as she waited for Amos to arrive, if anything it was becoming stronger. With all the plans that had been made and all the work that had been done it should have felt like a beginning, but it didn't, it felt more like the end of something, and Grace couldn't understand why. Perhaps it was just the inexorable passing of the weeks; the summer had swelled to its height and was now beginning its descent through August and, following that, the slide into cooler days. Autumn was a season that Grace loved, but she always felt a certain sadness at seeing the end of the summer coming closer. But that was weeks away yet and still the feeling persisted.

They had all been madly busy over the last few weeks, and none more so than Amos as he tried to fit in work on her house as well as on the farm. It wasn't really surprising therefore that today was the first day that he was actually going to get a look at the hives. There simply hadn't been time for any more visits, not together anyway, and Amos knew no more about beekeeping now than he did when he had first suggested the idea. Still, it was better late than never, and Grace knew that he was very excited to be finally meeting her bees.

She checked the kitchen clock again just as Amos appeared in the patio doorway, a bunch of flowers in his hand. He grinned when he saw her and placed a finger across his lips.

'Shhh,' he said. 'Don't tell anyone but I might have... erm, appropriated these on my way up.' He handed her the bouquet.

Grace laughed. 'You pinched them, you mean.'

Amos pretended to be hurt. 'I was merely tidying up. They're the stragglers from the ends of the rows, I'm afraid.' His expression softened as he looked at her. 'Still beautiful though.'

She blushed slightly and turned away on the pretext of finding a vase. There was no mistaking what Amos had actually meant, he wasn't referring to the flowers at all, and it was just the sort of lovely thing he would say. But he didn't mean anything by it, how could he, when he would be leaving in a matter of weeks? Unbidden, her hand went to her cheek as her nose began to smart and she took a deep breath to try and quell the rise of her emotion. Because that's what the problem was of course; Grace had got very used to having Amos standing in her kitchen, or sharing a meal with her, their laughter ringing around the room. She had got used to standing at her bedroom window for a moment before she went to bed, saying a silent goodnight to the man she knew would be sleeping somewhere in her garden. But, more than anything, Grace had got used to how Amos made her feel and she couldn't bear the thought of him going away.

She tried to gather herself. If she wasn't careful she would ruin the day by being maudlin and Amos was here with her now and that was all that mattered. She blinked rapidly and brightened the expression on her face before turning back around.

'Aren't they just. And they're not stragglers any more either, that role has fallen to the next in line. Now these are in pride of place, from zero to hero, just like that. I don't know how you do it, Amos, but you even make the flowers feel better.'

Now it was Amos's turn to blush. He looked away, embarrassed, no, not embarrassed… something else that Grace couldn't quite determine. She groaned inwardly. Oh, for goodness' sake, they had better get on or the day was going to go from bad to worse.

'Well then, are you ready for this?' she asked, deliberately grinning. 'I have told the bees to expect a visitor this afternoon and warned them to be on their best behaviour.'

Amos looked up and she was relieved to see he was smiling.

'And what did the bees say?' he asked.

'About time too,' she replied. 'So I guess we shouldn't keep them waiting, should we?'

'I'm ready if you are. Just as long as you promise that there will be no photographic evidence of me in a beekeeper's suit.'

Grace pulled a face. 'Spoilsport.'

*

Amos was more nervous than he cared to admit. And not just about the bees. It wasn't that he was nervous of getting stung per se, it was more that he worried that by doing something foolish he might cause a bee to sting him, thereby sentencing it to death. It was a thought he was finding increasingly difficult to keep from his mind. Coupled with the slight change in Grace's mood that he had noticed over recent days, he was beginning to find his thoughts freewheeling, and it wasn't a feeling that Amos enjoyed.

He was well aware that to others his life might have appeared chaotic, but he preferred the sense of optimism and possibility this gave him rather than the complacent or static existence that most people seemed to favour. By contrast, however, on the inside, Amos rarely felt chaotic. It had taken a long time to achieve this equilibrium which, over the last few weeks, had been sorely tested, and today he was finding it increasingly difficult to contain his thoughts. But, for Grace's sake, he must, and he drew in another deep breath.

It was understandable that Grace's anxiety was building. In just over a week her house would be full of guests for the weekend and, assuming everything went well, she would know that her future in the house was secure. It was her reward of course, but he wondered if she could see, as he could, that the penalty was in the loss of Grace herself. Whereas a few weeks ago she had begun to open up to ideas, to bloom under the energy created by possibility, now she was beginning to constrict again, her field of vision narrowing more and more with each passing day as all her thoughts became centred on her house and this one point in time. It was how she would be left when the weekend was over that worried Amos. But how on earth could he even begin to explain that Grace's absolute conviction that keeping the house would solve all her problems wasn't necessarily a good thing, not when everything they had done over the last few weeks would culminate with her attaining her dream?

He looked up and smiled. 'Come on then, let's go and say hello to the bees.' He pushed his shoulders downward, willing them to relax, and tried to clear his mind from rushing thoughts.

A few minutes later, once they were suited up, strangely Amos did begin to feel calmer. Perhaps it was the beekeeper's hat which helped. It made him feel a little like an astronaut, a stranger in a strange land, and he instantly became very aware of how he was moving and even breathing. Grace walked on ahead of him, but she paused once they neared the hives.

'How are you feeling?' she asked.

'Humble,' replied Amos, a little surprised by his choice of word. He had said the first thing that came into his mind, but now that he thought about his response he realised how perfect it was.

'Then we're good to go,' said Grace, smiling. 'And don't forget, if you need to back away at any time, just do so. The hive is very full and the sheer number of bees can be overwhelming. It's not a sign of weakness if you panic.'

Amos nodded, swallowing. 'So just how many bees would that be exactly?'

Even through the net of her hat, Amos could see Grace's eyes twinkling. 'Well, you know I've never counted them... exactly... but roughly? Getting on for close to a hundred thousand.'

Amos could feel his eyes widening.

'But don't worry, they won't all be at home,' Grace added. 'Now, once I lift the lid you can expect to have a few bees pinging at you. They're guard bees just doing their job, but ignore them and just stand still, okay?'

He nodded again, his mouth suddenly dry as he stood beside her.

'So this is what's called a top bar hive,' continued Grace, removing the lid. 'And inside are rows of slats, or the bars as they're called, and it's from these that the bees begin to build their comb – straight down, with any luck. So what we end up with are rows and rows of comb with a space between them just big enough for a bee to crawl. And, at this time of year, with a new brood raised and the numbers in the hive increased, the production of honey is being stepped up and up; it's what the colony will need to live off during the winter.'

He watched while Grace worked a metal tool under the edge of both sides of one of the bars to loosen it from where it was stuck to the hive. She waggled it experimentally to check if it was free.

'Are you ready for this?' She grinned and, as he nodded, lifted the bar straight up into the air.

The buzzing changed gear, becoming louder as a mass of bees was lifted clear of the hive, all clinging to the sheet of honeycomb they had made. For a second he felt a moment of panic, assailed by their sheer number, the power that emanated from within this giant machine, but then, as quickly as it came, the feeling disappeared and his discomfort turned to absolute awe. Amos was witness to a spectacle that few had seen and he did indeed feel humbled to be in the presence of such amazing creatures. His eyes feasted on their furry bodies, blurred in the movement of their dance, until it was hard to make out top from bottom, and he watched them for a moment, entranced by their industry in motion.

Grace turned the bar until it was facing her and she held it up so that Amos could see it.

'What do you think?' she asked.

Amos's eyes were still fixed on the comb. 'I think it's...' he began, trailing off, his head suddenly filling with adjectives, none of which seemed to accurately describe how he was feeling. 'Profound...' he said eventually, even then the word sticking in his throat.

Grace smiled. 'It gets you like that, doesn't it? And do you feel incredibly small, and utterly insignificant?'

Amos's mouth dropped open. 'Oh yes,' he sighed. 'That's exactly it...'

'And what if I were to tell you that each honey bee, in the whole of her lifetime, only makes about a twelfth of a teaspoon of honey... and yet they continue to do so, knowing that however little it is, their cumulative work is what counts. Every bee is a teeny tiny cog in a very big wheel, but they are a part of something far, far greater than they could ever be individually.'

Amos stared at her. 'If that were us, we'd give up,' he answered. 'No question about it.' His eyes were still searching the comb in front of him. 'I think that's the most inspiring thing I've ever seen.'

'Which is why, whenever I get to the bottom of a jar of honey, I make sure I use every last drop.' She shifted her grip slightly, pulling a face. 'It's getting heavy,' she added. 'And you can see where the honey is... all those cells which are capped with paler-looking wax, they're full and have been sealed by the bees.'

Amos peered closer, nodding. 'So, this is going to sound like a stupid question, but I'm going to ask it anyway... How do you get the honey out?'

Grace rested the bar on the top of the hive for a moment. 'I'll give you a clue...' She grinned. 'It's very sticky!' She picked up the metal hive tool and pressed one corner of the blade into one of the wax-covered cells. Immediately honey began to ooze from it. 'Go on,' she said. 'Stick your finger in it...'

He pulled off a glove and did so, finding he wasn't concerned about the bees at all, and brought his finger to his lips. He nodded at Grace. 'God, that's good.'

'The harvest is different every year,' explained Grace. 'And depends on the condition of the hive. The bees need the honey to survive the winter and so I only take the excess, judging what that is, hive by hive, and year by year.' She smiled. 'I think this year's going to be a good one, but the honey won't be ready for another month or so yet.'

Amos looked up, the unspoken sentence framed in the air between them. He would be gone by then.

Grace began to slide the bar back into the hive. 'The hardest part is getting the bees to relinquish their honey, as you can imagine. The comb is literally cut from the bar and put in a bucket before it's taken, mashed up, and sieved to strain off the wax, leaving clear honey. Although the bucket has a one-way valve on it so that the bees can crawl out but can't get back in again, it doesn't always work; I always end up with a few passengers.'

She frowned. 'I love my bees, but they can break your heart. Harvest time is wonderful, but it's tinged with sadness too, well, for me anyway.'

She sighed. 'It reminds me how opportunist the human race can be. Always looking to see how we can profit from a situation. I might lack the mercenary streak that some beekeepers have, but essentially I'm no different. I still sell honey.'

Her face was partially hidden by the folds of her veil, and Amos couldn't quite see her expression, but he could tell how she was feeling.

'Grace, the fact that you even think that way is testament to your true character. Your bees are lucky to have you.'

She smiled then. 'We're lucky to have each other,' she said. 'And I always feel inordinately proud and honoured that they choose to stay with me. Because, make no mistake, they do choose. I have three full hives but even if you provide the ideal conditions, there's no guarantee that the bees will accept them.'

She tilted her head to one side, looking across to Amos. 'Perhaps that's why I like them so much. When other things in your life seem so transient, or uncaring, at least I have the bees' validation.'

Amos badly wanted to hug her. To reassure her that everything would be okay but, apart from the fact that their beekeeping suits would make it next to impossible, he wasn't sure he could even provide that reassurance. It wasn't his to give.

'Well, I'm sure I've heard you say on more than one occasion that your bees know everything, and they are obviously an exceedingly good judge of character.' He touched a hand to her sleeve where a solitary bee was still crawling, hoping that it would climb on board his finger so that he could relocate it back to the hive.

'Come on, little one,' he said. 'Back you go.' To his amazement the bee complied, causing Grace to laugh.

'Well, would you look at that. I think you can now add Bee Whisperer to your list of many talents.'

Amos waited until the bee had crawled from his finger. 'Thank you for showing me your bees, Grace,' he said. 'I'm honoured to have met them. And who knows, maybe one day I'll be in a position to offer a home to some bees myself.'

Grace's face lit up. 'Do you really think you would?'

'Well, I'd like to; so really I'm already halfway there.' He was fudging the issue slightly. They both knew that for Amos to keep bees he would need to stop travelling…

Conscious that he wanted the mood to remain light, Amos looked back at the hive. 'So do we need to look at anything else?'

Grace began to prise loose another bar. 'I usually check a few combs at this time of year to see how the honey production is going and the overall condition of the hive. If everything looks okay, I'll leave them for a few weeks to get on with things. The brood bees have mostly hatched now and, although this hive is full, the risk of a swarm is probably passed.'

She looked at the new comb she had just removed, pointing at an area lower down where the colour of the wax capping the cells was slightly darker.

'See these, here? Those are brood cells, but as you can see the vast majority is capped honey. It's all looking just as it should this time of year.' She replaced the bar. 'I just keep a check on the numbers of dead bees as well,' she added, scouting the ground around the hive. 'Bees are very tidy, and any dead bees are simply dropped outside of the hive, so to find a few each day is normal. Large numbers would indicate something's wrong.'

'So what's killed them then?'

Grace smiled. 'Old age, the same as the rest of us. The worker bees born early in the season have the busiest lives. They've got lots of hungry mouths to feed plus new comb to build and they only live for six or seven weeks. Bees born later in the season, through into autumn, can live much longer.'

The more Amos learnt the more fascinated he became. He was also beginning to become aware of something else, a growing feeling that was sneaking into the back of his mind, but he wasn't ready to accept what it was just yet.

Grace replaced the lid of the hive. 'We'll just check the others quickly and then, sadly, I think we're done. Here endeth today's lesson.'

'Well it was worth waiting for,' replied Amos. 'Everything I hoped for and more.'

'You're a good student. I didn't see you flinch once.'

Amos grinned. 'I thought about it, several times, particularly at the beginning, but then I just got lost in the whole spectacle.'

'Well mind you're on your best behaviour with this next hive. They're not quite so even-tempered…'

It seemed only a few minutes later that they were standing back outside the shed at the top of the garden, where Amos stood patiently as Grace swept a few last bees from his suit with a soft brush.

'Can't be too careful,' she said. 'Seeing as how attached they've been to you previously.'

Amos watched as they flew away, and then repeated the process for Grace before helping her from her suit. The walk back up the garden had felt intensely poignant for some reason and he was wondering what to say next.

'Do you need to get back?' asked Grace, forestalling him. 'Or have you got time for a cup of tea?'

There was a huge amount of work still waiting for him at the farm, but he couldn't refuse. It would have felt rude to simply rush off but Amos was only too aware that his willpower as far as Grace was concerned was definitely on the wane.

'Always time for tea,' he replied. 'Besides, it would be good just to check where we are with everything for next weekend, so that I can make sure all the last-minute things are attended to.'

Grace gave a sheepish smile. 'I was hoping you'd say that,' she admitted. 'Only I've thought of something else that might need doing.'

She took his suit from him and, folding it up with hers, stowed them back in the shed, together with her other tools. They walked back into the house side by side. With their outer layer of clothing removed Amos was suddenly very conscious that only the thin cotton of their tee shirts separated them. He took a deep breath and tried to push the thought away.

He watched while Grace busied herself preparing the tea but, despite his best efforts, his head was still teeming with thoughts.

'Grace, can I ask you something?' He waited until she nodded, a slight smile on her face. 'Back out by the bees you said that the honey harvest reminded you how opportunist the human race can be, how we always try to profit from a situation… Something about the way you said it made me think, and I wondered whether you were perhaps drawing comparison with yourself?'

Grace turned from the counter, a mug in her hand, and gave a rueful smile. 'You got me,' she said. 'Guilty as charged.' It was a flippant comment, but her expression was sad. 'And the closer I get to next weekend the worse that feeling becomes. I know I'm supposed to look on it as a trial run for when this place becomes a guest house, but I can't shake the feeling that I shouldn't even be doing it. I feel like I'm prostituting myself whichever way I look at it.' She was about to say something else but then she stopped, instead holding Amos's look, an intense expression on her face.

Amos closed the distance between them in a moment, hugging her to him. A tight, fierce hug which took them both by surprise. Amos broke away, laughing.

'Oh God, I'm so sorry! I'm not entirely sure what came over me then. It's just—'

But Grace was laughing too. 'No, don't apologise...' She dropped her head a little. 'It's been a long time since anyone hugged me like that. It was rather lovely actually.' She smiled shyly. 'And I think, just what I needed. I'm sorry Amos, I'm in somewhat of an odd mood this morning. I'm not entirely sure why.'

'Understandable,' he replied. 'Given what's been going on lately, which does not under any circumstances mean that you are prostituting yourself, either. All that's been happening is that you are planning for your future, Grace, here, where you belong. Next weekend will remove the doubt you've been living with for so long, and that can only be a good thing.'

He was trying to make her feel better but, as soon as he said it, he felt something shift inside of him. Because Grace did belong here, but the very thought made him feel rootless and restless and that was something that had never concerned him before. Grace belonged, the bees belonged, but Amos didn't belong to anything. He didn't share his life with anyone, not really; he'd never depended on anyone, and he'd never had anyone depend on him. And he suddenly realised that he wanted those things more than at any other time of his life. And he knew why.

Chapter Seventeen

The house looked amazing. Even Grace couldn't remember a time when it looked quite so lovely and, although she hadn't really set out to achieve a particular look, everything had seemed to come together of its own accord, resulting in rooms which had their own distinct character but which also blended to give an overall impression. Somehow they had managed to bring the outside inside; the palette of colours mirroring those of the garden and, with the addition of some carefully chosen fabrics and finishing touches, every space was evocative of the summer countryside.

They had decided on a wash of gentle white on all the walls to give a unifying finish, and Grace had found the perfect colour which reminded her of the blush of velvety rose petals. The result was stunning. Its subtle gleam gave the rooms an airy look and was the perfect backdrop for richer-coloured blooms which Grace used as decoration and on the patterned soft furnishings. Some of the heavier, more architectural prints which Paul favoured had been replaced by Flora's botanical ones, and the bold colours and designs added to the theme rather than detracting from it.

And the favourite of all of these rooms was the one that Grace was standing in now, her new bedroom. She had relocated to a smaller room but, by adding some clever shelving and storage, she had just as much room for her things, exactly as Amos had promised. The room felt cosy and nurturing, and – most important of all – it was hers. It was not a room she had ever shared with Paul and neither would she. Their old bedroom, a much bigger room, was now available for guests and it was here that she was intending to put Zac, the man from America who they were all hoping to impress. His two colleagues would also sleep in newly redecorated rooms and Paul, although appearances would have to be maintained, would be sleeping in a smaller room next door to hers, but separate, and that was all she cared about. Paul would almost certainly not be happy about the new arrangements but that would be his problem and not hers.

She had thought long and hard about whether this was the right time to make all these changes, but she was conceding her house this weekend and it was the last concession for Paul she would ever be prepared to make. She couldn't get away with much, but she could get away with this and, small victory though it was, she claimed it. Their guests and Paul would be arriving with Dominic in about three hours' time and she knew that for the next two days she would have to act her socks off and adopt a persona she despised, in order to truly set herself free. She couldn't help wondering if the price wasn't too high.

Amos had seemed increasingly uneasy over the last couple of days and, although he had promised that he would be on hand over the weekend, she could tell that he was finding it tough. What she wasn't quite so sure about was why. And as more and more time went by, Grace also realised that this was bothering her a great deal more than she thought it would, or perhaps should. But the truth of the matter was that every morning when she got up, she thought of Amos, and the same was true when she closed her eyes at night. When she wanted to share something, it was with him, when she laughed, it was because of him, and when the room was empty of people it was him she wanted to appear.

She could hear Flora calling her from downstairs and went to join her. She would never have been able to do all that she had without her friends' help and even though Flora had a hugely busy weekend of her own ahead of her, as did everyone else at the farm, they had all worked their socks off to get the cottage ready.

'Oh, Flora…' Grace's hand went to her mouth as she entered the living room. Flora was carrying an enormous bowl filled with peonies, roses and sprays of eucalyptus.

Her friend grinned in reply. 'Where would you like this one?' she asked. It was the fifth display of flowers that Flora had created, having arrived with Ned about an hour ago, laden with blooms of every variety.

'The hallway, definitely,' said Grace, decisively. 'Having those colours there will give a stunning first impression of the house.'

'Right you are then,' replied Flora and beetled off.

Grace gazed around the elegant sitting room, before moving back through into the kitchen. It looked like a florist's shop at the moment, but the cut stems and fronds of greenery, unused flowers and vases would soon be tidied away and then the table would be set for their late supper. Simply dressed, it would provide the perfect informal setting for their meal. The night-scented stocks which stood in two huge tubs just beyond the patio doors provided ample invitation to explore the garden, and the lights which Amos was busy hanging now would add to the temptation.

She went out to join him, smiling at the sight of his bright-red boots halfway up a ladder. She would know those feet anywhere.

Waiting until he had finished tying off the length of wire he was holding, Grace looked across the lawn. Around its perimeter, lengths of small globe lights had been strung, looping through the trees. The light they gave was softer, more diffuse than fairy lights and, with careful placement, they seemed to disappear into the distance. Closer to home, on the patio, were two dozen jam jars, carefully hoarded over the last couple of weeks, each containing a small tea light candle. The rims of the jars were decorated with tiny sprigs of gypsophila and ribbon and, once lit, would be placed around the flagstones. Come the falling light of dusk it would look utterly enchanting.

'Amos, this is going to look incredible. I can't thank you enough.'

He stepped off the bottom of the ladder. 'Then all I ask is that you enjoy it.' He smiled, a little sadly Grace thought. 'But you're right, it's going to look magical. I only hope your guests appreciate the beauty that is around them.' His eyes held hers for a moment and she thought he was going to say something else, but then his gaze dropped.

'Well, there's no guarantee of that, I'm afraid, but at least there are six of us who think it looks amazing.' Hannah and Fraser had popped over during the afternoon to add their congratulations on how well everything had turned out.

'Have you heard from Paul?'

It was a casual enough sounding question, but Amos knew better than anyone how anxious she was. From the time Grace had first told Paul she wanted a divorce, she had only heard from him a couple of times. However, after ringing Dominic to tell him that she was agreeing to host the weekend, she had expected Paul to get in touch, but there had been nothing. It angered and saddened her in equal measure, but it also made her scared because not knowing what Paul was thinking was even worse than knowing what he was.

She shook her head. 'No, nothing. I just hope he isn't planning any nasty surprises.'

Amos touched her arm lightly. 'I don't think he would dare, Grace. The only one who would lose then, is him. This weekend has to go well and I'm sure he will do everything he can to make sure it does. And perhaps... well, he may be keeping out of your way to make it easier for you. Admittedly, given his track record, that doesn't seem likely, but Dominic doesn't sound like a fool, I'm sure he has Paul on a tight leash.'

Grace frowned. 'Let's hope you're right. I just pray I've done enough.' She looked to Amos for reassurance but he was silent, looking up at the sky, a peculiar expression on his face. Perhaps he was offering up a silent prayer of his own.

'Do you know what their itinerary is this evening?' he asked. 'Is Paul scheduled to be with them, or is he meeting them here?'

'No, he's with them, they're all supposed to be arriving together.'

Amos nodded, as if giving conclusion to his own thoughts rather than anything Grace had said. 'Right, what's next on the list of jobs to do?'

'I think we're almost there, actually. Once Flora has finished with the flowers then I need to set the table and make a few advance preparations for supper, but that's it. And get ready of course.' She looked down at her jeans and tee shirt and pulled a face. 'I can't remember the last time I wore a dress.'

'No, me neither...'

She looked up sharply to see Amos grinning at her. 'Come on then, let's go back inside and see if Flora needs some help.' He held out his hand, his fingertips just brushing hers and she was relieved to see he was looking more relaxed.

Back inside the kitchen, Flora was finishing up, collecting together the floral remnants she no longer needed. On the table in front of her were three low rectangular vases, each of them stuffed with fresh white Michaelmas daisies. No other adornment, just masses of the friendly heads, and running down the centre of the table they looked gorgeous. Grace crossed the room to give Flora a hug.

'I don't know what I would have done without you all,' she said, suddenly threatened by a wave of emotion.

Flora gave her a quick squeeze. 'You'd have coped beautifully, Grace, just like you have all these years. But look at the farm, nothing happens there without us all working as a team. People are better together, it's as simple as that.'

'Hmm… as long as it's the right people,' murmured Grace.

'Well that's okay then,' Flora replied firmly. 'Because we are the right people. Isn't that so, Amos?'

He grinned. 'You know I never disagree with you, Flora,' he said. 'Well, ladies, if you'll excuse me, I think the two of you are far better suited to adding the necessary finishing touches required, and I promised Ned I would give him a hand with the watering. I'll catch you a little later, Grace, if that's okay.' He gave a little bow and sauntered back out the door, disappearing into the garden.

Grace watched him leave. 'Is there something a little odd about him today?' she asked Flora.

'Who, Amos?' she replied, picking up some discarded greenery. 'I don't think so, why?'

'I dunno.' Grace shrugged. 'Can't quite put my finger on it.'

'You're just nervous,' replied Flora. 'After all, it could be a little awkward with him around, couldn't it, once Paul arrives?'

Grace stared at her. 'Could it?'

Flora smirked but didn't reply. She didn't need to – Grace knew exactly what she meant, she was just pretending she didn't.

Together they finished clearing up and setting the table until Flora too announced that she should get going, leaving Grace to get ready and collect herself for the evening ahead. And then, a moment later, it was just Grace left, standing in her kitchen watching the light turn golden through the patio doors. She wrapped her arms around herself and went slowly upstairs.

Her dress was years old, but didn't look it, and as her figure had scarcely changed over the years, it made no difference. Besides, it always made Grace feel good. Made from shimmering silk, in a soft sage green and gently fitted, it enhanced her slender boyish shape, the colour of the fabric slightly deeper towards the hemline. With her curling grey hair left loose about her shoulders, she looked feminine and elegant.

With ten minutes to go until everyone was due to arrive, she almost missed Amos as she came back into the kitchen. He was standing in the shadows by the patio doors, and it was only his intake of breath that gave him away. He stepped forward into the light, the sun making a golden corona around the black curls of his head.

For some reason Grace could scarcely breathe as he came to stand in front of her. He took both her hands in his, holding them lightly in the space between them. 'Is there anything I can do for you, Grace?' he asked, softly.

She closed her eyes and swallowed. 'No.' She faltered. 'Do I…? Do I look all right?' She hadn't wanted to ask him, but her nerves got the better of her.

He smiled, soft and slow. 'You do,' he said simply, holding her look.

The hairs on the back of her neck were beginning to prickle and she realised she was holding her breath. The pressure on her fingers increased slightly.

'And if you need me, I'll be here,' added Amos, leaning in towards her.

Grace closed her eyes in anticipation just as the sound of a key turning in a lock came from the hallway.

'Amos, wait, I—' But he was already pulling away.

She turned towards the front door and took a couple of steps, looking back to smile at Amos one last time, but he was already gone, slipping silently back out into the evening. She touched a hand to her lips as if she could feel him there and, blinking back sudden tears, went to greet her husband.

Grace could hear the burble of voices from behind the door as she plastered a smile on her face. Then, suddenly filling the hallway, was Paul, even bigger than she remembered, the flash of his suave good looks and expensive cologne sending her stomach into freefall.

She faltered for a moment, memories assailing her – good times, when all she wanted was to lie in his arms amazed that this intelligent, handsome and captivating man was hers. But then she pushed her thoughts away. It was all wrong; his bulk was too huge, domineering, even his bearing looked arrogant and overly confident. The charm was flowing as he ushered in their guests but all she could think was that his vulgar familiarity had shattered the calm equilibrium that was her home.

'Ah Grace, there you are,' he said, swooping forward and wrapping his arms around her. He kissed her full on the lips. 'Let me introduce you to everyone.' He stood back to allow them all to find a space. 'Firstly, this is Zac, who you've heard so much about.'

She had. Dominic had made sure he had sent her potted biographies of all three guests, together with photographs, although Zac was considerably shorter than she had imagined.

'It's so lovely to meet you,' she said stepping forward to receive the obligatory air-kiss to both cheeks. 'And I understand you hail not far from here originally. Do you get much opportunity to come home?'

He smiled and dipped his head in acknowledgement that she had done her homework. 'Not half as much as I'd like. My folks still live in Herefordshire, in the same house I grew up in actually, but I rarely get the time to visit, you know how it is. I've lived in the States for fifteen years now, but home is still home, so coming here this weekend is a real treat for me. A little slice of the England I always try to keep in my mind, and that's not always easy in the middle of New York, let me tell you.'

Tinkly laughter echoed around the hall and the tall man by Zac's side stepped forward, bouncing on the balls of his feet.

'This is my second in command,' said Zac. 'Riley Schwarz... far too young to be so incredibly talented, but there you go.'

Grace shook his hand. They were all impossibly young and good-looking, tanned, smooth-skinned, and with an air of money about them that couldn't be faked. Even the incredibly skinny chap standing tucked a little behind Riley was wearing top-to-toe designer wear. As Zac's assistant, Grace had no doubt he was required to look the part but she also had no doubt that his entire wardrobe consisted of similar clothes.

'You must be Scott,' she said, smiling again and moving forward. They all made Grace feel as if she were one hundred and two, on a good day.

Finally, introductions made, she was able to greet Dominic, bringing up the rear, who stared deep into her eyes with a look that left her in no doubt how grateful he was.

From her side, Paul opened his arms in an expansive gesture. 'Welcome to our home,' he said. 'Come through, everyone, and let's get some hospitality going, shall we? It's been a long journey for you all.'

Smiling at her cue, Grace led the way into the living room, which she knew would look stunning in the evening light. It was the perfect antidote to long stressful days.

'Please, sit wherever you would like and I'll organise some drinks.' She was pleased to hear collective noises of appreciation as they entered the room and even Paul had the grace to nod his thanks in her direction. 'Dominic, would you mind giving me a hand with the trays please?'

Everything was laid out ready; tea, a pot of the finest coffee she could find, and a jug of Hannah's homemade lemonade. All that was required was hot water and, within moments, they were carrying the drinks back through to the others. Paul was already deep in conversation, having pounced on the plate of sugary biscuits that she had baked earlier. The evening had begun.

*

'Well, well, well, someone has been busy...'

The voice, oily and snide, in marked contrast to how it had sounded earlier, cut straight through Grace. Startled, she whirled around in the dim light of the kitchen, trying to find its source, only just spotting Paul by the glow of his cigarette as he leaned up against the open patio door. He straightened once he saw that she had seen him.

'That didn't take you long,' he added. 'Had help, did you?'

She ignored his comment.

'I'm just getting a drink, Paul,' she replied. 'And then I'm going to bed.'

He moved forward into the room and she frowned at the smoke which wafted after him.

'Ah yes, your bed... which no longer seems to be my bed. Or indeed my bedroom. You could have told me, Grace.'

He was goading her, she knew that; he'd had too much to drink and even now, with three guests sleeping upstairs, was spoiling for a fight. She tried to distance herself from the memories of the last weekend she had hosted. It wasn't the same at all, *she* wasn't the same, and she lifted her head a little, feeling stronger.

'I did tell you,' she replied evenly. 'As soon as I could, but that was difficult seeing as you neglected to get in touch about any of the arrangements for this weekend. Or indeed to check if I needed any help.'

'Well, it could have been very embarrassing, not even knowing where my own bloody wife was sleeping.'

'I never know where you sleep, Paul. How does it feel?'

She took a glass from the cupboard and ran water into it from the tap. 'I suggest you get some rest. From the sounds of it you have a busy day lined up tomorrow. Goodnight.'

Her hand was shaking so much it was all she could do to keep the water from spilling and she had almost made it to the door when Paul's voice came again.

'So who helped you do all the work then?' he asked. 'All the painting, moving the rooms round… and don't tell me you strung all those lights up in the trees by yourself, Grace, because I know you didn't.'

She knew what he was asking: not who had helped her at all, but whether it was a man who had done so. She turned slowly, composing her face into a neutral expression despite the dim light. Amos had been an almost physical presence in her mind the whole evening. In fact, at times she was certain she had actually felt him close by, but she was damned if she would make any mention of him now.

'My friends helped me,' she replied. 'You know, our neighbours, Ned, Flora, Hannah… and Fraser too, who's doing incredibly well after his operation, thanks for asking.'

They had been his neighbours too for years and it irked her that he hadn't even thought to ask how they were doing, but she would have to be careful to make no mention of the business she was planning on running, or the fact that with her help, business at the farm would be expanding too. She inhaled more deeply, trying to get her breathing under control – his questions were beginning to irritate her intensely. What right did he have to question her, or anything she did?

'Well how public-spirited of them,' he remarked, drawing on his cigarette so that its tip glowed red. He blew out the smoke slowly, knowing it would annoy her.

Clenching her fingers into her palm, she waited a couple more seconds but, despite the sneering look on his face, he remained silent. Taking the opportunity, she turned and walked away, her face hot.

It was cool in her room, and she stood for a few moments barefoot on the carpet, trying to draw in the peaceful atmosphere the room exuded. The fact that Paul's behaviour didn't surprise her was no comfort. Despite the importance of this weekend, he still couldn't help himself. And the evening had gone well, in fact, it had gone brilliantly. The compliments had flowed for everything she had done; the simple supper of prawn and lemon linguine had been well received and, as the night stretched out and they retired to the patio, the atmosphere had been relaxed and convivial, the conversation tumbling and turning around a variety of subjects. Their guests were intelligent, well-read and charming, and she had even found herself enjoying their company, in spite of the occasion.

She crossed to the open window. Paul needed to be careful and, as a result, so did she. His behaviour could so easily backfire and she didn't want to be taken with it if it did. Wondering how on earth she was ever going to sleep, she'd begun to turn away when a slight movement caught the corner of her eye. She turned back, but all was still in the garden below. And yet...

She lifted her face to the moon and breathed deeply, a slow smile turning up the corners of her mouth. Amos might not be with her, but she was sure it had been him in the garden just now, keeping a watch; it was just the sort of thing he would do. She turned away, feeling his comfort wrap around her.

Chapter Eighteen

It was early when Grace opened her eyes the next morning to a still and silent house. She lay for a few moments listening to the sounds of the garden below her window and gathering herself for the day ahead. Despite her conversation with Paul the night before she had slept well. She could only hope that his bile would have calmed during the night and not be further inflamed by a hangover this morning; she didn't think she could cope with a repeat performance. Their guests would be out for most of the day but Grace still had a lot to prepare for and she would rather do so with a clear head.

Pulling on her usual jeans and tee shirt, she went soundlessly downstairs to freshen up the rooms and make a start on the breakfast preparations. Taking a tip out of Hannah's book she had decided to make fresh bread rolls and croissants and, although she had bought the puff pastry, she was making the bread from scratch.

The kitchen was flooded with sunlight and, after flicking on the kettle to make herself some tea, she opened the patio doors to let in the gentle morning air. The sky was already a cloudless blue and looked set to continue that way and, as Grace stared out across the garden, she couldn't help but wonder whether Amos lay sleeping somewhere just out of sight. She hoped so; just knowing he was around made her feel better.

She was turning out a ball of sticky dough onto the floured work surface when she heard soft footsteps behind her and turned in greeting. Like her, Zac had forgone the business dress of the day before and was clad in jeans and a soft shirt, worn loose. He was also barefoot.

'Good morning,' he replied, echoing her words. 'Another beautiful one too by the look of things.' His smile was easy. 'I hope you don't mind my interrupting,' he continued, showing her the book he carried. 'I hadn't expected anyone to be up just yet and I'm a sucker for a quiet spot of reading first thing in the morning.'

Grace indicated the table. 'Be my guest,' she said. 'I think that's a lovely idea. Or sit outside if you'd rather, it's probably warm enough already. What are you reading?'

He held up the cover which depicted a stack of books. 'Rereading,' he said. '*Stoner*, by John Williams, one of my all-time favourites.'

Grace held a hand to her heart and sighed theatrically. 'He should have followed his heart, don't you think? And given up everything for the woman he loved…'

Zac looked at her in surprise. 'You've actually read it? Blimey, I rave about this book to people all the time and they just look at me blankly.' He paused. 'Maybe that's why I like it so much, I feel like it's my secret pleasure. And yes, you're right, he should have.'

Grace laughed. 'Then don't let me keep you,' she said. 'I won't tell a soul.' She looked down at her floury fingers. 'Would you like a cup of tea or coffee to go with it? I won't be a moment.'

'Tea would be great, thanks… but let me – that is, if you don't mind?'

'*I* don't mind in the slightest but this isn't really the way it's supposed to happen. It should be *me* looking after *you*, not the other way around.'

Zac glanced over his shoulder. 'Then I won't tell a soul,' he said, eyes twinkling in amusement. 'Would you like another?'

'Yes please, I'll have tea too.'

Zac removed her cup from the side and instinctively opened the cupboard above the kettle, taking down a mug. He grinned. 'They're always in the same place, aren't they? In everyone's house.'

Grace smiled and started to knead the bread. Zac obviously didn't need help in finding his way around the kitchen. Moments later he placed her mug back down beside her.

'Are you all right with me sitting here?' he asked, indicating the table.

'Of course. And help yourself to a biscuit if you'd like one. Dominic asked for breakfast around eight thirty, but that seems like rather a long way away just now.'

Zac's eyes lit up. 'I shouldn't, but I'm jolly well going to.'

He took a couple of biscuits from the tin Grace indicated and settled himself in a chair, bending one leg up and resting his ankle across his knee.

'Can I just say how grateful I am to you for putting us all up this weekend, Grace. You have a beautiful house, and I confess this is just what I needed. New York can be the most amazing city to live in but, even after all this time, I still get a little homesick for the English countryside. It's good to be back.'

'Well then, it's my absolute pleasure,' she replied. 'And feel free to explore the garden if you wish. The views from the bottom are incredible.'

He dipped his head. 'I will, thank you.'

After that he fell silent, opening his book and losing himself in its pages. He leaned forward every now and again to drink his tea but, apart from that, was still. It rather surprised Grace, who had imagined that someone in his position would be rather more brash, not given to the pleasures of solitude and a good book, but it was rather nice having his undemanding company – not something she was used to at all.

With the bread dough proving, Grace turned her attention to rolling out the pastry, cutting it into triangles once she was done and rolling it up to make croissants. There would be tea, and coffee, obviously, and fresh figs, strawberries and pineapple along with either a full cooked breakfast or smoked salmon and scrambled eggs. Hannah had laughed when Grace had told her what she was planning on serving for breakfast. A convert to the healing properties of porridge and honey, she told Grace she should just make everyone do with that. It was tempting, certainly, but as Grace eyed the mountain of food in the fridge she reminded herself that if all went according to plan she would have to get used to cooking big breakfasts.

Having divided the dough into rolls, Grace was just popping them in the oven when a clatter from behind her announced Paul's entrance. Already dressed and reeking of cologne, he was about to say something when, looking past her, he realised that she was not alone. A smile lit his face and he loomed towards her, pulling her close and planting a kiss full on her lips. It was all she could do to keep from flinching.

'Hello, darling,' he said. Then asked, 'Can I get you a coffee?' before turning slightly and 'suddenly' noticing Zac.

'Good morning… another beauty, isn't it?' he fawned. 'I hope you slept well.'

'Beautifully,' replied Zac, getting to his feet.

Grace saw Paul take in the book, the casual clothes, the empty mug. 'I do hope Grace has been looking after you?'

'She has. It's been a peaceful and rather lovely start to the day.' He indicated his book. 'We seem to share a love of good literature too.'

Paul squinted at the cover and nodded, but Grace knew he would have nothing to add. Paul read one book a year, on holiday, and that was whatever he picked up at the airport.

As if realising that no further conversation on the subject would ensue, Zac put his book down decisively on the table and gave a massive stretch. 'I might take a wander now,' he said. 'And have a look at the garden. Then I guess I'd better hit the shower and get suited and booted, ready for the day ahead. I think Dominic has rather a lot planned for us.'

Grace caught his eye, smiling at the wry amusement in his voice. In that instant she decided that she really did like Zac. She was pretty sure he had already made up his mind about who would be getting his contract and this weekend would make absolutely no difference to his decision. Apart from admiring his integrity, she realised it took the pressure off her somewhat and for that she was grateful. Her whole future had seemed to be riding on this weekend, but maybe it wasn't going to be as bad as she had feared.

'Just be aware that I keep bees,' she said. 'Not everyone is a fan, but they won't cause you any problems. When you reach the slope and start to drop down, just keep to the right of the hives as you pass, that way you'll be out of their foraging path. It's worth it though, there's something of a surprise at the end of the garden.'

She smiled but wouldn't say any more despite Zac's arched eyebrows which invited further comment. He grinned and set off with a slight wave.

'What was that supposed to mean?' barked Paul as soon as Zac was out of earshot. 'What have you been saying to him?'

'Nothing, why?'

'Well you looked very cosy in here, and that comment he made about Dominic, what was all that about? I hope he realises that all this is for his sake.'

Grace hid her smile. 'I think he's only too well aware of that fact,' she replied. 'And to assume otherwise would really be insulting his intelligence. He's as much aware of the game you're all playing as you are.'

Paul's jaw clenched. 'This is not a game, Grace...'

'Isn't it? Oh, I do beg your pardon.'

'So, what were you doing in here then?' he asked, scowling at her.

'Well, as you can see, I've been making bread rolls and croissants and Zac has been enjoying a quiet cup of tea with a favourite book.'

Paul's eyes narrowed. 'But you must have been talking about something?'

'Not really, no. I rather think the point was that Zac wanted a little peace and quiet before the day got underway. And as such, we didn't chat, that would have defeated the object of the exercise.'

'So he just happened to come in here before everyone else was up, did he?'

Grace crossed to the sink to rinse her hands. 'It would appear that way, yes. But if you want a definitive answer I guess you would have to ask Zac.' She smiled sweetly.

'Yes, well, just don't do it again,' muttered Paul. 'It doesn't look good. I'm your husband for goodness' sake.' He picked Zac's mug up from the table and handed it to Grace. 'And that's another thing, do you think you could pretend to enjoy it when I kiss you? As far as our guests are concerned, we're supposed to be happily married, but it's like holding a cardboard box, you're so stiff.'

Seeing Paul's pouting expression was just too much and Grace had to turn away to hide her smile. His childlike manner had driven her mad over the years, but now she merely found it funny.

'I'll make you a coffee,' she said. 'But I've got things to do, Paul. Why don't you go and show Zac the garden?'

He almost shuddered. 'Why would I want to do that? You know I hate it.'

Fifteen minutes later Zac was back.

'You weren't joking, were you?' he said, brushing a greenfly from his sleeve. 'I've never seen anything like that before, but then I guess... well, how else do you grow flowers?'

'It's quite something, isn't it?' agreed Grace. 'My neighbours converted their dairy farm earlier in the year and that's the result.'

Zac nodded. 'There was a chap already working in the field, but he spotted me and came over, wondering who I was, I suppose. He explained to me what had happened.'

Grace checked her watch but it was only half past seven. 'Crikey, they're starting early today, business must be good.'

'That's what I said, but he was weeding before it gets too hot. A full-time job, I would imagine.'

'Well, rather them than me,' said Paul. 'I can't think of anything worse.'

Zac regarded him evenly. 'Oh, I don't know. I've always quite fancied the idea of an outdoor life.'

Paul looked uncomfortable. 'That's not to say I don't admire them,' he said hurriedly. 'I do, it's just not for me, that's all. I think I've worked out where my strengths are.'

There was a moment when Grace thought Zac was going to comment, but then he smiled. 'You're probably right. I suspect the reality is very different from the dream.'

Even if she couldn't hear it, Grace could sense Paul's release of breath.

Zac looked between the two of them. 'Well, thank you for the tea, Grace. I guess I'll go and get ready. When did you say you'd like us back for breakfast? I'll make sure the others are up and ready.'

Grace was torn. She sensed that Zac might like to set his own timetable and yet Dominic had been very definite in his requirements and she would hate to mess up his schedule.

'I think Dominic said half eight.' She looked at Paul for confirmation. 'As long as that's okay with everyone.'

'Fine by me.' Zac nodded at Paul. 'Excuse me, won't you?'

And then he was gone and it was just her and Paul alone once more. He stared at her, searching her face for a few seconds before turning away.

'I'll be in the study,' he said. 'Call me when everyone appears.'

*

Grace could tell there was a problem as soon as Dominic came back into the kitchen. He steered Paul to the window, taking his arm and talking softly. She watched them from the sink, seeing an agitated expression swiftly cross Paul's face and a minute later he strode off in the direction of the sitting room, presumably to talk to the others. Dominic beckoned her over as soon as he was gone.

'We have a bit of a problem,' he explained. 'In that I've just been out to put some things in the car and discovered it's got a flat tyre.' The car in question was a luxurious people carrier that Dominic often used for entertaining, allowing six people to sit comfortably. 'Obviously that poses a massive problem, given that we'll be using it all day.'

'Don't you have a spare?'

'Well yes, but—'

'So, I'll just stall everyone,' said Grace. 'Make more coffee, take them into the garden, I'll think of something to do while you change the tyre, don't worry.'

Dominic shook his head. 'I was rather thinking you could get someone to fix it for us,' he said. 'I don't think either Paul or I want to start behaving like bloody mechanics this morning. It's not exactly conducive to the type of day we need to have here, Grace.' He leaned into his last words, a sharper tone undercutting them.

She frowned at him, annoyed by his tone. 'Well, funnily enough I don't happen to have a mechanic on standby who can just drop everything and come on over. Or were you suggesting that *I* change the tyre?'

He tutted. 'No, of course not, but there must be someone. Paul rather thought someone from the farm might be able to help out.'

'Oh, he did, did he? Those people who he doesn't give a fig about from one day to the next… For goodness' sake he never even bothered to find out how Fraser was doing after he had open heart surgery following a heart attack. Do you really think they're going to drop everything to help him?'

Dominic didn't really know them either, although he had met them once or twice over the years, but he could see that Grace was telling the truth. His gaze sunk to the floor and, seeing it, she relented.

'But fortunately, they're *my* friends and they might do it for me,' she said. 'Give me a few minutes and I'll see what I can do.'

She picked up her mobile and slipped through the patio doors, dialling Ned's number. There was no reply and Flora's phone went unanswered as well. She didn't bother to leave a message but carried on down the garden, making for the field. If she was very lucky someone would still be working there and, if not, then the farmhouse was a short walk away. She had only gone halfway when she saw Amos coming towards her, swinging a basket.

'Morning!' He waved an arm in salute and hurried towards her, studying her face as he reached her. 'Is everything all right?'

Grace nodded. 'I'm fine, but Operation Impress the Americans has hit a snag. Flat tyre,' she explained. 'The end of the world, obviously, and neither Paul nor Dominic could possibly change it. I was just on my way down to the farm to see if Ned might have half an hour to spare.'

'He might have,' Amos replied. 'But I can come quicker.' He handed her the basket. 'I was on my way up as it happens – Hannah thought you might be able to make use of those,' he added. 'And of course I volunteered to bring them over simply because that way I'd get all the salacious gossip from last night first-hand.' He grinned at her.

Grace peered at the dozen or so eggs nestled inside, smiling at both the thoughtful gift and Amos's comment.

'I'm not sure gossip is quite the word,' she said. 'Although, actually, despite Paul being Paul, I enjoyed the meal. Everyone is impossibly young, of course, but for all that, educated and rather eloquent – not jumped-up, arrogant upstarts at all. It quite surprised me.'

'I met one of them this morning by the field,' replied Amos. 'He seemed genuinely interested in the flowers that are growing.'

'Oh, that was you. Zac did say he'd got talking to someone but I assumed it was Ned. You had an early start.'

Amos looked up at Grace through his lashes. 'Can I confess to having been in the garden and legging it when I saw someone coming. I only just made it into the field and pretended to be pulling up weeds. Actually, I was pulling up weeds but that hadn't been my intention.'

'Were you sleeping there…? Only I thought I saw you in the garden late last night just before I went to sleep.'

'Sorry, I was just… keeping an eye on things, I—'

'No, it's okay, Amos. I don't mind, it was… well it made me feel… better,' she finished lamely, not really sure how to explain how it had made her feel, or indeed if she should. 'Knowing you were around, I mean.'

Amos gave her a look she really couldn't fathom. 'It made me feel better too,' he said. 'Knowing I was around… So, you're okay then?' His voice was serious as he laid a hand on her arm. 'I couldn't stop thinking about you last night… wondering how you were all getting on. Wondering if Paul was behaving himself.'

Grace sighed. 'Well apart from chastising me for altering the sleeping arrangements without telling him, it's been okay.' She paused. 'I'd just rather he didn't feel the need to prove he's my husband by kissing me every time we're in the same room; it's beginning to make my skin crawl. I don't suppose anyone else is interested and besides…' She trailed off, not wanting to spell out to Amos how she felt having Paul touch her. 'Anyway, at least they'll be out all day, so it'll be fine, I'm sure.'

'Provided there's a car for them to go out in at all. I'll go and see what I can do.'

'Would you? Are you sure you don't mind? It doesn't really seem right to ask you, not when Dominic and Paul are both perfectly capable.'

'Grace, it's fine. If it makes life easier then I'm happy to help. The quicker it's done, the quicker they can leave.'

There was certainly a lot of truth in this statement and Grace hurried back into the house, leaving Amos to go and investigate the problem. 'I'll bring you out a coffee,' she said as she left him.

Dominic was still pacing the kitchen but looked up the second she walked back into the room. 'Did you get something sorted?' he urged. 'We need to leave in half an hour at the latest.'

'I would imagine you'll be leaving when the tyre's fixed,' she replied. 'But yes, a friend of mine has come to the rescue. You might want to go and give him a hand. At the very least say hello.'

A gale of laughter echoed from the other room. Paul's laughter. She doubted very much that whatever had been said was that funny and she was beginning to find his ridiculously over-the-top behaviour trying. Admittedly, she didn't know Zac or Riley at all well, but they had both struck her as pretty down-to-earth characters, not the stereotypical showbizzy types she had imagined they would be. And Zac was astute with it too; it made her wonder just how they really viewed her husband.

Reassured that conversation was still ongoing in the sitting room, she took a mug of coffee outside to see how Amos was getting on.

The boot on the car was raised and she could tell from its rocking movement that it was already being jacked up. She'd expected to see Dominic but was surprised to find Amos by himself. She walked around to the side of the vehicle, still holding his drink.

'Is everything all right?' she asked.

'Should be,' came the reply. 'It's straightforward enough. The tyre had picked up a gouge from somewhere, could have been a sharp stone, any number of things. It didn't puncture it straight away, but I reckon the air has been seeping out all night. There's a spare, fortunately, which looks okay. The chap who came out said it was a company car so it's been well maintained by the look of things.'

'Yes, that would have been Dominic. I'm surprised he didn't offer to help you.'

Amos looked up. 'Are you?' he said.

His words took her aback. Although it wasn't said with any particular undercurrent, Amos wasn't usually given to making sharp comments.

He was right though of course; now that she thought about it, she wasn't surprised in the least.

She smiled. 'I brought you a cuppa,' she said, holding out the mug. 'Shall I put it down for you?'

He nodded and she rested it on the gravel. With the car now jacked to sufficient height, Amos picked up the wrench and attempted to loosen the wheel nuts.

'Jesus...' The word hissed out from between his teeth, as he leaned all his weight onto the wrench. 'Whoever last did these up must have been a direct descendant of Thor.'

He tried a different nut, rocking his full weight onto the wrench to get it to turn, gritting his teeth and straining with the effort. Expelling air in a loud rush he stood up, panting for a few minutes before trying again. It was hard to watch him, obviously hurting from the effort.

Grace was about to stop him in case he did himself an injury, when she heard steps on the gravel. Turning around, she was amazed to see Zac walking towards them. His jacket was already off and he was busy rolling up his sleeves. He came to stand beside them.

'Hello again,' he said, looking at Amos. 'I saw what was going on from the bedroom window, can I help at all?'

Amos flicked her a glance, really not sure what the protocol was. Grace wasn't sure either, but Zac was offering to lend a hand, no one had forced him to.

'I'm obviously feeling particularly puny today, but I can't get the wheel nuts off,' said Amos. 'Either that or some Neanderthal tightened them before me.'

Zac pulled a face. 'I can have a go, if you like, but if you can't shift them, I'm not sure I'll be able to.'

Whatever the circumstances, it was a very generous thing to say. Amos smiled and handed him the wrench.

'I've probably loosened them for you,' he said with a grin, rolling his eyes at Grace.

But Zac grunted and groaned in just the same way that Amos had done and couldn't shift them either.

'Oh, thank God,' said Zac. 'That could have been embarrassing. Shall we give it a go together? I can't see how we're going to shift them otherwise and I think plans will be ruined if we can't change the tyre.' He caught Grace's eye and smiled. She was liking him more and more by the minute.

With one man either side of the wrench and a good deal of groaning and, in Zac's case, swearing, they finally managed to release the nuts so that Amos was able to ease off the flat tyre.

Amos offered Zac his hand. 'Blimey, that was hard work, and I really appreciate your help. I was going nowhere fast on my own. I can probably take it from here though, if you need to get back.'

But Zac shook his head. 'No, come on, let's get finished up. I rather think you're being kept from your work too, and your drink is getting cold.' He rolled the spare tyre across while Amos stood up to take a slug of his coffee.

'How are we doing?' It was Paul's voice from the front door. 'Are we nearly ready, do you think?' He began to march across the gravel.

Grace saw Amos look down as she too realised that Zac, crouched by the side of the car, was below Paul's line of sight and that therefore Paul was talking to Amos. It was, she realised, the first time the two men had met. She moved further to Amos's side.

'Paul, this is Amos who's helping out at the farm next door. It was very kind of him to come to our rescue.'

'Yes, yes, of course,' Paul replied, moving nearer. And then he stopped. 'Amos?' he queried. 'I know that name from somewhere...' He broke off, frowning. 'Yes, I know... You're the gardener chap, aren't you? The one who gave my estate agent the runaround.' He looked directly at Grace for a second, eyes narrowing and then back again. 'Only I don't remember employing you.'

Grace took a step forward, feeling utterly helpless. Zac had chosen to carry on working instead of revealing himself, replacing the tyre and slipping back on the nuts ready for tightening. If she wasn't careful this could all go very badly indeed.

'Actually, Paul, Amos doesn't work here, he's been helping out at the farm next door for the summer, and has given me a hand with some of the bigger gardening jobs, that's all.' She gave a light laugh. 'And all out of the kindness of his heart... and maybe the odd cup of tea.'

She wanted to give Paul the opportunity to offer some praise and to thank Amos for his generosity, but instead she could see from the expression on his face that he had taken it entirely the wrong way. Oh dear lord, whatever was he going to say now?

'Hmm, how very obliging of you.'

Grace's heart sank; he sounded like a pompous idiot.

'That's not it though,' Paul continued. 'That's not where I know you from. What's your last name?' It sounded more like an order than a casual enquiry.

Amos squared up. 'I don't think we've met, so just Amos will be fine. Like Grace said, I've been working at the farm so it was lucky I was around this morning to help out.'

'And you're pretty much done, I think, aren't you? Zac very kindly came to help as well.' She had to say something to alert Paul to his presence.

But even this didn't help. 'Zac did? Oh, for goodness' sake, whatever for? Well I suppose that explains why I couldn't find him earlier. Where's he gone now?'

Zac stood up abruptly and grinned at Paul. 'Right here actually.' He handed Amos the wrench. 'Just give the nuts one more turn for luck and we're good to go, I think. Thanks so much, Amos.' He looked down at his dirty hands. 'I'd better go and get washed.'

Paul's mouth was hanging open, and Grace could see his brain working frantically. He came swiftly around the side of the car, smiling broadly. 'Yes, thank you, Amos. I'm really not sure what we would have done without you.' He thrust his hand into his inside jacket pocket and pulled out the silver money clip he always kept there. He peeled off several twenty-pound notes in succession. 'Thank you,' he said again.

Amos stared at the money in his hand. 'I was doing a favour, Mr Maynard,' he said. 'Thank you, but that's really not necessary.'

'Nonsense, come on.'

But Amos made no move to either reply or take Paul's money, and the silence stretching out was embarrassing.

In the end it was Zac who spoke, patting Paul's arm in a way which Grace knew he would take for condescension. Whether it was meant that way she wasn't entirely sure.

'You heard the man, Paul, put your money away and just buy him a pint sometime for God's sake.'

He flashed them both a wide smile and led Paul back inside the house. 'Right, so run through this morning's schedule for me one more time,' he said, as they moved away.

Amos bent to double-check the wheel nuts, turning away from Grace so she couldn't see his face.

'I'm so sorry,' she said.

The seconds ticked by until eventually Amos raised his face to hers. 'Your husband needs to learn that not everyone can be bought,' he said, his face a mixture of sadness and anger.

And the unspoken words, *including you*, hung in the air between them.

Chapter Nineteen

The day ground by interminably slowly and Grace had wished for the evening to hurry up and arrive. Now that it had, however, she wished it had never arrived at all. After finishing up his checks on the car that morning, Amos had disappeared and she hadn't seen him all day. He had seemed okay when he left but she couldn't help feeling that something was very amiss and even, perhaps, that he was avoiding her. If she hadn't had so much to do she probably would have invented some excuse to pop over to the farm and see him, but it was not to be, and now she was a bundle of nervous, anxious energy.

Dominic and Paul were both in buoyant moods. Despite the slight bumpy start to the morning caused by the flat tyre, the rest of their plans had gone like clockwork and it was obvious from the confident swagger of both men that they were more than happy with the day's outcome. Grace didn't ask, she didn't particularly want to know; all that concerned her now was getting through the evening. And that was proving to be increasingly difficult.

The meal had gone well, and the atmosphere around the table was most convivial as the men relaxed after their food. But Paul was knocking back the wine at a pretty steady rate of knots and, although well able to handle his drink, was always more demonstrative when he'd had too much alcohol. He slid an arm around her shoulders, moving it inward so that his hand just caressed the back of her neck. It was a particularly intimate gesture and she could feel all her muscles tense in response. She eased herself away from the table on the pretence of fetching something from the kitchen. Strictly speaking it wasn't an excuse, she *had* bought some particularly fine truffles to have after dinner, but in truth she had only just taken away the cheese board and it was far too early to be bringing out more food. It was just that as time went by she was finding it increasingly difficult to stomach her husband's attention.

Their relationship had been on rocky ground for several years now, but it had been easy enough to miss each other in this spacious house and for the most part they had managed to live largely separate lives. But what was becoming increasingly clear to Grace was that during this time she had never had the opportunity to contrast her husband's behaviour with that of any other men. Now that she had, she was beginning to notice how loud he was, how gauche; showy and brash rather than displaying the quiet and cultured intelligence that the others did. Was this how they saw him too? And worst of all, she found herself contrasting his overbearing and possessive manner with that of Amos's kind and generous humility. Or simply just comparing him to Amos…

She pretended to tidy the already spotless kitchen; the dishwasher had long since been loaded and the few remaining pots and pans, washed, dried and put away. On an impulse she decided to make up a pitcher of what Hannah called her 'special water'. It was essentially just ice-cold water with fruit added to it, and a touch of lime or lemon juice, but was extremely refreshing and made a good non-alcoholic alternative. If nothing else, it might slow Paul down. His behaviour was beginning to feel far too similar to that of the last weekend they hosted.

Taking a lemon, some grapes and an apple from the fruit bowl on the table, she took a minute to cross to the open patio doors and breathe in the night air, relishing its verdant stillness.

'Looking for your gardener, are you?'

Grace whirled around to see Paul leaning up against the kitchen doorjamb. He had a glass of red wine in his hand and was holding it by the rim, swinging it loosely from side to side. She knew exactly who he was talking about.

'Taking the air actually,' she replied. 'Although if I was looking for my gardener, then I'm afraid I'd have to disappoint you. We don't have a gardener and I very much doubt that one would be working at this time of night, given that it's pitch black outside.'

'Don't try to be clever, Grace, it doesn't suit you.'

'I rather thought it was you who was trying to be clever.'

'Oh, come on, you were practically falling over him this morning.'

Grace sighed. 'Shall we just stop all this silliness?' she said. 'We both know you're talking about Amos, so let's just come out and say it, shall we? Just what exactly are you accusing me of here?'

'I'm not accusing you of anything, Grace, just making an observation, that's all. You said before that your friends helped you do up this place and it's very obvious which particular friend that was. I'm surprised at you actually; I really didn't think you had it in you. I mean, I've only been gone a matter of weeks and already someone else's feet are under the table.'

Despite having promised herself she wouldn't get riled, Grace could feel a flush of anger rising inside. She didn't much care what Paul said about her, but she would not let him talk about Amos in that way. He had done nothing to deserve it and would be horrified if he knew that someone could even think those things about him.

She fixed her gaze on Paul's. He was still leaning nonchalantly up against the door and his fake indifference was beginning to annoy her intensely.

'Shall we make something absolutely clear,' she began. 'First of all, Paul, you *have* gone... and you've gone because you have lied and cheated your way through the last few years of our marriage. So don't you dare question my actions or, worse, judge me by your own appallingly low standards. Amos is a friend, the same as Ned, or Flora, Hannah, or Fraser. He came to the farm just a few weeks ago, looking for work in return for his board and lodging, and that's what he's been doing ever since; working. And he may not have any money or fancy clothes but he's got more honesty and integrity in his little finger than you have in your entire body.'

Paul took a slow swallow from his glass, regarding her coolly as he did so. He was silent for a few seconds and then levered himself upright, away from the door. At first she thought he was about to turn and leave but then he took a few steps into the room.

'So where did he come from then, this Amos?'

'I'm honestly not sure. Like I said, he came to work on the farm. If you're that interested I'm sure Hannah can show you a copy of his references.'

'But from what you've said he didn't come invited, he just turned up, out of the blue, from nowhere in particular... Doesn't sound like something that stick-in-the-mud, Hannah, would allow. Or did he work his charm on her too?'

Carrying the fruit over to the work surface, Grace placed it on a chopping board. 'You know, you really are a pig,' she said, turning her back on Paul and slicing an apple in two.

She felt rather than heard the movement, realising that Paul had come to stand behind her. His breath was hot on the side of her neck, laden with wine fumes and casual threat. Every part of her stilled, waiting for his next move, wanting to recoil, to shrink from the touch that was surely coming. She felt his lips graze her skin and a wave of revulsion swept over her. She could barely even stand to be in the same room as him these days.

An arm stretched past her as he placed his glass down beside the chopping board, leaning in even closer. His lips moved along her shoulder, up her neck, until they just touched her earlobe.

'Well, when you want to know where Amos really came from, be sure to let me know, won't you?'

The words were a whisper, barely even a breath, but Grace heard them loud and clear. She froze, trying desperately not to give Paul the reaction he was waiting for. He pushed himself away from her and gave a low laugh as he turned and headed for the door. She turned too, at the last minute, fighting her impulse to know more. Staring at his back, the seconds ticked by and, despite herself, the question was on her lips when Dominic came through the door. He sensed the atmosphere in a second.

'Everything all right in here?' He looked straight at Paul, a challenging enquiry on his face.

Grace gave a vague smile. 'Fine,' she replied.

'Well, I hope so. We were just discussing one or two things which could do with your input, Paul, in case you've forgotten what this weekend is in aid of. Perhaps you could come back and join us? If you're done here, of course...'

'We're done,' said Grace and she turned back to the chopping board, heart pounding and ears roaring with the thoughts that were assailing her. She closed her eyes and breathed deeply, feeling the eddies begin to settle. She knew that Paul was trying to rile her, and she knew why.

The supposed jealousy he was displaying wasn't jealousy at all; she hadn't been the object of his affections for a long time and she knew the touches and kisses were designed only to make her feel uncomfortable, to remind her who held the power in their relationship. Paul didn't want her, but he couldn't stand being made to feel like he could ever be replaced either.

She stared at the fruit on the board, willing his words to stop their constant march through her head. *When you want to know where Amos really came from;* that's what he had said. *When you want to know...* but did she? And more importantly, *what* did Paul know? *How* did he know? Or was that just a ruse too, designed to make her question a man she trusted far more than her husband?

In reality Paul probably didn't know anything at all, but all the same his words touched a chord because Grace was only too well aware that she didn't actually know where Amos *had* come from, aside from the vaguest of details. And in all the time he had been at the farm, she and everyone else had respected his privacy, had accepted his way of life, because what else did you do with a man like Amos? Someone who was as kind and thoughtful as he was, generous and caring, and with a wisdom that went far beyond his years, must surely deserve not to have his very integrity questioned. But Paul had sown the seed of doubt and, just as he'd known it would, it had begun to grow.

Grace scooped up the fruit from the board and added it to a large glass pitcher which she then topped up with cold water from the fridge. Some slices of cucumber and sprigs of fresh mint finished it off and, placing the jug on a tray together with some clean glasses, she carried the whole lot through into the living room. Dominic's words rang in her ears; she too had to remember what this weekend was about, there was a lot at stake for them all. She felt as if she were on a runaway train, as if some process had been put into motion that she was powerless to stop, and she had no idea where any of them would end up when it did. But, for now, she would smile, and chat, refill glasses, offer tempting morsels of food and somehow make it through the rest of the evening.

She almost managed it. Zac and Riley were engaging company and even Scott who, much younger than the others, had been extremely shy to start with, had found his level and contributed as much to the conversation. It made the task of trying to keep Amos out of her head that bit easier and she made sure that Paul had no opportunity to catch her on her own and put him back there. Except that now, the evening was drawing to a close and Grace knew that in a short while she would be left with nothing but her own thoughts for company.

Dominic had been the first to retire to bed, followed by Scott and Paul. It was a political move, giving Zac and Riley some time to talk together on their own. She smiled as she carried the last of the glasses through into the kitchen and saw them sneak out the patio doors for one final cigarette and a sharing of thoughts. The candles all around the patio had been lit earlier in the evening, but with the lights on in the kitchen, Grace could see little of the outside. Every now and again a few words or the odd laugh would reach her, but that was all. She would have given anything to know what Zac and Riley were discussing. Tomorrow a leisurely breakfast would bring the weekend to an end and, if they hadn't made up their minds who they were going to award their contract to by now, she doubted very much that anything which happened tomorrow would change it. And, as far as she was concerned, she had done what she could.

She loaded the last few cups into the dishwasher and tidied away the stray bits and pieces that had found their way into the kitchen, leaving it neat and tidy for the morning. Then, having filled a glass with cool water to take upstairs to bed, she was about to go and say goodnight to Zac and Riley when the patio doors slid open and both men walked back into the room.

'Grace,' said Zac softly. 'I'm glad you're still up...'

She smiled a little nervously. His words didn't sound like the polite goodnight she was expecting.

Zac indicated the table. 'I know you're probably desperate to get some sleep, but we wondered if we might beg just a couple more minutes of your time.'

'And don't look so worried,' quipped Riley. 'We only want to heap praise and adoration on you, in case we don't get the opportunity tomorrow.'

She grinned at Riley's sense of humour, still very evident, and took a seat.

'We also wanted to make sure that you were alone when we did. We're under no illusion as to who has made this weekend possible, Grace, and we wanted to make sure that the right person received the credit.'

'Oh...' She didn't know what to say to that. It was extremely generous, but... She looked up and caught Zac's eye. He smiled.

'And yes, you're right, that's *not* what you were expecting to hear and it *isn't* especially complimentary as far as your husband goes. No doubt *he'll* be expecting nothing but compliments from us tomorrow, and we're not harsh people, Grace, he'll get them, but what he won't be getting is our contract.'

She stared at him in horror.

'You see, we're honest people too, Grace, which is why we've not only made the decision we have, but why we wanted to share it with you too. Otherwise you might feel that *you* have failed in some way and nothing could be further from the truth.'

Riley leaned forward. 'Your home is beautiful and your hospitality has been absolutely wonderful, perfect in fact. I wish every business trip could be like this—'

'Hell, I even found someone who loves my favourite book,' interrupted Zac. 'But I'm afraid that we were never here to pass judgement on *your* skills, Grace, and I think you know that.'

Grace felt sick to her stomach. Of course she knew that, she'd known it all along, and worse, now that she had heard the words from Zac's mouth, she realised that she'd also known that Dominic wasn't going to get the contract, Paul wasn't going to be their star. It had been obvious from Zac's small comments, from the glances he had shot Paul. She bit back her shock and managed to nod.

'Yes, of course…' She found a smile from somewhere and dragged it onto her face. 'And I'm very grateful to you, not only for your compliments but also for having the generosity to let me know that your decision has in no way been dependent on me.'

'You're in a very difficult position, Grace, we realise that…' added Riley.

She almost laughed. *You don't even know the half of it.*

'… And we're also a little concerned as to whether you're going to be all right.'

Her head came up in shock to find Zac looking at her, a gentle expression on his face. He smiled softly. 'The world of television is notoriously cut-throat, shallow and really not all that nice… although, I don't think I'm telling you anything you don't already know.'

He carried on without waiting for an answer. 'The other thing this business is, is full of gossip-mongering, and so your husband's… indiscretions, shall we call them, are not that much of a secret, despite what he believes. We've been aware of them for some time.'

She sat up a little straighter as the implications of Zac's words ricocheted through her.

'So it might surprise you to hear that there are still people who work in the industry who consider themselves honest, basically decent, and who at least know what the word integrity means.' Zac thumbed his chest. 'That's us by the way, in case you haven't worked it out. And so although Dominic can potentially offer us a very good home for our show, I'm afraid that Paul is not the right face to go with it. We had our reservations before we arrived, but I'd hate you to think we were taking advantage of you. This weekend was all about checking whether Paul was the right man, *despite* what we've heard. It was about giving him a chance to prove us wrong.'

'And he didn't,' muttered Grace.

'No, he didn't. I'm sorry.' Zac looked apologetic. 'We can't in all conscience go with someone who we don't believe in.'

'No, I understand that.'

'But, we also know that's going to come as rather a shock to him… and we don't want there to be any repercussions for you.'

Grace laughed, she couldn't help herself. 'Yes, it will be a shock,' she said slowly, lifting her chin a little defiantly. 'But don't worry, I can look after myself. And you know, perhaps it's time someone gave Paul a shock, he seems to be under the illusion that he can do exactly what he likes with no consequences.'

She met Zac's steady gaze. 'And I appreciate your honesty. In fact, since we *are* being honest with one another, I think it's only fair that you know I asked Paul for a divorce a couple of months ago. He moved out the same night and up until Friday night I hadn't seen him since.' She gave a sad smile. 'So, in a bizarre way it means even more that your decision hasn't been affected by anything *I've* done. Paul has brought all this on himself and, if there's any justice in the world, perhaps he's just had his served.'

Riley was watching her, an astonished expression on his face. 'Sorry… let me get this straight. You and Paul are separated and yet you still went to all this trouble for him? Why would you even do that?'

'Let's just say I had my reasons.' Grace wasn't about to share the details of the agreement they had made over the house. What was done was done and she wouldn't want them to feel in any way awkward about their decision.

Zac exchanged a look with Riley. 'Well, all I can say is that Paul is an even bigger idiot than I thought he was. But, for your sake, I'm glad that you're striking out on your own. You deserve better, Grace, I sincerely hope you find it.'

She swallowed. It was a lovely thing to say, and they had been incredibly kind and thoughtful to give her the consideration they had, but it was over for her now. The weekend had proved to be the final nail in the coffin as far as keeping the house was concerned, and the irony was that none of it was her fault. Dominic had made Paul agree to give her the house if she did nothing this weekend to his detriment, but she hadn't needed to – he had failed all by himself. What made it worse was that Paul was so arrogant, thinking he had the Midas touch, that he had even managed to place the onus for this weekend squarely on her shoulders, and she had been so desperate, she had let him. She had prostituted herself to keep her house, so what did that make her?

'Thank you,' she said quietly. 'I have some good friends. I'll be fine.'

'And I sincerely hope Amos is one of them,' replied Zac, a twinkle in his eye. 'He thinks the world of you, you know, and if I were you, I would make him a *very* good friend…'

Grace looked up, frowning. 'Amos?' He'd been in her head almost constantly throughout the day, but she was surprised to find him in someone else's.

Zac grinned. 'Yes, Amos. We got chatting after the palaver with the tyre this morning. I went to say thank you and to apologise for Paul treating him like a servant and he asked me if I was enjoying my stay.' He pursed his lips in amusement. 'I might have mentioned your many talents and he rather waxed lyrical in return. I could quote him if you like.'

'No, don't.' Grace put her hands to her cheeks, blushing. 'I get the idea.' She smiled at both men. 'I am still glad you enjoyed your weekend, just sorry it didn't turn out quite the way you wanted it to.'

'Don't be,' replied Zac. 'I don't suppose you'd like a job, would you?'

She stared at him. 'A job? Oh, come on… what would I do?'

He dipped his head a little. 'Forgive me, I'm being mischievous, but… what we do need from time to time is a good location somewhere in the UK – to use as a film or studio set. Admittedly I'm rather talking off the top of my head here, but have a think about it. If the idea interests you, get in touch.' He pulled a card from the inside pocket of his jacket and laid it on the table. 'You never know when these are going to come in handy.'

He flashed a grin at Riley. 'Right then, I think it's time we said goodnight and let Grace get to bed.' His face fell slightly. 'Not that you need your beauty sleep at all, but I hope we haven't said anything that will keep you awake. It was just important to us that you knew how things stood.'

Grace looked at the card on the table, the stark irony of what had just been offered almost making her laugh again, but she smiled instead. 'No, not at all. In fact, I don't think your decision is a surprise, not really, but I am grateful to you for your honesty and consideration, and of course, the heaping of praise, that was lovely too.'

Zac got to his feet. 'Then sweet dreams, Grace. I know I for one shall be dreaming about tomorrow's breakfast.'

Riley laughed. 'Goodnight, Grace. And thank you,' he said, rising.

Grace's thoughts were already racing far ahead, and in one direction only, but she dragged herself back to the present just in time before the two men disappeared through the door.

'When will you tell Paul?' she asked. 'Will it be before you leave?'

They both looked at one another. 'That would have been our original intention, yes,' replied Zac. 'But under the circumstances, I think it might be… easier, if we get in touch at some point afterward. It won't look unusual.'

She nodded. 'Thank you.' That weight at least now lifted from her mind.

And then she was alone. She waited a couple of minutes until she was certain that Zac and Riley would have made it as far as their bedrooms and then, as quietly as she could, she slid the patio door back open and slipped into the garden.

There was no way of knowing whether Amos would be there or not, but she had to find out. It was very late and it wasn't rational at all, but Grace didn't care. There was only one person who she wanted to see, had wanted to be with all day, and it had taken a virtual stranger to point out a fact she had been trying so hard to ignore, and worse she really didn't know why…

She slipped past the apple tree and began to drop down the slope where the beehives lay. If Amos was here, she was pretty certain she knew where to find him, but as she drew closer, her heart began to sink. The grass stretched out on either side of her, dappled in the moonlight and dotted with daisies, but otherwise completely empty of anything resembling the man she had fallen in love with.

Chapter Twenty

Despite herself, Grace was surprised to find she was full of energy the next morning. She hadn't slept particularly well, but that had nothing to do with the news that Zac and Riley had imparted the night before. In fact, if anything she was glad to have found out about the contract in advance; the knowledge brought with it a certain freedom and resolution of thought. Grace might not particularly like it, but at least she knew where she stood. It brought to an end weeks of uncertainty and, much to her surprise, the pain she'd thought she would feel on knowing that she had lost the house wasn't all-consuming at all.

She had half expected Zac to appear with his book again this morning, but there had been no sign of him and she had taken her tea alone. He was probably giving her a little space, she realised, but she didn't mind; making brunch would take up enough of her time, and soon everyone would be gone and she could do as she pleased once more. And now, she knew exactly what that was going to be. The sound of the shower running started over her head and she glanced at the clock. Paul would make sure he was up well before everyone else this morning, but today she wouldn't even mind his company. It had ceased to matter.

He appeared about half an hour later, reeking of aftershave and trying to look casual in a nonetheless very carefully chosen pair of chinos and a white shirt. He might have pulled off the more relaxed look if his face hadn't been set with a smug grin that showed no sign of leaving. Knowing full well what his movements would be, Grace had already made a pot of coffee and Paul crossed to it now, pouring himself a generous mug.

'Not long now, Gracie,' he said.

She winced at the use of his old pet name for her, one he hadn't used in a long time. However, as she watched him, she realised he hadn't meant anything by it; his mind was very firmly on himself.

'One final push, as they say,' he added. 'But that's obviously just going through the motions. They've already made up their minds.'

Grace nodded, turning her face away slightly so that he wouldn't see her expression. 'Yes, I guess so.'

'So, you were down here with them last night, did you catch anything?'

She flicked a glance back in his direction. 'No, they went outside for a cigarette. There was the odd laugh, but I couldn't hear anything else. Besides, I was clattering around the kitchen just tidying up, I wasn't really listening.'

He sipped his coffee, watching her over the rim of his mug. 'It all sounded pretty relaxed though?'

'I would say so, yes. They came in after a bit and said goodnight, all smiles, charming, same as all weekend really.' It wasn't exactly a lie but Grace was still keen to deflect the conversation onto safer topics. 'Do you know what time everyone is leaving?'

'Around midday, I believe. You've got everything planned for breakfast, I assume.' It was a statement, not a question, and she wondered what he would do if she said no.

'Then I'll aim to serve a bit before eleven, no need to rush.'

He nodded, looking her up and down. 'You will get changed though, won't you?'

She looked down at her jeans and tee shirt, which were clean and perfectly presentable.

'Yes, okay.'

She was fed up of being told what to do, but she didn't want to antagonise Paul either, there was still the tricky issue of his comment about Amos to be broached. Paul didn't say anything without reason, but even though she had spent a huge amount of time last night thinking about what he said, she didn't want to make a big deal over it. It was quite likely that there was very little to it, just Paul trying to be manipulative as usual.

'Good, I don't want anything to go wrong at the last minute.'

'Well, it's a beautiful morning. I thought I'd put coffee and a selection of pastries out on the patio table in a bit, and then as folks appear they can help themselves until—' She broke off as her phone began to ring and frowned before connecting the call, turning away from Paul for a little privacy.

'Morning, Flora, is everything all right?' She knew it wasn't early for her neighbour to be up and about, but it was early for her to be calling.

There was a pause at the other end of the line and Grace could hear a muffled voice in the background.

'Yes, it's fine... I just wondered if you'd seen Amos this morning?'

Grace was aware of Paul's eyes boring into the back of her head. 'No, why?' Flora was trying to be casual about it, but Grace could tell there was more to her question than just a simple enquiry. And there it was again, the voice in the background.

'I just needed a hand with something, that's all, and he doesn't appear to be around. He's probably gone for a walk or something, but I just wondered whether he might be with you.'

'I haven't seen him…' She paused, wondering how much she could say within Paul's earshot. 'But it's possible he's in the garden. Do you want me to go and have a look?' She declined to mention that he'd taken to sleeping there.

'There's no rush, Grace, I can wait, just if you spot him.'

Which was, of course, completely untrue. If Flora could wait and there really was no urgency, then why was she ringing?

Grace made her voice light. 'I'll pop down now, it's no bother. I'll ring you back, okay?' She cut the call without waiting for Flora's reply.

'Problem?' asked Paul as she turned back.

'No… just need to pass a message on, that's all.'

She moved past him and headed out of the patio doors, waiting until she was halfway across the lawn before ringing Flora back. She hadn't even checked to see if Amos *was* in the garden. He wasn't there last night and he wasn't there now; she could feel his absence, like a piece of her was missing.

The phone rang twice before it was answered. 'What's going on, Flora? I can talk now.'

There was a long pause, full of anguish. 'Oh, Grace… I think Amos has gone.'

Grace closed her eyes, feeling dread bloom in the pit of her stomach. 'What do you mean, he's gone?' She needed to hear Flora say it, so there could be no doubt.

'He didn't appear this morning, which is unusual, and at first I didn't think anything of it, but then it just began to feel… odd. I don't really know how to explain it. So I had Ned go over to the cottage, but his rucksack had gone... and he's taken my painting down from the wall...'

Grace was still marching through the garden and had reached the top of the slope. 'Come into the field, Flora, I'll meet you there.'

She ended the call once more and concentrated on moving as fast as she could. Why would Amos do that? Hadn't he promised he would never leave without saying goodbye? Besides, Amos would never just up sticks and move on without saying anything, not unless he had good reason...

She met Flora halfway across the field, running the last few metres until the two women stood looking at one another. Flora was the first to move, throwing her arms around Grace.

'I'm so sorry,' she said, hugging her close. 'I don't know what's happened. I thought he was a bit quiet yesterday, but I didn't read anything into it and I certainly didn't think he was planning on leaving.' She drew away, searching Grace's face.

It would have been impossible for Grace to explain to Flora previously how she felt about Amos, given that she had only just admitted it to herself, but in that instant she could see that she didn't need to. Flora was newly married, in the first flush of love, she knew what it felt like to have lost her heart.

'It's not your fault,' she whispered. 'It was nothing you did, it was nothing any of us did...' But the moment Grace said it, she knew she was wrong. Because there was someone who could well have done something. She turned and looked back up in the direction of the house. Her eyes narrowed. 'And you're sure he's gone?'

Flora nodded sadly. 'Everything he had, which admittedly wasn't much, has gone...' She trailed off. 'But even that doesn't account for it somehow.' She pulled a face. 'A lot more than just the man himself has gone, certainly more than what arrived with him. Does that make any sense at all?' It did, it made perfect sense.

'There's an Amos-shaped hole in Hope Corner,' replied Grace, feeling suddenly desolate. 'And I don't know what to do about it.'

'He can't have gone far, but I have no idea what time he left. Ned has already said he'll go out and look for him; drive the lanes and see if he can find him.'

Grace shook her head. 'I have a feeling that if Amos doesn't want to be found, then there's almost no point looking.'

'But we can't give up.'

'I didn't say that.' She looked back at the house again, feeling her despair turning to anger. 'I said there's almost no point looking, but if you know where he's gone, there's every point.'

Flora looked quizzical. 'But we don't know where he has gone... do we?'

Grace gritted her teeth. 'No, but I know a man who does.' She took hold of Flora's arms and gave them a squeeze. 'I have to get back,' she said. 'But I'll call you, soon, I promise.' She took a couple of steps. 'I think I may just have lost everything I thought I ever wanted, but in doing so I've found the one thing I really do want. I'm not going to let that slide through my fingers now.'

'Of course! Oh, Grace... the weekend... I never even asked you how it was going.'

Grace took a few more steps. 'I'll tell you later,' she said. 'But don't worry, I'll be in touch.'

She hurried back towards the house, giving a bemused Flora a farewell wave as she reached the edge of the field and began to climb the slope into her garden. Her breath was ragged as she climbed, anger fuelling the muscles in her legs, and she had just drawn level with the hives when she stopped. She could hear the steady thrum from within, the bees at their busiest, and she frowned, suddenly remembering how these bees had found their way to her – a phone call from a nearby farm to say that they were hanging from a tree and if she had room could she come and collect them. And she had, boxing the bees up in the age-old way and placing them at the foot of her empty hive. When she opened the box, she watched as the bees began to explore, instinct taking over until, as one, they began to move up the ramp, following their queen into the hive. These same bees had now grown in number and were busy and productive and happy. There was nothing special about her hive, no reason why the bees should choose it over any other. All she had done was provide the right conditions and the bees, knowing this, had made it their home. It could have been anywhere.

She ran the rest of the way, hurtling into the kitchen, praying that Paul was still there, and that he was alone. He looked up as she came in, sitting at the table, relaxed and utterly unaware of what was about to happen. She could see the expression change instantly on his face as he realised what kind of mood she was in, but this was Grace, who didn't usually say boo to a goose, and who certainly wouldn't cause a fuss now, would she…?

He recoiled as she placed a palm down on the table opposite him and leaned across, jabbing the forefinger of her other hand towards Paul's chest.

'What did you say to Amos?' she snarled. 'And don't you dare lie to me.'

A slow smile broke over his face. 'Why?' he said. 'Missing him?'

She had a sudden urge to hit him, to wipe the smug smile off his face. In the split second it took for the thought to flash through her mind, she saw an image of herself doing just that, the delicious surprise as she decked him one, and the total disbelief that she could ever be capable of anything like that. The thought buoyed her up – Paul had no idea what she was capable of. And truly, before that moment, neither did she.

'Answer the question,' she hissed. 'We both know he's gone, just as we both know that you're the reason he has. So, I'll ask you again, what did you say to him?'

'Moderate your voice, Grace. I wouldn't want anyone to think I was married to a fishwife.'

'No? Or that I'm married to a total bastard perhaps? Don't worry, Paul, no one has to wonder about that, they already know it.' She glared at him, chest heaving.

His gaze flickered to the door as he swallowed a little nervously. He wanted to ask her what she meant, but he wouldn't, not yet anyway.

'Very well then, have it your own way. I simply suggested to Amos that given his past, which no doubt he has taken great pains to avoid having to discuss, he might find it better if he moved on, just in case someone were to reveal all.' He smiled. 'Well I did tell you, Grace, that if ever you wanted to find out where he really came from, you only had to ask…'

'So tell me,' she said, the challenge clear in her voice.

'Really? You want to know?'

'I don't care what he's supposedly done, Paul. After all it can be no worse than anything you've done – the difference is that Amos has remained a decent, kind and caring human being. Besides, I don't suppose you do know anything about Amos – how could you? You're just resorting to your usual bully-boy tactics because that's what you do, Paul, it's what you've always done.'

He got slowly to his feet, towering over Grace. 'Well now, that's where you're wrong. I recognised Amos the minute I saw him, although it took me a while to figure out where from. It wasn't until I saw him changing the tyre that it jogged my memory; that ever so humble "*who me*" look he's perfected. *That* hasn't changed over the years, I can tell you.'

Unwillingly, Grace could feel herself being drawn in by his words.

'Because of course a few years ago, maybe five or six, I was still on the news desk and—'

'I don't care about that, Paul, just tell me where he's gone, where he came from, I know it's on the Worcestershire border somewhere.'

He baulked at her response. 'No, I think you'll want to know the whole story, Grace, just what you're letting yourself in for... After all, that is what this is all about, isn't it? An affair of the heart...? Well, how lovely, but I'm not so sure you'll think the same way once you know the truth.'

'Oh, this is ridiculous.' She drew herself up. 'Are you going to tell me where he's gone or not?'

His expression was snide. 'Well, I'm not sure I can remember, it was a long time ago...'

Her nostrils flared as she stared at him, wondering how on earth she could ever have thought she was in love with him. And then she spotted her handbag hanging on the back of the kitchen door. She marched across the room to retrieve it, checking she still had her phone tucked in her back pocket at the same time. It was time to go.

Returning to the table, she dumped her bag on it momentarily, fishing within it for her car keys.

'Where do you think you're going?'

'Out,' she replied. 'Following my heart.'

He stared at her, his mouth working. 'But what about brunch?' he asked, light dawning.

She took off her apron and threw it at him. 'Cook it your bloody self,' she said, backing away.

'Don't you dare!' he retorted, voice rising. 'Have you forgotten what this weekend is all about, Grace? What's in it for you?' He swallowed, taking a deep breath, visibly trying to calm down. 'Look, Grace, I'm sorry. And you're right, I was winding you up, I'm just a bit tense, you know how it is. We're so close to bagging this deal, Grace, so don't do this, please. I need you. You're the only one who can do this, you always have been. Just a few more hours.'

She held his look, taking in his softer expression, the way he thought he could just turn on the charm.

'Nope, sorry.' She smiled sweetly. 'There's somewhere else I need to be.'

His voice echoed across the room, laden with bile. 'Leave now and you can forget any thoughts you have about hanging onto this place. I'll sell it out from under you before you can say sold subject to contract.'

A throat cleared from behind him as Zac came into the room. 'Morning, Grace,' he said. 'Off out somewhere?'

She started, completely unaware that Zac had been standing there, and, worse, with no idea for how long. But then he gave her a thoughtful look and nodded at her in complete understanding.

'Don't let us keep you,' he added. 'Paul and I can take it from here, can't we, Paul?'

A smile lit up Zac's face as he met her astonished gaze. 'You go and enjoy yourself, Grace, and thank you, it's been a wonderful weekend.' He looked directly at Paul. 'Most enlightening.'

She dipped her head, and looked at her husband, no longer the cocky playboy or the threatening bully, but instead like a balloon that someone had let the air out of.

'Thank you,' she said. 'It's been a pleasure meeting you, Zac. You *and* Riley, Scott too, of course. Please would you say goodbye for me?'

'Of course.' He smiled. 'Goodbye, Grace. I hope you find what you're looking for.'

She reached the patio door just as Zac's voice floated past her. 'Sit down a minute, Paul. We need to have a little chat.'

Chapter Twenty-One

Grace gunned the engine slightly as her car shot around Hope Corner and moments later she turned onto the track that led up to the farm. Her head was awash with thoughts that were scattering her in all different directions, but mostly she was surprised at the complete about-turn her life had just seemed to have taken. She could even smile at the look on Paul's face as he realised that his sure-fire new contract had just gone up in smoke. While she wasn't a vindictive person, there was a rather pleasing justice to it all.

Mostly, though, her thoughts were centred on Amos and the absolute and overwhelming need to find him. She didn't doubt that there was something in his past that he wasn't proud of, but how many people had led truly blameless lives? What was important was that the man who had appeared out of the blue at the farm one day had made her feel like the Grace she knew of old, the woman who could be anything she wanted, and be any way she wanted. And she now knew that if she were very lucky it would include a life with Amos in it.

It would have been easy to ask Paul what he knew of Amos's circumstances and, no doubt, he would have delighted in telling her. But that wouldn't have been fair to Amos at all. If it was something he wanted to share with her, then he would, in time perhaps, but she needed to let him know he was among friends; there was no need for him to have run.

After parking up, she pushed open the gate into the yard, where she saw Ned walking up towards the house. She called out, waving her arm to attract his attention. He hurried over.

'Have you seen him?' he asked. 'I was just about to go out and look.'

Grace shook her head. 'No,' she replied. 'But I know why he left... well, not actually, but... Look, I'll explain. Where's Flora?'

'In the house.' Ned took hold of her arm. 'Come on.'

Flora was sitting morosely at the table with Hannah and Fraser. The teapot occupied the centre space but the mug of tea in front of Flora looked cold and untouched, a skin formed on its tepid surface. She got to her feet the minute she saw Grace.

'I can't even think straight,' she said. 'Goodness only knows what you're going through. There's a million and one things to be doing, and I can't bring myself to do any of them.'

'I know,' replied Grace. 'I'm afraid I've just taken off my apron and thrown it at Paul, telling him he could cook breakfast. That man has never cooked anything in his life before, but I don't care. There are more important things.'

Flora looked instantly horrified. 'Oh, God... but the TV thing! No, Grace, you can't, you can't let this opportunity go by. You'll lose the house.' She looked helplessly at Ned. 'There must be something we can do... Oh, this is the most horrible timing. Grace, you need to get back home, but we can't let Amos go, you can't... you need...' She trailed off, frustration jumbling her words.

But Grace shook her head. 'No,' she said. 'I don't. They don't need me there any more.' She smiled at the memory of Zac's words. 'In fact, even the bigwig from America turned out to be a really nice man; he gave me his blessing to leave actually. He said he hoped I find what I'm looking for. So, all things considered, I think that's what I should do.'

'I don't understand,' said Ned, frowning. 'It's all in the bag already, is it? Paul's got the contract?'

'On the contrary. I think right around now Paul is getting the shock of his life and finally having the arrogant grin wiped off his face.'

She quickly explained the events of the morning. 'So, you see, there really was no point in me staying.'

'But that's terrible!' said Flora. 'Grace, you'll lose the house…'

She nodded. 'Yes, I know… But it really is the most curious thing. I find I don't mind half as much as I thought I would.'

Flora sank back in her chair. 'But it's Paul's fault. From what you said he's the one who made Amos leave.'

'Yes, but in doing so, he also showed his true character, so he gained nothing either. Contrary to his belief, this weekend was not about putting the icing on the cake of the deal, but more about giving Paul a chance to prove that he was made of better things than they suspected. By trying to rubbish Amos all he did was prove them right, so he failed miserably.'

'Hah!' The triumphant exclamation came from the end of the table, and Fraser immediately apologised. 'I'm sorry, Grace, but we've been friends for a very long time, and I've watched you all these years, praying that one day someone would come along and give Paul his comeuppance. I can't pretend I'm not glad that someone has.' He pointed a finger at her. 'And now it's time for you to get your reward for putting up with him for all these years. Don't you dare look back.'

Hannah looked at him sideways. 'Fraser Jamieson, I couldn't have put that better myself.' She smiled at her husband. 'But what about Amos?' she added. '*Do* you think that what Paul said was true? That he recognised Amos and knows that there's some secret from his past he's kept hidden?'

'I'm pretty certain of it, yes,' Grace replied. 'Paul was trying to goad me about Amos all weekend but I don't think there's any doubt that he did remember him from somewhere. Once he figured out where, he was desperate for me to ask him what he knew, but that in itself means it must have been related to a news story. He mentioned it was five or six years ago, which would have been when Paul was news anchor, so it makes sense.'

'But it doesn't necessarily mean it was anything bad,' said Flora. 'People are in the news for all sorts of reasons.'

'Yes, but I can't see Paul being quite so manipulative if all Amos had done was win first prize in a national lemon-curd-making competition.'

'Hmmm.' Flora frowned. 'I know that makes sense, but I don't want to think badly of Amos, in fact, I don't think I can…'

'Me neither,' agreed Grace. 'And I absolutely refuse to believe the worst. Amos deserves better than that. So I will wait to hear whatever it is from his lips, or not at all.'

'He may not wish to tell you though,' countered Hannah. 'You have to think about that, Grace, hard as it may be. I think we all know how fond of you Amos has become, which is the very reason why he left in the first place – he obviously wanted to protect you from upset, and in my book that can only mean one thing. I think you need to prepare yourself for the fact that you might not like what you hear, however hard we find that to believe.'

Grace shook her head. 'I don't care,' she said. 'Amos has made me feel better about things than I have in a long while. Better about myself too. Apart from anything else, I owe him a huge debt of gratitude and, whatever else happens, I just want the opportunity to tell him that. And I'm a mature and supposedly responsible adult, not some lovesick teenager about to do something stupid.'

But then she stopped because that's exactly what she did feel like. Grace felt like doing something very silly indeed. And in that moment the perfect idea came to her.

She stared at everyone, catching Flora's eye, whose face split wide into a grin.

'Well, then,' Flora said. 'What are we waiting for? Come on, we've got to work out how to find Amos. What do we know about where he might have gone? Somewhere he might have mentioned before, or someone he might go to…' She looked straight at Grace, light dawning in the exact same moment.

'Maria!' they both chorused.

'It's where Amos was planning on going after he left here,' said Grace.

'And she rang here one time,' added Flora, thinking. 'Wait a minute…' Her face lit up with excitement. 'Amos wasn't around, so she left a message… with her number for Amos to call her back…'

'Yes, I took the message,' said Hannah. 'I wrote it on the notepad… What if—?'

But Flora had already got to her feet, rushing to fetch the pad of paper that was always kept on hand for messages. She brought it back to the table, leafing through previous pages, turning it this way and that as she tried to decipher the various entries. There wasn't a sound in the room as all eyes were trained on her every move.

Suddenly she gave a triumphant shout. 'Look!' she stabbed a finger on the page. 'There it is… Maria Holloway… and the number.' She slid it across the table towards Grace. 'Go and phone her.'

Grace's hand shook as she touched the paper. 'Oh, God… what do I say?'

Fraser leaned forward. 'You just say your name, Grace. I don't think you'll need to say any more.'

'What do you mean?'

He chuckled. 'Because I was here the day Amos called Maria back. I was in the dining room so as he passed into the hallway he didn't see me. I wasn't eavesdropping on his phone call as such, but it struck me that the way he was chatting with her was quite lovely... But then he said something a little odd which made my ears prick up. He said that the thing Maria had told him would happen to him one day – something that would change his life – *had* happened, and then he mentioned your name, Grace. Now I couldn't hear what Maria had said before Amos made that comment, but I'm sure he said it in response to a question from her, and it was the way he said it...' His eyes twinkled as he looked at her. 'So I'm sure Maria will know exactly who you are, Grace, and, more importantly, why you might be looking for Amos.'

Grace could feel herself blushing. 'Oh, I *see*...' She picked up the notepad, looking at the scribbled number, and took a deep breath. Then she grinned. 'Excuse me for just a minute, won't you?' she said. 'I need to pop outside and make a phone call.'

The phone was answered on the third ring.

'Hello?' The voice sounded a little breathless.

Grace opened her mouth to speak... and nothing came out. What on earth did she say to this woman, a complete stranger? She would sound a total idiot, or worse... She should have thought about what she was going to say, tried something out in her head, but now all the words she started to form dried in her throat, sounding stupid.

'Hello?' The voice came again. 'Is anyone there?... Amos?'

His name caught in Grace's throat. 'No,' she managed. 'It's not Amos, but—'

'Grace?' There was a noise that sounded a bit like a sigh. 'Oh, Grace... is this you?'

And despite herself Grace laughed. There was such hope in that voice, such longing.

'Yes,' she said. 'Yes, it's me.' She laughed again at the absurdity of the situation and was relieved to hear Maria laughing too.

'It's me, Maria,' she said. 'Amos's friend. Oh, how silly, you know that, *you're* ringing *me*... Oh, but it's so lovely to hear your voice. I wondered what you would sound like...' But then she broke off and Grace could hear the quick intake of breath. 'Is everything all right? Is Amos...?'

'He's fine,' reassured Grace. 'At least I think he is... It's so lovely to talk to you, I didn't know what to do... but we found your number and I...'

And from nowhere a rising tide of emotion threatened to engulf her. She swallowed, trying to gather herself.

'Maria, Amos has gone... he just upped and left and... I'm sorry,' she paused to wipe away a tear that had suddenly spilled down her cheek. 'I need to find him... I was hoping he was with you.'

'No, but oh, Grace, you don't know how happy that makes me, hearing that. I've wanted someone to find Amos for such a long time...' There was real emotion in Maria's voice too. 'And he's spent so long trying to avoid being found he hasn't realised yet that it's the one thing he wants... more than anything.' She paused to think. 'Where are you?'

'I'm at home,' Grace replied. 'Well, at the farm where Amos was staying, but we don't know when he left exactly, or which direction he went in. All I know is that when he had finished working here he said he would make his way back to you.'

'Yes, he told me that too. It was the day he rang me to tell me about you. And I've been wondering about it ever since, hoping... Well, if he is on his way, he's not here yet, so… But I'd love to meet you. Can you come here, Grace? Come and stay with me and we can wait together.'

Grace could feel the warmth of Maria's words wrapping itself around her and she couldn't think of anything she would rather do. 'I can come straight away… Would that be all right?'

'Perfect, let me tell you how to get here…'

The call ended a few minutes later and Grace hugged her phone to her chest. She had no idea what was going to happen next but, for once in her life, not knowing where she was going or what she was doing felt completely and utterly wonderful.

Her head was awhirl with things she needed to think about, but most of them could wait. There was just one other thing she needed to do now.

She found the contacts list in her phone and dialled another number.

'Hello, Grace…' Bill's voice was hesitant with worry. 'Is everything okay?'

'Yes, I'm fine, and I'm so sorry to call you on a Sunday, Bill, but something rather important has come up. I'm really sorry but I won't be able to come into the shop tomorrow. It's hideously short notice, I know, but…'

'No, no, don't worry… but you sound a little… I don't know, anxious? Are you sure you're all right?'

'Bill, I'm honestly fine, I'm sorry to have to ask.' She smiled to herself at the thoughts in her head, wondering what to say next. 'And the thing is, well, I'm going to visit someone, only I'm not sure how long I'm going to be away…'

'Grace, you never take any holiday, I'll manage. Take a week, two even if it helps, and—'

'Bill, you're a darling, thank you so much.' She could almost see his cheeks colouring down the phone. 'Erm, there is just one more thing… You know how you've always said you'd do anything for me, I only had to ask?'

'Yes?'

'Well, I wondered if I might ask a massive favour…'

*

Maria's directions were wonderfully precise and not quite two hours after they had spoken on the phone, Grace pulled up outside her house. Her head had swivelled from left to right as she drove, scouring the lanes and the countryside for any sign of Amos, but there was none. Once or twice her heart had quickened at the sight of someone walking but, within seconds, she'd see that the person's gait was different, that they were the wrong height, or with a dog, but it still didn't stop a rush of excitement from churning her stomach.

The door to Maria's cottage opened as Grace was still walking up the path and she suddenly realised that it was in fact, Amos's house. She stopped to look at it, feeling odd to be seeing something that was such a part of Amos without him being present.

Maria laughed, opening her arms wide. 'Isn't it beautiful?' she called. 'Just like Amos!'

The cottage was red-brick, low and perfectly symmetrical, almost like a child's drawing. A bright-red front door stood between a window on either side, both upstairs and downstairs and a chimney pot stood on the right-hand end of the roof. The garden was beautiful, filled with waving stems of hollyhocks and roses, and a small bench sat to one side, surrounded by pretty tubs. It was friendly and welcoming, and absolutely perfect.

Maria herself was probably in her late twenties, with rich auburn hair that bloomed in a cloud around a petite face. It was tied back with a vividly coloured headscarf, the ends of which trailed onto the tops of dungarees printed with an equally loud pattern. Grace could see instantly why she and Amos were friends. She held out her arms as Grace approached and the two women hugged as if they had known one another their whole lives.

'Come in, come in,' beamed Maria. 'And no, he's not here yet,' she added in response to Grace's unspoken question. 'But I'm sure he will be.' She squinted up at the sky. 'It's such a beautiful day.'

It was cool and dim inside by comparison and it took Grace a moment for her eyes to adjust. The front door opened directly into the living room, a space that was filled with plants against a backdrop of soft creams and mellow yellows, and Grace felt instantly at home.

'It's so lovely to see you, Grace,' said Maria, still holding her hand, Grace realised. She clasped the other one, holding her at arm's length and looking her up and down. 'And you're everything I hoped you would be.'

Grace blushed at her frank assessment, but strangely, coming from Maria, it felt like an entirely normal thing to say.

'You're just like Amos,' she replied. 'I don't know a thing about you, but I can see why you're such good friends.'

'Then you approve,' said Maria. 'That makes me very happy.' She looked at her watch. 'Now, have you eaten? I've a fresh batch of scones straight out of the oven, so have one of those at least, even if you can't face anything else.'

Maria led her from the lounge through an archway into a dining room, and on into the kitchen which ran along the back of the house. Two things struck Grace straight away: the first was the sudden light in this room, and the second was the smell. There was a glorious scent of baking, but also something much earthier, greener and, looking up, Grace realised that the ceiling was hung with bunches of herbs strung from a line across the room. A sewing machine stood on the kitchen table along with heaps of colourful cotton fabric.

'Have a seat,' said Maria, 'if you can find a space, and then I want to know everything about you.'

And so, surprisingly, although she had only just met Maria, over the most delicious cheese and chive scone and a pot of strong tea, Grace did tell her. Except that she didn't tell her about the Grace of old, she told her about the person she had become since she had met Amos.

Chapter Twenty-Two

Somehow the afternoon slipped into the evening without either of them really noticing. More tea had been drunk, both the house and garden explored, and Maria had told Grace all about herself and the small business she ran from the cottage growing and selling herbs and making fragrant pillows and other herbal remedies. In fact, the two women seemed to have so much in common that Grace couldn't help but wonder aloud why Amos hadn't fallen for Maria's considerable charms. It was the first time the young woman's face fell during the whole time Grace had been there.

'He hasn't told you what happened, has he?' she asked.

Grace shook her head. 'No, he left before I had the chance to talk to him about it. But I know it must have been serious.'

'I thought as much, because if he had told you, you would understand why he and I could never be a possibility.' Her face brightened a little. 'Of course there's a huge age gap and we'd have to fancy one another as well, which we don't. But even if we did it would never work, we're too much of a reminder for each other. Amos and I are the best of friends, and I am glad to have him in my life, but that's as far as it goes. But you, you're a different matter... You're just as special as Amos if I'm not much mistaken and I'd hate to see you slip through each other's fingers.'

Grace blushed slightly at the compliment and chose her words carefully. 'Was the thing that happened something… bad? I feel awful even asking. I mean, here I am, miles from home, waiting for a man who in all honesty I barely know, and yet I *am* here… I'm not entirely sure why, and yet I can't believe that anything will change how I feel about Amos.'

Maria considered her question for a few moments, her lips pressed together. 'That's not a question I can answer, I'm afraid. The judgement you make must be yours and yours alone.'

'Yes, I can understand that,' replied Grace sombrely. 'And I appreciate your honesty.' She smiled, trying to lighten the mood once more. 'I just wish he'd hurry up and get here, that's if he's coming at all. I'm beginning to feel a little like a lovesick teenager.'

Maria nodded in acknowledgement of how Grace was feeling. 'He'll get here, I'm sure of it, but you might have noticed that time doesn't seem to hold the same constraints over Amos that it does over most people. The spare bed is made up anyway though – you will stay, won't you?'

'Oh…' Grace stared at her. 'I hadn't even thought about what might happen if Amos doesn't arrive today. I don't have anything with me… no nightclothes, clean underwear, not even a toothbrush.' She pulled a face. 'I'm afraid I was in a bit of a rush to get going when I left home. I wasn't exactly thinking straight.'

Maria grinned. 'Then it's a good job I have some spares. Don't worry, as long as you don't need anything fancy, you'll be fine. Now what say we open a bottle of wine and get some food on the go? The garden is just bursting with delicious stuff to eat at the moment and I rather like the idea of picking our own dinner.'

Grace followed her out into the garden, grateful to her for keeping the mood light. It was bad enough waiting for Amos without dwelling on the reason why he left in the first place. Together they gathered some lettuce leaves, fat juicy tomatoes, a pepper, some green beans and handfuls of fresh basil, the smell clinging to Grace's fingers. She inhaled deeply, feeling the peace that pervaded the place. She tried to draw it down deep, as if she could store it up for the future.

Scarcely a half hour later they were back outside, eating a simple salad dressed in homemade pesto. With another scone to mop up the juice, it was one of the tastiest meals Grace could remember eating. Or perhaps it was the company. Maria seemed to instinctively know how Grace was feeling and, as she poured another glass of wine, she sat back and squinted into the evening sun.

'Change is never easy, is it?' she said.

Grace twiddled the stem of her glass. 'No,' she replied. 'And there seems to have been rather a lot of it lately. But I think that's one thing that Amos has taught me – that I shouldn't be so concerned with the destination that I forget to enjoy the journey. I've been trying to remember that, but it's not always easy.'

Maria smiled. 'That's just the sort of thing he would say, but you're right, we all have an intrinsic need to be settled, don't we? Even when the change happens for a good reason, we strive to get to the point where things stand still again. Yet even though it's the passage between the two points that gives us problems, it's where our greatest learning comes from, and also the greatest reward.'

'It's a lesson I think I'm finally beginning to learn,' said Grace, somewhat ruefully. 'Although I fear it's come a little too late. I've been so fixated with keeping my house that I haven't seen the possibilities that lie outside of it. And, worse, I think it might be one of the reasons why Amos left.'

'How so?'

'Because he's such a free spirit, and I was convinced that I couldn't exist without my house around me, its comfort, its security, but also all the things that I thought were me. I'd wrapped it so tight around myself like a cocoon, no one else could get in. Amos could never stand to be so constrained and, unwittingly, I think I gave him the message that if he didn't live by my rules there was no room for him in my life.' She stared out across the garden, the last rays of the golden light sinking below the horizon. 'He's not coming, is he?'

Maria leaned forward to take her hand. 'Don't give up hope, Grace. You're not the only one who's beginning to realise a few things. Amos has been on a journey of his own these last few years, one he's trodden unwaveringly, but I've a feeling he's coming to the end of it. That's a scary feeling for anyone, as well you know, but he'll get there – he already knows who it is that's changed his course…' She gave Grace a very direct look. 'But he has to forgive himself first before he can even think about taking a step in a different direction, and that might take some time.'

'Forgiveness,' said Grace quietly. 'Perhaps the most powerful quality we humans can bestow – to be able to offer forgiveness, either to another or to ourselves. I'm not sure I've ever been that good at it, but I recognise the sacrifice involved, to lower all defences and put aside our prejudices and sometimes expected behaviour too, so that we act out of the simple and honest truth of what is right. It can take extraordinary courage to do that.'

Lost in her own thoughts, it took Grace a moment to realise that Maria hadn't replied. When she looked across at her, she was horrified to see her eyes had filled with tears.

'Oh my goodness... Maria, I'm so sorry. I didn't mean to upset you.' But to her even greater surprise, the young woman got to her feet and threw her arms around Grace, hugging her tight. When she finally drew away, her eyes were shiny bright but her face was lit by something that came from very deep within.

Maria wiped under her eyes. 'No, you mustn't be sorry, Grace. I can't tell you how much it means to me to hear you say that. And you haven't upset me, you've offered me the greatest kindness anyone has shown me in five long years. You've understood me, Grace, you've finally confirmed that what I did was right, when everyone else has spent that entire time telling me how wrong I was. It sounds silly, but you've made me feel whole again.'

Grace was shocked to see how affected Maria had been by her words. The young woman had shown Grace such kindness since she had arrived and, naively, she had assumed that everything was perfect in Maria's life. She lived in this beautiful cottage, surrounded by a beautiful garden, making beautiful things for a living. And yet now that Grace really opened her eyes, she saw the truth of the situation – a young woman, clearly living alone, in a house that belonged to someone else and who had made the best of what she found around her, probably because she'd had no choice. And she was a friend of Amos too, which was particularly telling because Grace knew full well how that happened... usually when someone had need of help. Suddenly she understood.

'So what was it that you forgave Amos for?' she asked gently.

Maria looked up, a tender expression on her face. 'Oh, Grace. I wasn't sure I should be the person to tell you any of this, but now I think perhaps I should. It might help you to understand what Amos has been running from all these years, but also why he might finally be ready to stop.'

Grace swallowed a slug of wine, feeling as if a thousand butterflies had suddenly taken flight in her stomach. 'Tell me what happened,' she whispered.

'You're right when you said that I forgave Amos, I did. Although, in truth there wasn't really anything to forgive. He was as much a victim in what happened as the person who…' She broke off, pouring herself another glass of wine and taking a long swallow. 'As the person who died,' she finished. 'Her name was Bethany, and she was my sister.'

The breath caught in Grace's throat, a sudden lump of emotion forming, and she reached out her hand in comfort. Maria took it, giving it a squeeze.

'Amos was just in the wrong place at the wrong time and I truly think that if it had been anyone else driving that day, they all would have died. It's just that Beth was in the wrong place at the wrong time as well, and whatever Amos did he knew he couldn't save her too. He had a split second to make a decision, and I absolutely believe he made the right one, but it's a question he has asked himself every day of his life since then.'

'Go on…'

'It was a day in the middle of January, five years ago, a beautiful, bright, but bitterly cold morning. I've often thought over the years that this was why it happened at all; the sunshine belying the freezing temperatures, making it seem warmer than it was, and the driver therefore heedless of the icy road. His name was Maurice Green and he got in his car in the morning to pay a visit to the post office, a journey into the local town which took all of ten minutes. Except that this morning he was rushing to get back home to wait for the engineer who was coming to mend his boiler. He shot around the bend at the top of the hill into town, braked rather sharply and, instead of slowing down, skidded on some black ice. He went straight down the hill, gathering speed, until he ploughed into the back of Amos's stationary car, sitting in the road as he waited to turn right.

'At that moment Amos became a lethal weapon and there was only one possible outcome. As Amos's car shot forward towards the pavement he was faced with an impossible choice – hit the group of young mums with their pushchairs, or try and steer in the other direction, pushing him into the path of the single pedestrian who was just crossing the road. He had a split second to make his choice and there was no guarantee that he would even be able to bring the car under any kind of control, but he had to try. The rear end of his car missed the mothers by inches as he swung around, but Beth was hit head on. There was nothing anyone could have done.'

A single tear rolled down Maria's face as she stared out across the darkening garden. The birds were still singing and the scent of flowers warmed by the sun still hung in the air, but it seemed to Grace as if the world was frozen in time, holding its breath. Her own cheeks were wet, as she concentrated on getting breath in and out of her body; the ability to do so naturally seemed to have totally deserted her.

And then, suddenly it all made sense – why Amos had felt the need to leave his home, why he always looked for the person who needed saving, why he constantly denied himself comfort as if punishment was all he deserved. The guilt he had carried with him ever since that horrific day had dictated his every move. Amos was a hero and yet someone had died. No, not someone, Maria's sister had died, and Amos had killed her. How on earth did you ever move on from that? But then Grace realised she knew the answer to that too.

'And you forgave him?' she whispered.

'Yes, when no one else around me could. Least of all Amos himself. My family hated him for what he did, still do. They made his life a misery, and mine for sticking up for him, and yet even though he saved the lives of three women, three toddlers and a baby of just seven weeks old, all they could see was the life of the one he killed.'

Grace was still holding her wine glass and she put it down gently, her hand trembling as she did so.

'But how did you end up here?'

'Because I couldn't stay at home listening to my parents' raging, and their grief, which was so different from mine. I loved Beth with all my heart and there isn't a single day that goes by when I don't think of her, but I grieved for Amos too, whose life had ended just as surely as Beth's. In the end I couldn't stand being there for any length of time and I began to visit Amos a couple of times a week. Inexplicably I felt lighter when I was with him, as if, even though it was so different in texture, we were able to share our grief. I think it helped Amos too, to start with anyway. There was a storm of publicity immediately after the accident, most of it portraying him as a hero and, as you can imagine, while this didn't sit well with him either, at least it helped him to focus on the good that had been done. But, as with all things, people move on. The kind comments stopped, the women he had saved got on with their lives and the contact they had with him initially dwindled to nothing, until all he was left with was the fact that Beth had died.'

'I can't imagine what you both must have been going through. I am so, so sorry, for your loss, Maria, but also so very glad that you were there for Amos. I can't bear the thought that he could have been on his own.'

'In the end Amos decided to take a break for a few days and I offered to look after his house while he was away. When he came back he seemed lighter – the local pub in the village where he stayed had just been taken over by a young couple who were in the throes of renovation. A chance conversation with them revealed that they'd just been let down by their builder and so Amos offered to give them a hand in return for a meal and a pint each evening. He was gone three weeks altogether.' Maria smiled. 'You can imagine what happened after that…'

Grace nodded. 'And he's been travelling ever since.'

'He sold his business and—'

'Wait, I didn't know he'd had his own business. What did he do?'

'Build houses…'

Grace looked heavenward. When Amos had arrived at the farm he had produced a bunch of references for Fraser and Hannah, mentioning nothing about his past. They didn't know the half of it. 'Well that explains a lot of things.'

'Yes, I thought it might.'

'And so, you stayed to look after things here for him?'

'I did. Things had become unbearable at home. It was probably about the right time for me to move out anyway, but with everything that had happened, naturally my parents decided I must be having an affair with Amos. There could be no other reason for my scandalous behaviour and it didn't matter what I said, they didn't believe me. We had a furious row one evening, and I moved out. I've been here ever since. Amos put things on a proper legal footing so that I am officially his tenant, and the rest, as they say, is history.'

Maria took another swallow of wine, her words swirling around them as Grace sat quietly trying to take in everything. She felt utterly humbled to be in the company of this young woman who had shown so much courage and dignity, even when she herself had suffered enormously; it made Grace feel quite ashamed to have been so fixated with the material things in her life. And, as for Amos, Grace couldn't even begin to piece together all the different emotions she was feeling about him.

The minutes ticked by until Grace became aware that Maria was watching her. The young woman smiled. 'It's a bit of a conversation killer, isn't it?' she said.

'I don't know what to say first,' admitted Grace. 'Except that I am very grateful to you for telling me. That can't have been easy.'

'It's a whole lot easier telling someone who I know will understand.'

Maria's eyes were clear and bright as she held Grace's look and, impulsively, Grace got to her feet, her eyes filling with tears as she hugged Maria to her. The two women stood like that for quite some time until, beginning to laugh, Grace wiped under her eyes and gently pulled away.

'I'm not sure who that hug was for, me or you,' she said.

'For us both. Thank you, Grace. It's been a while since anyone hugged me.'

And suddenly Grace realised that the last person who had hugged her had been Amos, right out of the blue, and she had felt just the same way. It had felt so good to be held. A wave of longing swept over her; she was aching to see him, talk to him, touch him, but more than anything to let him know how special a person he was. She gave a sudden shiver.

Noticing, Maria took her hand. 'Come on, let's go back inside. It's too cool out here now and getting late.' Her smile turned into one of sympathy. 'And perhaps you might like to have a bath or something? A little time to yourself.'

Grace returned her smile gratefully. It was as if Maria had read her mind. Gathering up the glasses and plates, they went back inside, Maria switching on lamps as they went. Moments later they were standing in the spare bedroom.

'This is Amos's room, of course,' said Maria. 'Although I guess you've probably worked that out.' She stroked a hand across the homely patchwork throw on the bed. 'I don't know why I always keep it made up really, I mean he usually sleeps in the garden.'

Grace's hand went to her heart, warmed by their shared knowledge. It felt absolutely right that she should be here, in this room, and the thought was like the softest of blankets settling around her.

'Help yourself to whatever you need,' added Maria. 'I know that Amos won't mind in the slightest, and if you need anything else, just say. I'm going downstairs for a bit so take your time.'

She stood by the doorway for a second on her way out before turning back to Grace. 'Sweet dreams,' she said.

The warm water of the bath felt like silk against Grace's skin and she lay, letting her tears fall peacefully without even attempting to wipe them away. Maria's story had left its mark and, as Grace relaxed, she let go of her emotions too. Shortly after, feeling cleansed and calm, she wrapped one of the huge towels around her and padded back into the bedroom. The curtains were still open and the moonlight shone onto the lane below. She wondered what it would feel like to see Amos walking towards her.

Crossing to the wardrobe, she took out one of Amos's shirts, soft white cotton that felt delicious against her skin as she pulled it over her head. His presence was palpable in the room as she climbed into bed and, minutes later, she was fast asleep.

Chapter Twenty-Three

Grace left after breakfast the next morning.

She'd known as soon as she woke that Amos wasn't coming back. She had slept well until about four in the morning when she came to with a start and, without even thinking, crossed straight to the window to look down into the lane beyond. As soon as she saw the empty road she understood the turmoil that must be filling Amos's head. He couldn't come home, not just yet anyway. He had left the farm because he was terrified that his secret was about to be revealed but, from what Maria had said, Amos was also realising that he couldn't outrun his past forever, and that maybe the time was right to finally face and lay down his guilt. That being the case, would his home really be the place to do that? Maria was here, someone he trusted and cared about, but so were all the memories and emotions that he had run from in the first place. They would crowd his head, giving him very little space to think things through rationally.

Grace had tried to put herself in his shoes, to understand how he must be feeling, but all she could think was that he would need to be in a place where he could reflect and put things into perspective. But where? And then it had come to her. Amos had spent years travelling from place to place, criss-crossing his path back and forth, but if you were going to finish a journey, to bring it full circle, what better place than where it all began? Particularly if there was someone else from whom you sought forgiveness...

As soon as she'd put her idea to Maria, she could see her eyes light up in agreement, and she dashed off to find a map.

'It's near here,' she'd said, pointing at a collection of lanes on the map that made up the nearest town. 'Go straight through, past the market square and just after, turn right towards Marcle. The village isn't huge, so you'll find it easily enough, just stay on the same road and you'll drive right by.' She folded up the map and gave it to Grace. 'Take it,' she said. 'I'll make us some breakfast.'

It had been all Grace could do to sit still and eat it. Every part of her was itching to get on the road, and the delay felt excruciating. The more she'd thought about it, the more she was certain that the village was where Amos had gone and she was desperate to race after him, but she couldn't refuse Maria's kindness. She ate as fast as she could without seeming rude, until, in the end, Maria just laughed, whisked Grace's plate out from under her and cried, '*Go, go!*'

They hugged fiercely and Grace knew without a doubt that she would see Maria again, very soon.

'I'll ring you,' she said. 'As soon as I know anything.' And with that she was gone, navigating her way carefully down the narrow lane away from where Amos had made his home. It took several minutes before Grace's heart stopped its ferocious pounding and she was able to relax and settle into the journey without crunching the unfamiliar gears. She had a feeling she was going to remember every mile of it.

Even with stopping briefly in the small town, it took Grace just twenty minutes to get there; she hadn't driven fast, crawling along to see if she could catch sight of Amos along the way. Her stomach was tying itself in knots. She was so close to her destination but, despite her earlier desire to race ahead, now she just wanted to slow everything down.

At the moment she still had hope. There was still the possibility that everything would turn out all right. But what if Amos wasn't there? Or what if he was there but didn't want to talk to her? A sob caught in her throat. She thought of the time they had shared together since he arrived at Hope Corner; his kindnesses, his quirky sense of humour, his wisdom and the ability he had to make Grace feel so alive. She couldn't bear the thought that all that could be over, that she might never get to share those things with him again. How misguided she had been over the past few years, and now, just when she had realised how to set herself free, she stood to lose everything.

Heart pounding as she drove, her eyes scoured the countryside for any sign of him, but the road ahead stayed empty and, as she pulled into a small layby, there were neither people nor cars in sight.

The sun was warm on her arms as she pushed open the lych-gate and walked inside, following the path that led off to the left, just as Maria had described. She was vaguely aware of birds singing, of flowers along the path, but she scarcely registered them, intent on her search. Her feet carried her forward, not caring where she was walking until suddenly she stopped, one hand moving to rest against her heart.

She looked down at the flowers in her other hand, and with tears welling in her eyes she took the final few steps of her journey until she was kneeling beside Amos.

Gently she laid the roses she'd been carrying beside the young woman's grave. 'Hello, Beth,' she whispered, 'I've heard so much about you.'

She thought at first that Amos hadn't heard her. His head remained bent, his hands loosely clasped in his lap. But then he looked up, turning slightly, and his eyes went straight to hers, widening and then shining in delight with a warmth that wrapped itself around her as a slow smile lit up his face.

'Grace,' he said. 'You came.' And then he stood, pulling her with him, pulling her closer, and his arms welcomed her in as he cradled her head against his chest. 'You came,' he whispered again.

Around them the world continued to turn, the birds sang, the breeze rustled the trees at the churchyard's edge, but for Grace there was just a quiet and peaceful, perfect calm. She was home.

They stood that way for a few minutes, Grace revelling in the warmth of his skin through his tee shirt, but then she pulled away and stood, looking at Amos, drinking him in; his hair, his dark eyes, his red boots. He looked the same, but different. Or perhaps it was just the way she was looking at him, or he her. They stood for a couple more moments until suddenly Amos laughed and it was just like the day they first met when he came into the village shop and she had rescued a bee from his shoulder. A bee that hadn't wanted to be rescued at all. She now knew exactly how it felt.

'How did you…?' he began, but then he touched a hand to her arm. 'Maria. Of course.'

Grace nodded. 'How else would I know where you were?'

There was a pause while time seemed to stand still again as Amos's eyes searched hers. His face softened. 'And do you love her just as much as I reckoned you would?'

'I do.'

She slipped her hand inside Amos's and rested her head on his shoulder. 'And although I've never met Beth, from what Maria said, I think that I'd have liked her very much too.' She lifted her head. 'Maria told me how close they were, so very different in looks but in all other respects two peas in a pod.' Her eyes searched Amos's, and he nodded, just slightly. 'And she told me what happened, on the day that Beth died.'

Amos's fingers wound tighter in hers. 'I'm sorry,' he said simply, head bowed.

She stared at him. 'Whatever for?'

He didn't answer but gazed out across the churchyard.

'What, Amos? For leaving? For keeping your past a secret from me? Or for killing Beth?'

He flinched but held her look. The seconds ticked by and he still didn't answer. He didn't need to.

'And how long are you going to continue being sorry for? Your whole life?' She sighed and touched a hand to his face. 'Let it go, Amos,' she added. 'You've suffered enough.'

'I know…' His voice was barely above a whisper. 'But I don't know how.'

'By setting your guilt free, Amos…'

'Grace, I—'

'No, let me finish. I can't begin to imagine what that time must have been like for you, or how you ever move on from something like that, but what I do know is that you've let your guilt be your prison. You couldn't see a way to live without it, so you took it with you everywhere you went, like a snail sheltering inside his shell, praying that some blackbird wouldn't crack it wide open.'

He gave a rueful smile. 'I never pictured it quite like that,' he said. 'But you're right, I know that.'

'So then you also know that every once in a while it's okay to put down your burden and take the weight off your shoulders. Or let someone else carry it for a while… someone who knows how precious it is and will care for it just as you do…' She touched a hand to his cheek. 'No one can wave a magic wand, Amos, and these feelings aren't going to leave you overnight, but Maria is right, it's time to forgive yourself. And, knowing how alike Beth and Maria were, I know that Beth wouldn't have wanted you to live your life like this either, Amos, she'd have wanted you to *live*...'

Amos closed his eyes and swallowed hard. Grace brought his head to rest against her chest and they clung together, a shuddering sigh giving way to quaking sobs as Amos finally released the pain he'd had tethered inside him for so long.

When Grace could feel his breathing start to ease, she straightened slightly. There was a question she needed to ask, although she was rather afraid of what the answer might be.

'Amos... I know that Paul recognised you from his time on the news desk and that he threatened to reveal what he knew, but why did you leave the farm? Was that the only reason, because you were scared?'

He was silent for quite some time before answering, lifting his head to look at her. 'I was just listening to your heartbeat,' he said, finally. 'And I think I'm finally beginning to listen to mine... but that's a scary place for me, Grace. I've travelled all over the country, some beautiful places, some run-down, desperate places, but I've never been anywhere as daunting as the place that's inside of me. In fact, I've tried to deny it even exists, but since I came to Hope Corner Farm I find it's been poking at me, inviting me to visit, and there's only one reason for that, Grace. And it's you.' He looked around him, spotting a bench a little distance away and motioning towards it.

Grace waited until they were seated before continuing. 'That didn't quite answer my question,' she said.

Amos hung his head. 'No, I know... I *was* scared about what Paul would tell you. I was terrified actually. That's why I left in such a hurry, something I promised I'd never do. But you've been let down enough and… well, I couldn't bear the thought that you might think I'd let you down too. That everything you thought about me was a lie, and in a way it was.'

'You never lied to me, Amos. In fact, everything about the way you've acted only points to the goodness of the man inside, not the other way around. But that wasn't the only reason, was it?'

'No,' said Amos quietly. 'I wanted to stay… I wanted to stay with *you*, but Grace, you've seen the way I live. I can't remember the last time I slept in a bed and I've got used to that, the freedom, the open road and the possibilities that opens up. What started off as a means to assuage some of my guilt has also allowed me to discover who I really am, and I enjoy that way of life – not being tied to one place – the materiality of possessions but I—'

'I've lost the house,' said Grace, abruptly.

Amos's head shot up, his eyes full of apology. 'Oh my God, the weekend…'

'Yes, it seems our friends from America were rather more perceptive than I gave them credit for. Amos, the weekend was never about putting the icing on the cake of the deal as everyone had assumed. It was really the other way around – to check if what they thought about Paul held water, or whether he would prove them wrong. Sadly, it didn't turn out quite that way.'

'And I was one of the reasons for that… I'm so sorry, Grace.'

'No! Zac didn't like the way Paul treated you, it's true, but you didn't make them change their mind, it was already made up. They were lovely about it, actually, I really liked them and I'm not sorry about their decision. It's about time Paul was taken down a peg or two. He behaved appallingly and now he's realised that maybe he can't get away with it after all.'

'And you're certain that's the only outcome? Is there no way Paul would change his mind?'

A ladybird was crawling along the back of the bench and Grace watched it for a moment, feeling a little unsure of herself.

'I don't know for certain, because when Flora rang to tell me you'd gone, I'm afraid I rushed off...' She broke off, blushing slightly. 'I was so desperate to find you, I threw my apron at Paul and told him he could cook breakfast by himself. Believe me, it was worth it just to see the expression on his face... But that was the deal, Amos, you know that... I can't see why Paul would change his mind now. It was his last threat as it happens, just before I left...'

Amos was quiet for a moment. 'You know, Grace, your home is not four walls and a roof, it's what you carry inside of you that makes it so. You have a peace and serenity, an inner state of being that fills any space you occupy. It's one of the reasons why I fell in love with you...'

He looked up, smiling, the same depth of emotion shining from his eyes as she hoped was shining from hers.

'But you make the mistake of thinking that way of being comes out of your home. It doesn't, it never has. It has always come from you. You could make your home anywhere and the effect would be the same. You just need to realise that whatever is within you flows outward too.'

She opened her mouth to speak, leaning forward in her eagerness, but Amos held up his hand to stop her.

'I didn't finish just now, when you asked me why I left. It's true, I *was* feeling that I would find it difficult to stay in one place all the time. Your way of life is very different from the way mine has been but, bizarrely, as soon as I left I realised I no longer felt that way. Perhaps it's just that I've finally realised it's time I stopped running, that I no longer need to, but I suddenly find myself, if not exactly longing for comfort and security, at least being able to appreciate its merits.' He smirked. 'I think I might be ready to settle down, Grace, is what I'm, very badly, trying to say.'

Grace could feel her heart thumping in her chest, its beat quickening as she listened to his words. Because if Amos was saying what she thought he was saying then… She stared at him and then burst out laughing, getting to her feet and dragging a bemused Amos with her. She took hold of his hand and began to tow him back down the path.

'Come with me,' she said, mysteriously. 'Don't say anything,' she added. 'All will be revealed in a minute.'

She began to lead him out of the churchyard, still holding his hand. 'Can I just check something?' she asked.

Amos dipped his head, a slightly cautious smile on his face.

'Am I right in thinking that you've just spent the last few weeks helping me come up with a business plan to try and save my house, or at least allow me to carry on living there, and in the process just might have fallen a teeny bit in love with me…?'

Amos blushed, but nodded.

'And that this was a bit of a problem because you couldn't imagine anything worse than having to live in one place, or being with someone whose whole life revolved around her house and garden…?'

Again, a small nod.

'But that now you might have changed your mind, and might want to come and live with me, after all?'

'That's pretty much the size of it, yes,' agreed Amos.

She stopped as she reached the gate. 'I thought so,' she said. 'Which is a bit ironic really, given that I drove here in this…'

She looked towards the layby where she had parked and pointed at the camper van she had borrowed from Bill.

'You see, I find myself in the curious position of not caring that I've lost the house. I've realised that it's not what's truly important in my life any more. I'm just like you, Amos, except that instead of guilt, I made my house my prison, locking myself inside so that I almost became a part of the furniture. I couldn't see a life without it, and therefore no one else could see a life with me that didn't include the house...'

'And now you think differently...?'

'Yes,' she said simply. 'Now I see differently. You were right about me, Amos, and it's you that's given me the courage and the strength to see that. I can be anyone I want to be, and anywhere I want to be. And where I want to be is with you...'

She looked up at his expectant face, his expression changing as he took in her words. He looked between her and the camper van as a slow dawning crossed his face and the radiant smile she had come to love lit up his eyes.

'You really came here in this?' he asked, pulling her into his arms.

'I really did...'

His eyes rested first on her hair, and then on her lips. His head bent slightly. She closed her eyes and breathed in as his hand travelled until it just brushed the back of her neck. She breathed out. And then, ever so gently, standing by the side of the road, with only the wind and birdsong as witness to their joy, Amos kissed her.

'Oh, Grace,' he whispered. 'What are we like?'

Chapter Twenty-Four

Once Amos was settled and his rucksack stowed safely on board, Grace started the engine. He hadn't said a word the whole time, just grinned at her, but now, as she prepared to pull away, she paused.

'So, where are we going?' she asked.

'I think we should head home, don't you?' replied Amos. 'But there's someone I reckon we should call in on first…' He indicated the road up ahead. 'Turn right just around this bend and the road will take you back towards the town.'

'I wonder if she'll be expecting us,' said Grace.

Amos just laughed. 'This is Maria we're talking about. Of course she'll be expecting us!'

Fifteen minutes later his words were borne out. Grace had only just climbed down from the van when she heard Maria's shout of welcome.

'Oh, my God! I knew it, I knew you'd find him!' She rushed up to Grace and threw her arms around her, her cloud of bushy hair almost covering Grace's face. She broke away, laughing. 'I've been watching from the upstairs window,' she confessed. 'I can't tell you how happy I am.'

'I'm pretty pleased myself,' said Grace, grinning. 'I nearly had heart failure on the way there, mind.'

'Nah, I knew you'd be okay. You're The One you see, I knew it the minute I set eyes on you.'

'So did I actually,' said Amos quietly, coming to stand beside Grace. 'Except that it took me rather longer than you to realise.' He held out his arms. 'Hello, Maria.'

Neither of them needed to say any more, their warm hug said it all, as did the dancing light in their eyes. Despite Amos having been on the road so much, Grace could see how close he and Maria were. They had shared their journey, travelling the path that their grief had taken them together, not always side by side, but in every other way that was important. And in many ways this would mark a new beginning for Maria too.

Grace took the young woman's hand. 'Thank you,' she said simply, knowing that without her she wouldn't now be standing by Amos's side.

Maria took hold of Amos's hand as well and gave them both a hearty squeeze, before abruptly dropping them. 'Right, wait here,' she said, and dashed off back down the path.

Grace gave Amos a puzzled look.

'I have no idea,' he said, just as bemused as she was.

They didn't have to wait long; within a minute, Maria had returned, carrying a wicker basket.

'Now, I know I haven't seen you in ages, Amos, but I think I understand all I really need to, and the proof of it is standing right in front of me.' She looked at Grace. 'Correct me if I'm wrong, but I'm guessing that you don't usually drive around in a camper van, so there must be something significant about your choice of transport.'

Grace grinned, beaming at Amos. 'You could say that...'

'I thought so.' She handed Amos the basket. 'You may come in if you need to use the bathroom, otherwise it seems to me you've wasted quite enough precious time together already, so I've packed you a picnic – for wherever you're going...'

'Oh, Maria...' said Amos, warmly. 'You've been the best friend I could ever have hoped for.'

She grinned at him. 'What do you mean *been*... None of this past-tense rubbish. I still am your friend, you ninny, and don't you forget it. And once you're done travelling for a while, I shall expect a visit so that you can update me with tales of your adventures, so mind you have some.'

'Oh, we intend to,' replied Grace. 'Thank you, Maria, that really is the kindest thing.'

'And make sure you look after Grace,' she added, directing a look at Amos. 'Or there will be trouble.'

'Yes, Ma'am.' Amos swung the picnic basket. 'Well, are we ready then, Grace?' He took her hand and led her back to the van. 'Ready for the rest of our lives?'

Grace nodded and sighed with happiness.

By the time she had climbed inside the cab, Maria had already walked back down the path and was standing by the cottage's front door. Grace waved. 'Thank you so much,' she called. 'For everything!'

Maria blew them a kiss. 'I'll see you next time you're passing.'

Grace settled herself back behind the wheel and waited for Amos to join her.

'You know, my head is spinning with the thought that we can go anywhere and do anything. It's the most delicious feeling. I ought to be terrified but...' She took Amos's hand, unable to say any more.

'You heard the lady,' he replied. 'We've wasted far too much time already. Come on, let's hit the road.'

*

It seemed as if a lifetime had passed since Grace had pulled away from Hope Corner Farm the day before, but now, as she drew up in front of the gates, she was excited to be back, even if it was only for a short while...

She gave a couple of toots on the horn before climbing from the cab, looking around to see if she could spot anyone. They had decided against phoning ahead, instead wanting to spring a surprise on everyone at the farm, but it was late afternoon and she knew that everyone would be busy.

It was Brodie who spotted them first. The elderly dog gave a half-hearted woof as he raised himself up from where he'd been lying in the shade of a tree. Moments later, as he walked towards them, tail wagging, Grace spotted Flora at a distance, walking alongside two other people. She was about to rush forward when she realised that they could well be prospective customers and so she hung back a little, looking at Amos; perhaps they should go to the house first. She was about to suggest it, when there was a gleeful shout and Grace looked back to see Flora hurtling across the yard towards them.

Flora was moving so fast she almost bounced off Grace, crushing her in a hug before letting go and doing the same to Amos.

'Oh my God, you're here... both of you... together!' She laughed, jiggling about in an excited fashion so that her wild curls bounced about her shoulders. But then she stopped suddenly, her face falling as her hand went to her mouth.

'Oh... is everything okay...? Are you...?' She stopped, she couldn't say any more.

Grace took her hand. 'Yes it is... and yes, we are...' And then she pulled Flora into another hug.

'Oh, I'm so happy!' Flora pulled away, unashamedly wiping under her eyes. 'It's been agony wondering how things were going. I didn't know if you'd found Amos, or if you had, well, you know… whether you'd be together. I nearly called Maria so many times to see if she knew anything.' She grinned at them both.

'I know, I'm so sorry,' replied Grace. 'We were going to call, and then we thought we should just turn up. It's been a bit mad, to tell you the truth. Utterly wonderfully, gloriously mad, but mad all the same.'

Flora nodded. 'None of that matters, it's just so lovely to see you. Come on, we need to go and find everyone else.'

Grace peered over her shoulder at the two figures who were loitering hesitantly a little distance away. Noticing, Flora slapped a hand to her forehead and turned towards them, beckoning them over.

'This is Huw and Kitty,' she explained, gesturing at the two young people. 'You might remember when you first arrived, Amos, that I was due to have a couple of students come and work for the summer but they decided to go to Greece for a bit… Well, it would seem that things didn't work out quite the way they hoped and so… well, here they are…' She broke off, peering at Amos. 'You didn't have anything to do with that, did you? I wouldn't put it past you.'

Amos laughed. 'How could I possibly have anything to do with it?'

'Hmmm…' Flora's eyes narrowed. 'I don't know, but I still reckon I'm right. I always said there was something about you…'

They all shook hands before Flora asked Huw and Kitty to go and fetch Ned from the field. Then she turned back to Grace and Amos.

'Cup of tea?' she asked. 'I bet you're dying for one. And I need to hear everything that's happened, come on.'

They followed her back inside the farmhouse, where her loud shout brought Hannah and Fraser into the kitchen. Ned arrived soon after, and it was some minutes before their excited chatter died down enough for Amos to speak.

'I am sorry for just taking off like that,' he said. 'But…' He trailed off and Grace remembered that she was still the only one who knew about his past. She wondered what he was going to say when Fraser leaned forward, cutting him off.

'I've said it before lad, but I told you that as long as you looked after us here you were entitled to keep your past to yourself until you were ready to tell us, and the same is still true. We couldn't ask for more from you, Amos, and, as far as we're concerned, the only reason you left is because of the way you feel about this wonderful lady here.' He paused for a second, looking at Grace, a huge smile on his face. 'And really that's all we need to know. So, I don't reckon that today is the day to tell us, after all. Besides, the smile on Grace's face has told us all we need to know.'

Amos smiled gratefully. 'My head *is* a little all over the place,' he admitted and then blushed a deep red. 'But then I've never been in love before.'

Ned gave a low whistle and clutched hold of Flora's hand. 'And I thought it was just me that was a soppy idiot.'

'Romantic,' said Flora, firmly. 'Not soppy.' But her smile was as bright as her husband's.

'So, what are you going to do now?' she asked them both.

Grace glanced at Amos. 'Well, I have the van for two weeks,' she said. 'So we're going to do a little driving, and a little thinking… but mainly we're just going to enjoy what life seems to have brought us.' She took hold of Amos's hand. 'Isn't that right?'

He nodded. 'But we'll be back… I don't know how long we've got before the house is sold, but there's all the work to finish here and—'

Ned held up his hand. 'Don't you worry about that,' he said. 'That's not going anywhere and we don't need to rush, we've plenty to keep us going for the time being. Our dreams aren't going anywhere.'

'No,' said Flora, smiling. 'No, they're not. And we'll sort something out for you two, one way or another. The universe isn't going to let us down now,' she added. 'It wouldn't dare.'

Hannah smiled. 'I went and checked over the house once everyone had gone yesterday,' she said. 'Everything was fine, although there was this letter left for you on the table.' She got up to fetch it from the countertop. 'But we'll keep an eye on the place for you while you're away, so there's nothing for you to worry about.'

'And you'll check on my bees for me?' asked Grace. 'Tell them what's been going on.'

'Of course we will.' Flora drained the last of her tea. 'So that's it then,' she said. 'We've got work to do and you two need to frankly bugger off and start enjoying yourselves.'

She caught Grace's eye and grinned. 'Just send us a postcard, when you get to wherever you're going,' she added. 'Or I shall be very upset…'

'But we don't even know where we're going, do we?' replied Grace.

'Nope,' said Amos. 'But that's half the fun.'

Ten minutes later, after copious hugs and goodbyes, Grace pulled the cab door shut for the fourth time that day and began to turn the van around.

'I just want to pop to the house,' she said. 'Just for a minute.'

'Of course,' replied Amos. 'If only to tell the bees to make life hell for any prospective purchasers.' He studied her face, his eyes soft on hers. 'It's not goodbye though, Grace, not just yet.'

'I know,' she said. 'But I once told Hannah that I never knew what it was to love someone so much you couldn't bear to be parted from them. So you see the house is not really what's important any more. We'll just make a new home, you and I, and wherever that is will be perfect.'

Amos said nothing, merely smiled.

*

Grace pulled up in front of her house, the place where she had lived for most of her adult life. It was a house full of memories, some good, some not so good, but all of them had one thing in common – they belonged to her old life, and it was time for something new. She pulled Amos towards her and, just as their lips were about to touch, she broke away, laughing.

'Wait here,' she said. 'I won't be long.'

'Hang on, aren't you going to open your letter?' he asked. He had held it on his lap the whole way over. Grace had scarcely looked at it.

'No. It will be from Paul and I have no desire to hear what he's got to say. You can read it if you want to but then I suggest we throw it away.'

It took her less than ten minutes to gather together the things she needed, running back down the stairs before skidding excitedly to a halt in the hallway. She trailed a hand through the bright blooms of the flowers that still stood on a table and laughed as her eyes filled with happy tears.

'I'm not sure when, but I'll be back,' she whispered as she closed the front door behind her, pausing slightly as she corrected herself. 'No, *we'll* be back, for one last song…' And then she walked down the steps to where Amos was waiting for her.

'What?' she asked when she reached him. He was leaning up against the side of the van, squinting in the sunshine, his whole face lit by an enormous smile.

He handed her the letter. 'I think you might want to read this.'

'Why, I can probably guess what it says.'

'Grace, it's not from Paul…'

She looked at him, confused. 'Then who—?'

'It's from Dominic.'

She stared at Amos, her lips working as she took the single sheet of paper from him and began to read.

Grace, you were right.

By the time you read this I'll have left for the States where I hope I'll be able to put the finishing touches on the deal I've secured with Zac. You already know he doesn't want Paul as the star of his new show, but it seems the network still does have what it takes after all, as do you…

See, the thing is, Grace, I have been guilty of overlooking the truth. It's been staring me in the face for quite some time, but this weekend has finally brought home a few things. The main one of which is that Paul may be a wow with the ratings, but he's also a liability and, in reality, if he carries on the way he has been, only inches away from becoming the biggest disaster the network has ever faced. I have told him that in no uncertain terms… He still has a job but, well, let's just see, shall we?

Which brings me to the small matter of your house. I promised you a watertight contract if you agreed to host the weekend for us, and that's exactly what I gave you. But didn't anyone ever tell Paul that you should always, always read the small print? He signed a contract to the effect that should the network be successful in gaining Zac's contract then he would give you the house. And Paul being Paul he just assumed that meant with him as star, but in fact the contract made no mention of that. Oops, I must have left that part out…

So, when push comes to shove it seems I can do the right thing after all, and I'd like to thank you for giving me the opportunity to do just that. I think I rather like it.

It looks as if you'll be keeping the house after all, Grace...

Be happy.

Dominic x

A bubble of laughter broke free from Grace's lips as she felt Amos's hand slip into hers. 'Well,' she said, puffing out her cheeks. 'What do you make of that?'

Amos grinned. 'Seems as if he's a nice chap, after all,' he said.

Grace held his look, a rush of happiness building within her. She looked at the house and then back at Amos, at the camper van behind them. Then she pulled Amos towards her and this time she did kiss him, thoroughly and unreservedly. It was just the way she wanted her life to be lived from now on. Moments later she drew the van to a halt at the end of the driveway, staring at the road in front of them, as she looked first to her right and then to her left.

'Which way?' she asked.

There was a pause for a moment as Amos considered the question before he turned to her, grinning, a delicious twinkle in his eye.

'That way,' he said, pointing to the left. 'Just follow the sun.'

A letter from Emma

Hello, and thank you so much for choosing to read *The Beekeeper's Cottage*, I do hope you enjoyed reading it as much as I enjoyed writing it. In fact, I'm so sad it's come to an end! I really hope you'd like to stay updated on what's coming next, so please do sign up to my newsletter here and you'll be the first to know!

www.bookouture.com/emma-davies

This book is particularly special to me because I've been able to bring back possibly my favourite character of all time – Amos. We first met him in a novella I wrote several years ago, called *Merry Mistletoe*, and I fell in love with him then. I'm even more in love with him now! Amos arrived in my head one day, almost fully formed as I drew up behind a motorbike at a set of traffic lights. The bike had a personalised plate and yes, you've guessed it, it was Amos Fry. It struck me that it was such a wonderful name for a character and, seconds later, my Amos appeared in my head, begging for his story to be told. The only problem was that Amos was also a little bit of a mystery and so he never got to tell his story in *Merry Mistletoe*. However, I always knew that one day I would find a way to give him the story he deserved and, in Grace, to find his perfect partner. I'm so glad he stuck around long enough for me to make it happen!

Having readers take the time to get in touch really does make my day, and if you'd like to contact me then I'd love to hear from you. The easiest way to do this is by finding me on Twitter and Facebook, or you could also pop by my website where you can read about my love of Pringles among other things…

I hope to see you again very soon and, in the meantime, if you've enjoyed your visit to *The Beekeeper's Cottage*, I would really appreciate a few minutes of your time to leave a review or post on social media. Every single review makes a massive difference and is very much appreciated!

Until next time,
Love, Emma x

 @EmDaviesAuthor

 emmadaviesauthor

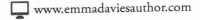 www.emmadaviesauthor.com

Acknowledgements

I had such a wonderful time writing this book as it indulged all my loves in one go! Not only did I get to learn more about bees and flowers, but in Flora I was able to dream about printmaking too, something else I'm keen to try my hand at. To this end I am indebted to Clare Ashcroft of The Flower Farm in Lancashire (*www.theflowerfarm.co.uk*) for her advice on planting schedules and all things flowery. I would also like to thank Helen Jukes for her wonderful book, *A Honeybee Heart Has Five Openings*, and Alys Fowler and Steve Benbow for the delightful *Letters to a Beekeeper*, just two of the many books I read to accompany the writing of *The Beekeeper's Cottage*.

I have also spent a good deal of time walking over the last few months, not only to try and ensure that I do move around at least for some part of the day, but also just to immerse myself in our wonderful countryside – there is truly nothing better for the soul. I am fortunate to live close to Attingham Park, an estate now owned and managed by the National Trust, without which this book would not have poured from me with the ease that it did. I am so very grateful that we still have organisations that preserve and protect our woodland and meadows and Attingham has both in abundance. I have walked there in all weathers, and now in all seasons, and every day has been a joy.

Finally, huge thanks, as always, go to the wonderful team that are Bookouture, for getting as excited about this book as I am (that's you, Jessie!) and for making it happen. Writing for them is just like belonging to a huge and happy family and, as we writers spend a good deal of time alone, that's incredibly important.

Made in the USA
Columbia, SC
07 July 2022

63021703R00171